KIT'S MINE

A
Daring California
Novel

Ann Bridges

Also by Ann Bridges

The Silicon Valley Novel Series:

PRIVATE OFFERINGS

RARE METTLE

Kit's Mine: A Daring California Novel
Copyright © 2014 by EndSource Management, Inc.
2017 Revised Edition
All rights reserved

Cover photos provided through Creative Commons license:
Las Médulas Roman Goldmines courtesy of Karsten
Wentink (via Wikimedia); Chinese Girl, courtesy of
Andoni Garcia (via Google+ and blogspot.com)

For Mom,

who lived loving,

and loved living.

MAP OF NORTHERN CALIFORNIA

Sacramento●

KIT'S MINE
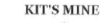

San Francisco

Angels Camp

San Jose

CHAPTER 1

San Francisco, California - June 14, 1870

All manner of property traded hands at this bustling intersection of Market and Montgomery Streets. Ship captains, newly arrived from the far-off Celestial Empire, hastily unloaded their cargo onto haphazard wharves extending into San Francisco Bay's frigid waters. The fact that today's commodity was human made no difference to the men making a fast dollar on each transaction.

Peeking around the corner of a ramshackle building in the murky afternoon light, Kit Lee swiped tears from her cheek. The sound of hammering by willing hands erecting the temporary auction stage was audible blocks away, and had bombarded Kit earlier as she went about her endless morning chores. Distracting her. Terrorizing her. She had to see for herself that importing Chinese slaves still thrived.

"Sold!" The auctioneer pushed the naked woman to the edge of the crude scaffold and tossed a ragged blanket after her.

Kit drew a quick half-cross over her chest. There but for the grace of...fate? Luck? God? She didn't much care which, as long as she still had her freedom.

The portly buyer marched forward. He dug under the filigreed watch chain displayed across his chest, lobbed a gold nugget to the auctioneer, and averted his face. Undoubtedly, his purchase stank after eight weeks crammed into the ship's hold. Stumbling off the platform, she lagged behind her new owner up a steep hill, passing house after house with scalloped bay window frames and easy-to-construct flat-topped roofs.

Kit bit her lip at the poor girl's welcome to this supposed land of the free. A pitiful existence, with no prospects or dreams—and with no one to help her escape, either.

The gavel cracked. Its death knell to another person's freedom sent apprehensive shivers down Kit's spine. She could be up on that block, sold to the highest bidder. Her identifiable cascade of straight black hair and ivory skin labeled her a Chinese Undesirable, even though she'd inherited Mama's Irish eyes. In this town, female Undesirables were either slaves or whores—or both.

When Mama and Papa encouraged her to finish her schooling at the Mission in San Francisco, they hadn't warned her of the deep-seeded prejudice she faced as a mix of races. After years living farther east in the rugged mountains, perhaps they believed attitudes had progressed since their arrival at California's far western port. Kit soon learned that instead of more tolerance towards the flood of immigrants, there was less.

The days of this minor hamlet's adherence to Spanish Catholicism had long disappeared. Mission Dolores, once a hub for devout villagers and earnest priests, supported itself with gambling, not tithes or offerings. Intent on hosting popular horseraces and bullfights, the priests overlooked the exploitation of those seeking safe haven. Kit had barely escaped a slave trader while living on the streets in Chinatown. Somehow, she'd managed to yank herself free and run.

Shunting aside the distressing memories, she tugged the oversized shawl over her damning features and searched the goggling spectators for the ideal man to shepherd her from this cesspool.

Not too old, but at least her father's age. Papa will forgive traveling with an older gentleman. A kind face, strong body—and clean. Lord, she was tired of serving drinks to filthy miners. She swore that dirt filled every crease of their clothes and skin. She needed shrewd eyes to see her dilemma, and broad shoulders to vanquish unexpected trail dangers—adept with a rifle or knife would be perfect. A newcomer to the gold fields suited best, so she could barter her talents in return.

A newspaper sheet danced in the cold wind, embracing her exposed ankles under the threadbare skirt. She untangled it and scanned the front page, sprinkled with fantastic tales of gold strikes and high-stakes venture funding. Buried at the bottom was the official reminder of the Foreign Miner Tax on all discovered gold. She shook her head. Papa despised those laws targeting Mexican and Chinese miners, decrying the race-based injustice blocking aspiring, talented men from contributing to the prosperity of his adopted home.

Flipping it over, she winced at the editorial complaining of the influx of deceitful Chinese Celestials with the completion of the transcontinental railroad. The writer advocated a return to San Francisco's infamous vigilantism in order to persuade foreigners to leave—including the

Mexicans who settled here first. Revolted, she read on. A single paragraph denounced the passage of women's suffrage in Wyoming Territory last week, decrying it as a foolish precedent for California. Exhilarating hope surged through her. Someday she might vote, too, and abolish these cursed laws.

Crumpling the paper in her fist, she peered again at the faces in the crowd. Her heart raced. Every beat reminded her of time racing by, the few hours left to find the proper man to escort her to Papa. She must leave soon. It will take days of grueling travel to reach their mine for her eighteenth birthday reunion. She didn't dare be late. Nor journey alone. Trusting in luck once more would be foolish.

From the corner of her eye, she noticed a younger man joining the spectators. He stared up at the platform, his swarthy features contorted in dismay. Will he be courageous and step forward, reminding these people that America fought a war on the other side of the continent over this barbaric practice of slavery, and outlawed it seven years ago? No, he was without doubt apathetic.

Or was he? His head swiveled back and forth, his thick black brows raised as if he sought a fellow sympathizer. As if he cared. Maybe she should talk to him. Perhaps he knew an older man who could protect her. She moved toward him, but he maneuvered to the opposite side of the street, hat pulled over his face, mixing with the crowd. Giving up.

The auctioneer yanked another naked Chinese girl forward. She wrapped spindly arms around her frail curves, her futile efforts merely calling attention to her exoticism. Knee-length black hair cascaded over her shoulders. The bay's cool breeze whipped her undulating mane, exposing her privates to the leering onlookers.

"Let's start the bid at forty for this beauty." Waggling his gavel at the crowd, the auctioneer began his hypnotic cadence. "I hear forty. How about fifty? Fifty? Yes! I have fifty from the lady in the rear. Do I hear sixty? Sixty?"

"One hundred dollars." A woman's loud bid rang out from the left. The crowd fell silent, necks craning to identify who would offer such an outrageous price.

The auctioneer hammered his gavel. "Sold!"

Elbowing her way to the platform, this buyer wore a pink and white striped dress with a plunging neckline, a bold advertisement for her whorehouse. No doubt, she expected to earn a high profit off her unique slave's nubile body from eager clientele.

Kit blinked away sudden moisture, cringing. Remembering.

The crowd shifted. Kit spied Madame Bonita scowling as her competitor hustled along her purchased slave. Kit shrank into the awning's shadow. Ever since hiring Kit, Bonita pressured her to shift from housemaid to whore. Apparently, she intended to buy a different victim today, and lost.

Nauseous with premonition, Kit wondered what additional coercion a frustrated Bonita might exert on her tonight.

A man's lanky body crowded against her spine, jamming her breasts against the wooden doorframe.

"Wha'cha doing here, girlie?" His heavy weight forced the breath from her body. She gasped for air, muscles frozen. "I got back from Gold Country today, and ain't had no woman in months. But I got gold in my pocket fer you."

Gagging on the sweet tang of liquor on his breath, her knees sagged. Horrifying memories of Father Angelo flooded her brain. Shoving them aside, she fought the suffocating, threatening blackness, and squirmed free.

Wait.

Shifting an arm's length from the miner, she stared him straight in the eye and notched her chin high. After all, possibly he planned to return to Gold Country soon, or would for the right price. She'd clarify what she would—and wouldn't—offer as payment.

"I'm not for sale!" She gripped the thin shawl's front edges over her gaping bodice. Remembering Mama's endless scolding, Kit kept her posture straight and her tone aloof. "Maybe you're interested in a different kind of proposition—or know a friend who is."

The homely drunk squinted down the alleyway. "You got a friend somewheres?"

"No!" Kit planted a fist on her hip. "Listen to me. Please." She drew a steadying breath. "I need an escort to my land in Gold Country."

Disbelief painted his wrinkled face.

"I'll pay for the trip," she said. Kit prayed her pitiful hoard of coins stashed under the kitchen floorboards was sufficient.

He chortled. "Girlie, I can't figger what you want to pay me fer! There's no chance you got land anywheres."

"I do, too."

"You're not even a growed woman yet, and you're a Chinee to boot." Wagging his head, he hooked his thumbs into filthy dungarees and puffed out his chest. "I mebbe ain't got much learning, but I know California don't allow no Chinee coolie to own land."

Hearing the familiar recitation of the restrictive laws, Kit gritted her teeth. "I'm American, just like you, and I have land to get to in Gold Country. I can guide us there, in return for protection on the trail."

His skeptical gaze swept over her, lingering at each gap in the folds of her tattered dress.

Kit strove to keep an open mind. An older man was a more appropriate escort. Perhaps he wasn't a habitual drunk. A bath will surely help. An ignorant man might take her guidance better. Negotiating with him was possible...or maybe she was too hopeless to be particular.

"Are you interested or not?" she asked.

"I reckon I am, girlie." Bony fingers snatched her arms.

"In taking me to Gold Country?" Her heart thudded in frantic rhythm. She pulled against his surprising strength, but not very hard. She couldn't afford to ruin her last chance.

The gavel's loud rap penetrated the heavy mist. His eyes narrowed, his manner became calculating and hard.

"Mebbe I'll sell you fer my next stake." He hauled her tight against his frame. The fetid stink of his unwashed body filled her nose. Bile shut her throat. "That last Chinee girlie fetched a hundred dollars."

Kit aimed her knee squarely between his legs and jerked high. He sank into the muddy street cupping his privates, red-faced and gasping.

Spinning away, she edged along the crowd's fringe and spotted the young man for a second time. Kit hesitated. Maybe he...no. He won't be any different. Better travel alone than risk being enslaved.

She dragged in a shaky breath and pushed aside gnawing fear. Despite her careful planning, Bonita will surely turn her onto the street with nothing except the clothes she was wearing if she didn't become Bonita's whore soon. She'll leave tonight, and put this past year of sheer survival and misery behind her.

Hastening down Market Street toward the brothel, Kit avoided the horse-drawn trolley lurching in and out of the hardened ruts. She wound through a band of emaciated children playing on the wooden sidewalks while their parents bargained for damaged scraps at the closing food stalls.

At least they still had parents.

At the final corner, she shivered in the inevitable afternoon wind blasting through the thin shawl. Maybe pregnant Penny would give her an old dress that no longer fit. Didn't she deserve at least one pretty gown?

Not that she could wear it anywhere. She held men at bay by having them consider her ugly, ready to swat away the unavoidable gropes that came with working in Bonita's brothel. Until she was safe, she would keep her guard up and her femininity disguised. Someday, a man might actually find her attractive for more than a night. Then, hopefully soon, she'd dump these rough and cast-off clothes in return for owning something that was wholly hers. Something nobody could take from her.

She'd accomplished her flight to San Francisco alone. She simply had to reverse her path. This time next week, she'll celebrate with Papa at her namesake gold mine.

But she had better hurry if she wanted to locate Papa ever again.

CHAPTER 2

Michael grimaced at the rapid-fire exchange of bids across the crowded San Francisco marketplace. As far away as his hometown of San Jose, rumors abounded describing traders selling imported Chinese girls, but he hadn't believed it. Until today. Clearly, his fellow citizens of California disregarded their new state's commitment to follow the laws of America.

He scanned the crowd, appalled that anyone would purchase a slave. A few short years ago, Californians staunchly contributed to the Union cause. Yet now, young men and old, Chinese and white, rich and poor, scrutinized the thin, shivering bodies as no more than livestock. Passersby rooted for the bidder to hold out for the greatest bargain. The auctioneer surely didn't fear a lawman would halt the illegal bidding—his booming voice carried for blocks. Most likely, the residents of San Francisco paid the sheriff handsomely to ignore scofflaws.

Michael clenched the pouch fastened at his waist. His small number of gold coins wouldn't buy even one poor soul her freedom and leave him adequate means to live. The auctioneer's hammer crashed down. Its loud thud slugged at his conscience. How could he protect a defenseless woman when a mob cheered her demise? He turned away in disgust. Evidently, his stepfather wasn't alone in ignoring the laws. Hypocrites always won. Better to remember that hard truth.

Adjusting his wide-brimmed hat, he headed southeast. The fog's chilly arms enveloped the sun, robbing his warmth. A putrid stench from muddy sewers offended his nostrils every time he inhaled. He quickened his pace toward the wharves and clean sea air.

He had spent three days in the stifling courthouse with other disillusioned Californios, Spanish- and Mexican-Americans like himself, battling the arcane mix of laws that purportedly established rightful ownership of land they had worked and lived on for decades. So many had already lost their abundant ranch lands to the flood of Eastern settlers, unable to cope with changing rules that favored a different faction every few months.

Jamming his fingers into his trousers' pocket, Michael patted his lawful title of land in Gold Country, officially documented in his new identity, not tied to his stepfather at all. Any association to Diego Salazar and his infamous cold-bloodedness repulsed him.

He marked off the time in cadence with his footsteps. Twelve years to escape from under Diego's thumb. Six years to win his inherited land in Gold Country, in spite of Diego's loathsome tactics. Two years to fulfill his deathbed promise to his mother. Just a mite longer and he could finally step foot on Father's bequeathed land, free to start a new ranch as he saw fit.

"Michael Rivers. Michael Rivers. Michael Rivers." He practiced the new moniker under his breath. Americanizing his name still honored Father's heritage. He'd insisted his son learn perfect English to adapt to their latest government. Miguel de Los Rios no longer existed.

He navigated the notorious Barbary Coast district, an apt name for its whiff of land-based piracy. Hoots of laughter rang in the night air. Recent arrivals of varied nationalities jammed into the street, sailors' pockets bulging with just-issued pay, easy targets for criminals who thrived on their unworldliness.

Michael ignored the riotous swarm, and shot a challenging glare at those approaching him as a potential mark. They veered aside quickly, looking for easier pickings among strutting gold miners flaunting the white silk top hats and gleaming nugget watch chains of freshly minted wealth. Despondent failures loitered in the dusty alleyway, sniggering as the winners' clothes dirtied and thin-soled shoes wrenched on uneven stepping-stones.

With one last task to complete before his departure tomorrow, Michael returned to where he stabled Midnight, counting off the remaining hours. He gave the stallion his evening feed and added fresh straw, glancing across the street at a packed bar advertising liquor and whores.

After decades of panning and digging by California's newcomers, there were no longer any easy mine fields to exploit. Thwarted men returning from Gold Country probably sought drinks and female companionship before setting off again into the wilds. Michael was as likely to hire a guide in a tavern as at the ferry building in the morning.

The last time he frequented the cantina and native girls near San Jose was months ago. Long nights alone stretched before him. Why not enjoy a last bit of pleasure mixed with business? Mood lifting, Michael walked into the Friday night din of Madame Bonita's.

Laughter and smoke billowed in thick waves through a crush of bodies. Crudely-painted arches decorated mud walls dotted by speckled mirrors. The tinkle of lively piano music overlaid boisterous whistles. Men jostled to capture the attention of the few women for hire, whose plastered-on smiles didn't mask their boredom. Tangy sweat and cheap spirits permeated the air.

Rough miners in worn dungarees grouped together swapping recent stories from the gold fields. In the far corner, three well-dressed men stood aloof in a tight circle, appearing to assess which miner might be worth a fresh stake of cash to seek another golden lode.

Elbowing to the scratched redwood counter and lifting his foot onto the lower rail, Michael caught the barkeep's attention and motioned for a whiskey.

"Know anyone leaving for Gold Country tomorrow willing to contract out as a guide?" Michael asked. "Someone experienced, preferably."

"For a gold cache, they'll clear out pronto." The bartender plunked a sloshing glass down and palmed Michael's coin. He gestured to a knot of wizened miners hunched over beers. "Most of those are losers who never found nothing except the end of a dream. I expect they'll vamoose right quick to Nevada and Alaska. If you're desperate…" He shrugged.

Gulping the liquor, Michael prayed their fate wouldn't become his. Their scrawny bodies couldn't endure the rapid pace he required, yet he would bet they were scarcely older than he was.

"Searching for a guide to your lucky strike, Californio?" A hand landed on his shoulder, pressing hard. "Got a chart someone sold you and need to get there fast?"

At the disparaging tone, Michael fingered the knife hilt protruding from his boot. Too bad he didn't bring his rifle. He never figured on needing a firearm in a civilized tavern. No animals to keep at bay. His mistake.

He shrugged off the weight and turned, raking his glance over the intruder. One thick arm blocked his way forward, the other hung close to a pistol belt. Struck by the man's combination of aggressive focus and hungry greed, Michael judged him to be pushing middle age, down on his luck, and darn pissed.

"I have land perfect for a ranch." Michael hoped the truth would encourage this stranger to leave him alone. He wasn't in the mood for another senseless battle. "No gold. Just grass for my horses."

"You Californios don't know beans." The man snorted. "Been sitting on this gold hidden under grass for years, and never once noticed it until you lost the territory. Your cattle rodeos kept your bellies full, your señoritas warmed your beds, and that's all you cared about." He shoved his ruddy face forward, and the smell of whiskey assailed Michael. "Why not employ me? We'll unearth your gold together."

Yeah, and as soon as we arrive, you'll kill me and claim the land as your own.

Michael sidled a step back. By the time he pulled his knife free, this drunken scum might pin him. He shot a fleeting look at fellow Californios observing from a nearby table. The rhythmic cadence of their Spanish tongue diminished to a murmur. None rose to help.

"We're not so dumb we can't recognize a loser when we see him," Michael said. He rammed the man's shoulders with restrained force, tumbling him backward.

Enough. He didn't need to hire a guide. He'd proceed to his new ranch alone. He could decipher Father's hand-drawn map if he studied it longer. Maybe. Just a matter of taking the first steps toward his future. Michael noticed a backdoor tucked in the opposite corner. He plunged through the throng and exited into a foul alleyway.

The damp air cooled his temper. He leaned against the rickety fence separating this run-down property from the next, knocked mud off his boots, and propped a foot on top of a weathered slat. Opening the top button of his worn cotton shirt to catch the breeze, he scraped days-old stubble along his neck. He'll order a shave tonight. And a bath. Then a woman. It might be a while before he indulged in such civilized pastimes.

Closing his eyes, he pictured the eight tavern flirts he'd noticed earlier, all smiles, giggles and winks. Each promised a different indulgence—playfulness, sultriness, enthusiasm, daring—except none sparked his interest.

He ignored the accustomed yearning for a wife and lifelong partner. A casual hour with a female he'd never see again would have to suffice. No sane woman would marry him and settle in an unknown wilderness. Not without a home and a solid means to provide for a family. Isabel's callous rejection taught him that. And Father praised him for learning lessons fast. What was that phrase from Mother's treasured book by Miguel Cervantes? *"A bad year and a bad month to all the backbiting bitches in the world!"* Yes, that Spanish author, long dead, summed up perfectly his farewell to Isabel.

Michael shrugged off any remnants of discontent for the lonely times ahead. He should be satisfied with the occasional prostitute. The girls inside were at least honest about what they did and why. Not like Isabel, taking a man's hard-earned money to spend on worthless fineries, even as whispering lies and tender endearments.

Pushing himself upright, he wandered down the alleyway toward the kitchen door. He'll order a bite to eat before cleaning up, and then choose a bedmate.

Melodious laughter drifted from an open corner window. Curious, he skirted the shadows and followed the sound, coming from the upper story. Stepping onto the rickety bottom-floor casement, he peered over the top sill.

A delicate female back filled his vision. Straight black hair fell past a slender waist to an enticing swell of hips. Pale skin peeked at him from behind that sumptuous waterfall. She wiggled into the top of a black dress capped by tiny lace sleeves. Reaching fingers tugged at the short bodice and struggled with the lowest button.

Muttering under her breath, she stopped fastening halfway up and stepped closer to the window. She hummed a popular dance tune and held the skirts aloft, exposing slender calves and knees. Preening, she curtseyed to the mirror. He caught a glimpse of high cheekbones and rosebud lips curved into a winsome smile.

He forced a deep breath and dropped to the ground with a growing smile, jiggling the coins in his pocket. She'll be mine tonight.

"FIRE! FIRE! FIRE!"

CHAPTER 3

Torn from wistful dreams of elegant dresses and a fine-looking husband, Kit froze, hands outspread within the gown's folds.

"FIRE! FIRE! FIRE!" The cry rang from the brothel.

"Where is that heathen Chinese bitch?" Bonita's shrill voice split the night. "It's her fault."

Kit peeked out the window. Inebriated patrons poured through the kitchen doorway and clustered around Bonita, who kept her back to her smoldering establishment. All Kit saw through the smoky haze was her elaborate bun, not garish, painted features.

"That lazy coolie girl set the fire!" said Bonita.

Kit winced at Bonita's loud, blatant lie, blaming Kit yet again. Bonita's complaints and punishments had escalated over the weeks, almost as if setting a trap for Kit.

"She'll pay for this," Bonita cried, pointing to the black smoke pouring from the window. "I'll own her!"

Bonita would earn ample money to rebuild if she converted Kit into her special Chinese whore. What better method than to scapegoat Kit for the brothel's destruction, instead of organizing a bucket brigade to spare it?

Time to leave.

Kit ducked inside, thankful she'd anticipated Bonita's craftiness and organized her few belongings earlier.

A thunderous crackle of burning wood filled her ears. Kit reached for the slippery dress buttons. Smoke drifted into her puny room, enveloping the bed in moments, streaking toward the window.

No time to change, just to retrieve her savings from the hidey-hole. Groaning at her misfortune, she yanked open the ill-fitting door, ran into the narrow hall, and flew down wobbly stairs to the kitchen. A cloud of blackness engulfed her.

Feeling blindly along the far counter, Kit smacked into the table. She squatted and groped underneath for the burlap sack, coughing. There! She tugged it free, and buried her nose in the rough folds protecting everything she had left in the world. Gasping, she ran from the kitchen. She dodged flames licking from tinder-dry panels, singeing her skin, blocking her exit.

Only one way out.

Bounding over the red-hot lower steps, she tore upstairs on stinging feet to her room, three strides ahead of the leaping inferno. She slammed the door on the racing blaze and dashed to the open window. Gulping fresh air, she hoped for fortune's smile one more time.

"Jump! Hurry, now. Jump!"

The command drifted up from below the windowsill. Darkly outlined against the billowing smoke, a man waved her down, bracing himself. She hesitated. Could she trust a drunk to catch her?

Searing heat scorched her uncovered spine. No other choice. She draped both legs over the sill and clutched the bulky sack to her chest. Closing her eyes, she kicked free and tumbled into outstretched arms. As soon as her toes touched the ground, she pulled loose.

"Where is that Celestial?" Bonita yelled. "This is exactly her coolie style. She'll pay for this the rest of her life."

Kit shuddered at her boss' censure, her strident tones competing with the clang of the approaching fire wagon's bell. Calls for water mingled with fascinated gasps from the assembling crowd.

Cowering in the alley's shadows, she gauged the distance to the barn. She could push her mule into a fast pace if she kicked him hard—and he cooperated. Her optimism plummeted. She had to get away fast before Bonita convinced the sheriff Kit owed a lifetime of work on her back for starting the fire. The stabled animals' ruckus would soon bring everyone rushing into the alley.

She took off at a run, her rescuer shadowing close. Why was he hounding her? Perhaps Bonita sicced him on her already! She increased her speed. He split off to the left and crossed the street.

Thank goodness.

Kit darted into the smoky barn and sprinted to the rear, ignoring the frightened horses. The panicked mule brayed, pulling at his ties. She dumped her parcel, approached his side, and wrestled with the thick, taut ropes. He skittered from her grasp, lashing out with his hind legs. Crooning nonsense syllables, she tried once more. The mule battered his feet against the confining wooden wallboard, creating a large, jagged gap. Twirling, he kicked at her. She released the ties and barely evaded his flailing hooves. He pushed through the hole in the stall and bolted for liberty.

"There goes her mule. Catch her!" Bonita cried, sounding triumphant.

Five men stumbled through the alley, peering into the shadows and windows.

Searching for Kit.

Scooping up her burlap sack, she shrank alongside the stable wall and hugged her dearest possessions close. Mama's voice whispered in her mind—*Use the brain God gave you and think!*

She could escape hanging for arson if she turned her body over to Bonita. But living as a slave—was it worth it? Could she escape tomorrow? Next week? Ever? Or should she take her chances with tonight's mob, instead? She breathed a hasty prayer under her breath. Would God even listen?

CHAPTER 4

The fire's roar overwhelmed Michael's cajoling whispers to Midnight. His mount reared on hind legs, fighting his inflexible hold on the reins. For once in his life, Michael wished for spurs. Another Chinese girl faced a jeering mob—and this time he could help her escape a reprehensible future.

Flames spat from the brothel's kitchen window across the street. Crimson tongues devoured the dry timber with each taste of fresh air. The wooden roof glowed orange against the inky sky, and a rushing whoosh reached his ears as the front corner crumpled into ash.

Excited voices joined the bell's clanging. Volunteer firemen barked orders to help or move out of the way. A line of men passed sloshing buckets in crooked procession. They ignored the doomed saloon and doused the neighboring building instead, managing the fire with easy conversation and rehearsed expertise.

Michael forced the stallion to a quivering halt at the stable entrance, and squinted between Midnight's flattened ears. He glimpsed a slender streak running toward him, her lacy skirt fluttering against exposed thighs.

"Get up here, quick." Michael leaned low to the young prostitute and extended a hand. The other gripped the reins fast. Disciplined composure would see them through the crowd unharmed—he hoped. "There's no time. They're coming!"

She stopped, checking right, left, and behind. Impatient with her dithering, he waved his fingers in front of her nose. Finally, she put her bare toes on his boot. Michael hoisted her up and settled her in front of him. Her slight weight rested against his chest, her legs tucked up and captured by his arms. He draped his multi-striped poncho over both of them and pulled the neck opening shut. Nosing Midnight toward the stable exit, he sauntered through the door, pretending he hadn't a care in the world.

"Have you seen a Chinee girl hiding in there?" A stewed man staggered along the fence, eyeing the spooked horses pummeling the stable partitions. "We're helping Bonita catch her before that girl runs into Chineetown."

Michael's human bundle stiffened.

"No." Michael tautened his arms in reassurance. "Hope you find her, though. Anyone destroying someone else's property sure should be punished."

"That's the law, all right," a second drunk said, tipping a half-empty bottle to his lips.

A sharp whistle pierced the air. Bang! The roof collapsed. Midnight started, his terrified whinny adding to the din. The soused patron stumbled, barely eluding a blow from Midnight's restless hooves.

"I'll keep a lookout," Michael said. "Have you searched the crowd? Fire-starters sometimes blend in and watch."

"Good idea." They rushed off in the direction they came, bloodlust complementing their bloodshot eyes.

The girl between his arms squirmed. He ignored her, searching the quickest route to safety. A sharp elbow dug into his stomach, demanding attention, and Michael eased the poncho's neck open less than a hand width.

"Keep still." He restrained her wriggling body and kept his voice low. "They'll come back when they can't trace you."

"Let me go" she murmured. "I'll capture my mule and ride out of town before they ever catch me. He's fast."

"That thing?" Michael chuckled. "He sure moved fast getting away from you. Not fast enough to outrun a mob, though. Midnight can."

Flames sputtered toward the rear of the tavern. A clearing appeared through the thick miasma. Starting along the vacant alleyway, the steady rumble of Midnight's hooves mirrored his own stark purposefulness.

"Let me down!" The muffled command, louder this time, carried overtones of distress. Pointed toes wormed from underneath the poncho, exploring Midnight's withers, reaching for the ground far below. "I've been taking care of myself for ages."

Michael glanced into the air hole. "Does that mean you've had run-ins with the law before?"

"No!" Her soot-stained face twisted in his direction.

"Because those drunkards told the truth. Whoever set fire to Bonita's place has to pay her for it. It sounds like she's blaming you."

"I didn't start the fire! I wasn't even in the kitchen at the time."

Michael could vouch for that—dancing in front of a mirror didn't bear much resemblance to someone planning a quick escape.

"I-I should have been, I know," she said. Her quiet tones carried the tiniest shade of guilt. "I only left the kitchen for a few minutes—honest."

"I may believe you, but who else does? Better yet, who else cares?"

Her toes retreated under the poncho, and the weight between his arms steadied. Her head moved against his collarbone as if in silent denial. Fine tremors transferred from her arms to his.

"Bonita sure has it in for you," he said, gentling his voice. "Unless you have friends hiding in that crowd, I'm the best hope you've got."

Only Midnight's alarmed snort in the smoke-laden air answered him.

Michael cursed under his breath. Why should he shield this willful girl? Except he knew—he wouldn't deny his attraction. Tonight, she was his alone. As an honorable Californio, just as Father lectured, protecting his woman and keeping her safe was his chivalrous duty.

"Fine." She sniffed. "Please leave me a way to breathe before I die of suffocation instead of hanging. Nothing personal, but maybe you should have taken a bath at Bonita's before the fire."

"Lady, if you'd been doing your job instead of taking a break, whoever started the fire couldn't blame you," he retorted. "And I'd be enjoying my evening at Bonita's, including a bath, instead of hiding an ill-mannered fugitive."

His poncho did stink. He used it as a blanket in the stables, bedding down in dirty straw and keeping watch over his prime thoroughbred stallion. Michael raised him from a colt, always intending him as stud for his beginning herd. Of course, that was before Diego blustered his ultimatum. For all Michael knew, Diego already informed the sheriff in San Jose that he stole Midnight—Michael hadn't stopped to ask for Diego's explicit permission before he left San Jose. Sleeping near manure was worth the hardship rather than risk losing Midnight to Diego's henchmen intent on filching the stallion back—or to San Francisco's infamous horse thieves.

They exited the passage onto the hot street, eerily illuminated by the fire's golden aura. Michael reined in and felt her spine tauten. He scanned the milling crowd for danger.

An elderly sheriff with a ready shotgun questioned intoxicated patrons, who followed Bonita's example by pointing out every black-haired woman spectator. That roughneck from the bar touched the sheriff's shoulder and motioned in Michael's direction. Michael tensed, praying the sheriff wouldn't shoot him on the spot as a horse thief—or an arsonist.

"Stop right there, mister." The sheriff's loud order cut through the clamor. "And take off that hat—let me see you clearly."

Michael lifted his hat free, letting it hang from its ties against his neck. Taking a settling breath, he ran his fingers through his hair and waited.

The lawman advanced, scowling. "You one of those Californios here to instigate trouble?"

"No, sir. I'm here to enjoy a drink and female company, same as everyone else. Unfortunately, my evening got interrupted."

"Who are you and where are you from?"

"Name's Michael Rivers, from east of San Jose, down south approximately 50 miles."

"What's your business in San Francisco? We don't take to those rabble-rousers from San Jose stirring up riots here over land claims." The lawman stepped closer, eyeing Michael's rifle secured behind the saddle. With the power of law backing him, the sheriff might confiscate it, even for the most absurd reason. Michael wouldn't stand a chance if he resisted. Nor would his scrap of a runaway.

"I came to San Francisco's court to pick up my legal title for land I own in Gold Country." Careful to keep his tone polite and respectful, Michael replaced his hat. "After I engage a guide, I'll never set foot in your town again, as much fun as I've had tonight." Truer words he'd never spoken. San Francisco held no charms for him.

"You get going now, and acquire a guide elsewhere. We got our hands full rousting coolies, as you can see from Bonita's troubles."

Michael exhaled in a silent whoosh. "Thanks for your advice, sheriff. I sure do hope you catch your fire starter. I'll be moving on."

He cut through the crowd, towering above the gaggle of bystanders. Nudging Midnight forward, they jogged through a neighborhood of modern buildings neatly stepping down the slope toward the busy wharves.

The ferry building graced the far end of the street, in the opposite direction the sheriff decreed. The morning ship would leave for Sacramento without him, his expedition postponed indefinitely until he hired a knowledgeable guide.

The warm bundle nestling against him served as a constant reminder of the reason for his delay. Butting in was his choice. It wasn't her fault. She had merely accepted his help.

He scowled and chose the southwesterly path, which no longer hugged the uniform houses packed within the center of town. Instead, it wound near scattered, listing shanties at the base of tall hills. He ventured a quick look over his shoulder. A fog bank glided through the harbor entrance, shrouding the tethered ships and deadening the night insects' usual serenades.

Not a soul in sight.

"All clear," Michael said. Curiosity intensifying, he slowed Midnight to a walk and unfastened the poncho from his throat.

CHAPTER 5

The reeking cape opened wide. A spurt of cold raced across Kit's face.

"My goodness, why didn't you ride away without saying a word? If I had my mule, I would have skirted to the outside so no one could stop me." Kit unbent her cramped body by inches, mindful of her precarious balance. Falling off this massive horse would be the crowning touch for her ruined plans. "Get this stinking thing off me before I choke!"

"Is that any way to thank me? And after I saved you from the sheriff. Didn't your mother teach you manners?"

"Your name is Michael, is that correct? Michael, please remove this, and I'll give you whatever gratitude you're due." She flapped the rank cloth and wheezed.

The horse came to a standstill and the heavy garment lifted. Surprised by the frosty air's punch, Kit listed sideways. She seized his wrist to steady herself and took three deep breaths.

Alive and free.

Bitter wind plowed through the half-buttoned, thin black dress. She cursed the damp fog. Who willingly lived where mid-summer was colder than mid-winter? Teeth chattering, she released him, pressed her meager possessions to her chest, and burrowed her feet under the horse's mane.

"Want the poncho on instead?" His palms scrubbed the length of her arms. "What on earth were you thinking, hightailing it out of there in this get-up?"

At his mocking drawl, Kit pulled back, cautious. She peeked up at him.

Moonlight pierced the ghostly fog and highlighted bristly cheeks under a tipped-down hat brim. He looked familiar. A regular saloon patron? She didn't think so. Of course! She saw him at today's auction—the young man with the scruples. The lone individual who seemed knowledgeable that slavery was illegal.

Thank goodness he was at Bonita's tonight. He was right. Nobody else would have rescued her. Not a single person would have cared.

"I planned on wearing my traveling clothes," Kit said. "They will keep me quite warm, thank you kindly." She lifted the bag from her chest. "If you would please help me dismount and turn away for a moment, I'll dress in something more suitable."

"Suitable for what—a hanging?" Michael laughed. He lifted her off the horse with easy strength and set her on the ground. "If this fog isn't dense enough for your privacy, those cypress trees might serve as a ladies dressing room."

Ignoring his sarcasm, she trudged through white mist toward the indicated grove.

Ouch!

She flexed her stubbed toe, and kept her balance but little of her dignity. Muttering under her breath about invisible tree roots and difficult men, she stripped off the troublesome dress in a hurry. She didn't dare risk him abandoning her.

What a mess. How will she ever meet up with Papa? She stepped into her sturdier garb. A whole year of planning wasted, journeying in the opposite direction with a man she just met, who probably expected to buy her services as a prostitute. Was that better than becoming Bonita's slave?

Oh, yes.

Despite tonight's setback and Michael River's opinionated comments, she still had her dream, the means to get there, and the will to go after it. Mama said that's what success required. She will make it happen. Somehow.

She quickly plaited her hair, balancing the straw hat on top. Swiping the grime from her face and neck, she squared her shoulders, feeling much less exposed and quite a bit warmer. Kit hastened to where Michael waited on his black horse, a welcome silhouette against the austere backdrop of sheer hills. He stared at the winding road leading back into San Francisco, searching for...what? Miles distant, orange flames exploded high at Bonita's, warning of her fate if she returned.

Hell.

CHAPTER 6

Sensing her presence, Michael turned. He rubbed his eyes and gawked. What happened to the lovely young prostitute seeking shelter in his arms? She now sported manly blue cotton trousers instead of provocative frills. A shapeless jacket hung off her shoulders with too-long sleeves falling over her knuckles, and she wore wooden-soled shoes covered with—socks? A woven cone-shaped hat hid her striking face, her hair plaited into a thick braid. With those baggy garments, she might be any Chinese—man, woman, child, young or old.

"Yeah, I'd say you sure are dressed for a hanging. No wonder those drunks thought you would slip into Chinatown unnoticed." The hairs on the back of his neck itched. She might ply miners with drinks and kisses at Bonita's. Or sell information regarding the latest gold strikes to the highest bidder. Was he so stupid that a pretty woman manipulated him a second time? He squinted at her features, the dim light giving him pause. Maybe she wasn't as pretty as he remembered.

A wry smile curved her mouth. Was she laughing at him?

His shoulders tightened and he scowled. "Who are you anyway?"

"My name is Katherine Lee. Please call me Kit." She executed a curtsy, looking ridiculous in those pants. "Personally, I cannot stand this fog-cursed city, including Chinatown."

He compressed his lips, too unsettled by her mysteries to agree.

Kit planted her feet in front of Midnight's nose. "I heard you tell that sheriff you're going to Gold Country. Since I'm heading there as well, I have a proposition for you."

Wary, Michael scraped his memory for his exact words to the sheriff. She heard about his land in Gold Country—yet he only knew her as a saloon girl who didn't perform her job. Her allure must be due to those fantasies he had in the alley, not a real attraction to this skinny escapee dressed in unflattering, masculine clothes.

Perhaps she set the fire. She probably intended servicing him before robbing him blind, then buying new frocks and putting her hooks into the next guy for money. Just like Isabel. Why did he adopt trouble?

Unwelcome recollections assailed him. Flames nipping at her shoulders. Wrestling the mule despite her fear. Her stony hush riding through the mob. Her trust in him to spirit her from danger—and Bonita's unjust punishment. She had guts, and probably fought her share of battles alone.

Hands clasped at her waist, chin up, her brows lifted in expectation—not pretend helplessness. Tonight, she coped with real dangers. He should give her the benefit of the doubt and at least hear her out.

He coiled the reins around the pommel and dismounted, looming above her. He placed his fists on his hips.

"Listen here, honey. I had my choice of propositions at Bonita's." Michael chucked her under the chin. "Nothing you can offer would tempt me."

An unbidden image of her dancing at the mirror clouded his vision. What a lie!

He continued. "If you think I'm taking care of you all the way to Gold Country just to save your hide from the law, think again. I've got better things to do."

Kit glared up at him, lips pursed. "Listen, Mr. Michael Rivers, there's not much I know about you." She mimicked his stance. "I realize that because you helped me, your plans got side-tracked—as did mine. I thank you for your help. Right now, I'm simply trying to return the favor and benefit us both. However, not in the manner you're suggesting. I'm not one of Bonita's fancy ladies."

He eyed the ruffle protruding from her burlap sack. "Really?"

A pistol shot resonated from the valley below. Muffled hoots and hollers followed.

Dread zipped across her features. Kit's pleading gaze met his.

Numerous torches lit the hillside through the mist, snaking upward, tracking their path from Bonita's. If his stepfather's influence spread this far north, they might be stalking Michael, too, determined to repossess Midnight since now Diego couldn't claim Michael's inheritance.

He swung into the saddle, grabbed her forearm, and hoisted her up behind him. She wrapped an arm around his waist and jammed her lumpy belongings between them. He kicked Midnight into a full gallop. They'll ride these coastal hills until dawn and put distance between themselves and their pursuers.

Long minutes blended into hours. Blinking scratchy eyes into focus, Michael followed the constellations tilting across the sky in measured lockstep. Kit's slight form fell heavy against him, her arms slackening around his belt. Had she fallen asleep? Just in case, he grasped her wrists and anchored her, slowing Midnight to a canter as smooth and easy as a rocking chair. He anticipated a protest. Instead, a barely audible snore reached his ears.

He marveled at such fragile hands. Rough and callused on one side, they fit in his with room to spare. Removing his glove, he skittered fingertips across her slender wrist, mesmerized by its silkiness. He recalled in vivid detail how he itched to explore her alluring back. However, in these preposterous clothes, that opportunity was unlikely any time soon. And not as tempting.

Silvery moonlight pierced the clumps of thickening fog. Faint outlines of oak-studded valleys fell away in every direction. Michael swiveled in the saddle, getting his bearings and taking stock.

Now what?

Neither could risk returning to San Francisco. He didn't employ a guide, and the lone ferry up the Sacramento River left from San Francisco's wharf. His sole option—ride back the fifty miles south around the bay and then veer northeast to Gold Country. That would take days longer. He growled at the delay.

The trusting weight of Kit's sleeping body gave him pause.

Father insisted on nobility as a man—to guard and care for women belonging to him. Tonight, that meant helping a young girl escape from an angry mob and horrific injustice. As a youth, he was unable to protect Mother from Diego. Now, he could shield Kit from undue hardship. And at present, intriguing Miss Kit was definitely his.

He won't throw her aside yet. He wanted additional time with this enticing woman, as well as to get at the truth of her plight.

Besides, what kind of proposition did she intend? Her exhalations through his shirt heated his blood in ways he never imagined possible. All while running from the law. His thoughts swung between resentment for the delay and curiosity about its cause until weariness muddled his brain.

He pulled Midnight to a walk, cooling the horse from their swift pace. Calm darkness beckoned, whispering of restful slumber. Spying a grove of eucalyptus trees, hidden among thick redwoods drinking from the cool mist, he halted under the low-hanging branches.

Kit stirred. She tightened her grip around his waist and sighed. Michael was loath to disturb her. She seemed childlike and trusting while asleep. Better yet, she didn't argue every step.

With great care, Michael extricated himself from her unconscious embrace and slipped to the ground, keeping her balanced. She tipped over like a full sack of corn. Catching her close, he snagged the poncho and carried her to a lush pallet of ferns. He spread the thick garment over their lacy branches and folded it around her, hoping it would ward off the night chill.

Removing her ludicrous cone hat, he tucked the poncho alongside her jaw and chanced a final stroke of her skin. He had to face the facts. This unfortunate girl was an encumbrance to starting his new life. Come morning, he'll take her to someone else for assistance, no matter her protests. No matter his reluctance.

He removed the saddle and her burlap package from Midnight, leaving the blanket on the winded horse. Yawning, he shivered. He didn't mind sleeping on a leather pillow—he often did. However, in cold weather he burrowed into his warm poncho. Not tonight, he thought with real disappointment.

Stacking her belongings within her reach, he stretched full-length, his spine touching hers, seeking her body heat as a buffer from the ground's cold seep.

Michael warmed up fast. Ignoring her soft breathing with determination, he shut his eyes. He needed to get on his way and forget her altogether.

CHAPTER 7

Kit drifted half-awake in dawn's glimmer. Smoke permeated her every inhalation, yet damp, cold air brushed her cheeks, not acrid heat.

Loose hair blinded her. She huffed it from her face and strained against the cloth binding her tight. Had Father Angelo awakened and tied her up, primed to take advantage of her?

No!

She stifled a scream, tore her arms free, and bolted upright. Panting, she scraped her hair aside.

The tranquility of a eucalyptus grove calmed her nerves. Birds chirped from nests high in the fragrant branches, their songs muted by the wispy fog.

A light snore whistled behind her. She eased her head toward the sound and braced her palm flat on the ground. Should she flee?

Michael's prone form lay next to her. A well-worn saddle cradled his neck. The rise and fall of his stomach lifted interlaced fingers in mellow rhythm. Lowering her guard, Kit ran her gaze the length of his wiry body. Muscled, clean clothes and nails, smelling of horse and the outdoors. Nothing to remind her of Father Angelo, or the disgusting patrons at Bonita's.

Nothing to fear. Everything to hope for.

Someone to trust? He already saved her once. Actually, twice.

Kit nibbled her lower lip, recalling his conversation with the sheriff. If Michael's destination was Gold Country, she could guide him in return for protection on the main trail. After a hundred miles or so, they'd part company. The worst danger would be near settlements, not in the wilds. She'd survive the occasional coyote or docile bear sniffing around at night, but sneaky two-legged varmints worried her. Was this man one of them?

Michael grunted and tilted his weathered hat. He rubbed his cheeks and sat up, massaging his neck. Suspicious deep-set eyes met hers, tempered by what looked to be regret.

"I've no coin to pay you, gal." He yawned and rose. "But I'll drop you off at a backroad heading home to Chinatown."

"I'm not going anywhere near Chinatown again," she said. That insular community shunned her for inheriting Mama's independent streak. It would never be safe for her.

"All right." He stepped toward his horse, grazing at the misty crest. "I'll take you to the Mission Santa Clara. Hurry up and pack your things."

A dizzying roar filled her ears. She trembled, breathing in shallow gasps. Scrambling to her feet, she caught his arm.

"No!" Birds scattered from the treetops at Kit's yell. "Never. Not a mission."

Michael shook off her grasp and cocked his head, studying her. She met his questioning stare. Her heartbeat stuttered and accelerated. Rising on her toes, she flexed her leg muscles. She'll run like the dickens if he as much as threatens.

"Maybe you'd better enlighten me on why the thought of being protected by the Church scares you." His untroubled voice mollified her, and she sank onto her heels. "We'll pass near it on our way. The priests I've met there seem harmless."

"Not for people looking like me. At least that's what Father Angelo said." Her throat constricted uttering the name.

"Father Angelo? Never heard of him."

"Trust me. You never will." Images of the priest's sprawled body— forehead bloodied against the fortuitous rock, thick tongue lolling from between cold lips, dried spittle tracks flecking his chin—pummeled her brain. She shook in an uncontrollable spasm, fighting the memory, fighting gut-wrenching fear. Fighting for freedom.

She met his confounded gaze. "I won't ever go to a mission, but I may be able to help you, instead."

"What makes you think I need help?" He set both hands on his waist, hips tilted in a belligerent stance.

"I know you tried to hire a guide in San Francisco and couldn't."

"Because I was busy saving you," he grumbled.

"I'm sorry for being a burden, and I appreciate your rescue. If you let me, I'll make it up to you," she said. "I'm traveling to Gold Country to meet my father, and need a trustworthy escort. I'll serve as your guide until our paths separate, if you're willing to be my trail protector."

"How convenient a harlot just happens to be going my direction. I hate to disappoint you, honey. I'm planning on ranching my property, not digging for gold."

"I am not a harlot, or whore, or fancy lady, or whatever label you choose," Kit retorted. "I worked as a maid scrubbing floors and washing up after the likes of you, not rolling about in bed day and night."

The sun shattered the fog with the abruptness of a thunderclap. A strong ray illuminated his skeptical expression.

"See these calluses?" Kit asked, twisting her palms upward. "Do they belong to someone who spends time on her back, or on her knees?"

"Honey, some men enjoy women on their knees. True, most don't like it so hard that you'd build up calluses." He chuckled, tugging at his hat brim. "I'll listen to this hare-brained scheme of yours. We have to ride extra miles south around the bay, anyway. Eat some of that jerky and grab your things if you're coming." He sauntered toward his horse.

Relieved, she stuffed her belongings into the poncho and rolled it tight. Watching his efficient movements readying their mount, she sipped water from the canteen and stuffed a bite of tough jerky into her mouth. He accepted her word—that was a first.

She remembered his disdain at the auction. Hadn't she determined that would be the sign of a true gentleman—someone who cared? He seemed the finest man she ever met, both helpful and courteous. Too young, of course, but downright handsome.

Convincing him that traveling together was in his best interest might take some doing, yet she looked forward to the debate.

She could trust him. She hoped.

CHAPTER 8

Michael swung his leg over the saddle and trotted Midnight into the clearing. Kit clutched the bulging poncho to her chest, looking like an abandoned calf instead of any whore he'd ever seen. Her almond-shaped eyes gave him pause. Chinese people didn't sport green ones like hers, did they? None that he ever saw.

Then why else would Bonita call her Chinese? Dressing in those ridiculous clothes sure made her akin to what they called Celestials, and would cause big trouble if they ran into anyone else, especially if that sheriff helped Bonita with runaways on a routine basis. He might even order a posse down south to San Jose after them, and give Diego yet another forum to accuse Michael of wrongdoing. Diego tossed troublesome facts aside to wield his power. No doubt, in front of a sheriff, Diego would expediently forget Mother gave Midnight to her son years ago and add to his woes.

Diego's glib tongue, first developed as an aspiring politician under Mexican rule, then perfected by his career as a lawyer, would render any false allegation regarding Michael believable. Aiding a runaway in addition to horse theft should stick Michael in jail for a few months. Then Diego would have all he needed to overturn the San Francisco court and claim legal title to Father's land in Gold Country. Michael wouldn't let that happen. Not after what he suffered. Diego had already taken his childhood ranch in San Jose away from him by marrying Mother. No more.

However, he needed to stick Kit in a safe place—and get her out of his life before Diego twisted Michael's chivalrous impulse into a scandalous one.

Freeing his foot from the stirrup, he gripped her forearm and set her in front of him. He lifted the poncho from her grip and tied it behind the saddle. With a light tap of heels, he guided Midnight into a rolling canter southbound, away from San Francisco. Snitching a length of jerky from her fist, he chewed slow and deliberate.

Where should he leave her if not with the Church? True, most of the Missions were destitute and desperate. The decades-long contributions from Catholics in Spain and Mexico disappeared when California fell under American rule. He doubted the elderly priests at Mission Santa

Clara presented real danger to a young girl. Or did they? Whoever Father Angelo was, he'd scared Kit to death.

His father's friends had resettled in Mexico once war with America broke out. After he died and Mother remarried, her remaining neighbors bowed before Diego's ruthlessness. Michael suspected Diego's influence among the powerful in San Jose and beyond started with opportunistic land dealings. They continued through unethical arrangements taking advantage of ever-changing leadership, as California became America's golden child. Not one person would risk financial ruin from Diego's or his cronies' retribution, not even as a favor to Michael.

His last fight with Diego surely gave the gossips hours of merriment at the local cantina—their livid shouts carried to riveted eavesdroppers in the barn. Michael swore he would never return, yet here he was, advancing on San Jose, putting his future in jeopardy.

Kit swayed to Midnight's gait, not relaxing an inch toward his chest. A faint smoke smell clung to her hair, mixed with her sweet, feminine scent. Michael shook off the distraction.

"OK, Kit, let's assume for a moment I'm considering your proposal." He injected a facetious note into his voice so she would understand the absurdity of her suggestion. "What proof can you offer that you will guide me straight to my land?"

"Proof? What kind of proof?"

"Let's begin with how you know the land in Gold Country precisely enough not to get lost."

"My father is—was—a cartographer. That means he drew maps for a living." She sounded like a patient schoolteacher tutoring a thickheaded student.

"I know what the word means," he griped. He was no uneducated lout. He spent hours learning from Father and his extensive collection of books. Too bad Father hadn't taught him about the hard existence outside his library, too.

"Papa worked for Spanish Jesuit priests in China before coming to California," she said. "When the railroads employed Chinese, they took on Papa to translate, and log the track's progress from Sacramento across the mountains. The Chinese workers asked him for help documenting where their gold mines were throughout California."

"Why? They couldn't return to their property without getting lost? Do Chinese have bad memories?"

"No more than other men," Kit said. "However, their land was basically pilfered from them after that terrible Foreign Miner's Tax law passed. They were blocked from getting legal title to their claims, and any gold they mined went toward the high taxes—"

"So it wasn't worth mining." He recalled hearing the complaints at the cantina. "It is plumb unjust taxing only the non-white foreigners."

"Unfortunately, that's the law." She released the top buttons of her jacket, flapping the edges. A flash of smooth, ivory skin arrested his focus.

"Papa drew an enormous drawing of Gold Country based on each man's description of the surrounding landmarks—major rivers, distinctive rocks, approximate distance from Mount Diablo." She pointed northeast to the well-known peak rising above the rolling hills. "His is the lone document registering Chinese properties. He considers it our family treasure."

Michael wished he had such a record with him. Father's diagram was hardly more than hieroglyphic scribbles detailing the boundaries of his property in relation to the neighboring lands. He had a general sense of where it was, yet without a guide he might spend months wandering, looking for the exact match to Father's cryptic notes.

"Papa worked on it every evening. Mama and I joined the others, and they would swap stories about their properties." Leaning forward, she braided the mane, her lithe body moving as one with the stallion.

"Obviously your father can make it to San Francisco without getting lost. Why isn't he coming to your aid?"

Kit rocked upright. Long seconds passed in silence.

Michael tilted to the side. Multiple tear tracks marred her cheek. This girl's life was full of misery, he was certain.

"Papa doesn't know where to find me except at Mission Dolores or Chinatown." With a soggy hiccup, she dabbed her eyes. "Last summer, Mama and I were to continue to San Francisco so I could finish my schooling at the Mission, while he went to Sacramento to fight for our land. We planned to meet at Kit's Mine—"

"Kit's Mine? What's that?"

"My parents named their gold claim after me, kind of a play on words. They promised someday it would be mine. They promised..." She trailed off, and yearning marked her features.

"Where is your mother?"

Her face crumpled. "Mama convinced Papa a priest would be a safe travel companion for us—she was very devout. After Papa left us and headed north, Mama died of cholera on the trail..." She bent her fingers into claws. "...and I ended up facing a journey alone with Father Angelo."

"I gather he wasn't a sterling example of the good Catholic Church." Baffled how to express sympathy for her loss, Michael opted for grasping her shoulder.

"He attacked me the first night..."

Attacked? Michael leaned closer, barely able to hear her whisper.

Quivers shook her. "He tore my clothes off, and pawed at me, and...he was so heavy I couldn't breathe...and then...finally, I shoved him away. When he stayed on the ground, I figured he was too drunk to move. The next morning I found him dead, his head fractured from a sharp rock." A sob wracked her slender body.

Michael pulled Midnight to an abrupt halt, wanting to lift her into his arms and cradle her against his chest. However, she was doubtless leery of men and uninvited contact. Torn between pity for Kit and fury at the lecherous priest, he drew off his gloves and wiped her unending tears, imagining the horror of a young girl, entirely alone, no one defending her virtue. No wonder she was fiercely independent. And keenly aware of her need for a trustworthy escort.

"Your father doesn't know of the...incident?" He wouldn't use the blunt word of rape, yet that's what it was, pure and simple.

She shook her head, sniffling. "I didn't dare go to the mission. Father Angelo said Chinese girls...did that...with the priests. Once I reached Chinatown, I sent Papa word about Mama. Except I couldn't stay there, either." Her voice dropped even lower. "Father Angelo spoke the truth. Chinese girls become either whores or slaves."

Her straw hat fell askew, bathing her hair in sunlight. Should he simply leave her, an open invitation to another attack, or protect her and hope she knew the trails?

With a resigned sigh, he tugged on his gloves, and nudged Midnight into an easy walk. "Kit, I am truly sorry that happened to you. But...how does that prove you know the route to your property, let alone mine?"

"Are you relying on directions of some sort?"

"Of course. I'm not wandering around to stake a claim—it was my father's."

"If you get us to the outskirts of Gold Country, I promise I can lead us the rest of the trek. I memorized Papa's sketch." She regarded him over her shoulder, her reddened eyes sparkling as brightly as Mother's emerald ring. "Mama and I promised to meet Papa at Kit's Mine next week for my birthday celebration. Do you want a guide to your property or not?"

Respect and a tinge of awe swept through him. Just like him, fire ran in her blood. She carved her individual path—even as a woman, overcoming her Chinese heritage, besides. She had no guarantee her father would meet her. Michael wouldn't rest easy until he assured her safety, and the obvious options of sanctuary in Chinatown or at a Mission were impossible. He prayed her father hadn't met with disaster already. California politicians and lawmen applied more pressure on Chinese than Californios.

"On one condition, Kit."

Jubilation brightened her face. "What's that?"

"We get you a decent pony and clothes to wear. Midnight can't carry us both for the long trek, and the way you look..." He clicked his teeth with his tongue. "Strangers will assume you're either my slave or my— what did you call it?—fancy lady. I won't stand for either reputation in my new home."

Big boasts, yet where could he obtain the mount she needed? Kit doubtless possessed scarcely a dollar to her name. His paltry coins represented all he had in the world. And returning to his childhood ranch begging for another horse from Diego was chancy. Even if Diego were in a good mood, groveling to him stuck in Michael's craw. Besides, what price might Diego exact for publicly flouting his will last week? No, there must be a better approach.

She held out her hand. "You've got yourself a partner, Michael Rivers."

He swallowed with difficulty. What had he gotten himself into with this woman?

CHAPTER 9

The afternoon sun scorched their backs in merciless intensity. Sycamore and willow trees clung to sluggish creeks' life-giving banks, marking a trickling path through undulating grasslands and into the bay.

Michael tore off his sweat-drenched shirt. "Sorry if this offends you. Dying of heat stroke won't protect you much, or get me to where I'm going, either." He mopped his torso dry and stuffed the top into the saddlebag. Opening his canteen, he sipped, and offered the tepid water to Kit. "Of course, the guide suffering heat stroke won't help, either. Drink up—you must be as hot as I am."

Kit swallowed a long swig. Her rounded cheekbones contrasted in sharp relief against the turquoise sky. She looked downright pretty. It's too bad that abominable priest triggered distrust of any man's honest attraction.

Well, it didn't matter beans to him.

However, even with her hat's protection, an alarming ruddiness stained her cheeks.

"You got anything on under that jacket of yours?" he asked.

"Nothing I can show." She followed the direction of his pointed glance and her cheeks tinted a deeper color. "I'll be fine."

"In the interest of your health and not some silly propriety, you may consider at least opening your jacket to cool off." He tucked the canteen into place. "Not a soul can see you, including me. I'm merely enjoying the scenery."

"I guess I'll heed your advice, since I'm going to instruct you when it's my turn to lead." Her lips twitched. "Lord knows I'll expect you to follow it."

Kit unbuttoned her jacket and parted the edges. His rejoinder died unborn. A sheen of perspiration clung to the gentle swell of breasts rising above a modest camisole. His nerve endings tightened.

How did this woman get to him so fast? Even if he conceded her fanciful tales, it still didn't add up. He'd better dig out the truth, and soon.

"Why did your father work for the railroad, instead of starting over elsewhere? A lot of miners came home and ranched for a living, instead." He recalled the old men at the San Francisco bar, stricken by gold fever. They would chase dreams promising easy wealth until their last breath.

Was Kit's father like them? Is that why he asked to reunite at the family mine, despite the onerous tax law still in place?

"Where else could Papa go if he couldn't own land? The laws say Chinese aren't allowed to bring their families to settle here, or to become citizens."

"Oh, that's why they're called sojourners," he said. "I never understood that distinction. Californios and their families lived here for generations, and most of us elected to become Americans after Mexico lost the war."

"You were lucky. People everywhere harassed Papa, whether mining, trading or farming. He had to care for his family, and at least the railroad paid him a decent wage. The other Chinese men accepted railroad jobs with long hours partly because they were all alone."

"Sounds like the railroads got the best of that deal."

"Over time it became almost slavery. Fortunately, Papa avoided the backbreaking labor. He translated both Chinese and Spanish, and in addition mapped the construction. Mama helped by cooking and doing laundry to earn money. In the evenings, even though they were exhausted, they schooled me."

"Ah, that explains it." He prayed his banter would erase her crestfallen mood. He didn't want his conscience haunting him.

"Explains what?"

He paused, considering how best to poke her into leaving bad memories behind. "I believe a regular schoolhouse would break most girls into polite young ladies and teach manners that would be second nature."

She faced him and glowered. As soon as she opened her mouth, he grinned. A tremulous smile appeared on her face.

"I hope you're not saying I'm ill-behaved," she said. "Mama grew up in a distinguished Boston family, and tried mightily to teach me social graces and decorum."

"I'd never say such a thing." He kept his solemn gaze fixed on hers. "If you'd been brought up too respectable, you wouldn't have survived that priest or living alone in San Francisco. Actually, I compliment your parents on a fine job. They educated you to reality, not to an ideal world like I was promised."

Kit had good reasons for her unorthodox journey. Nobody would fabricate that story. He disguised the pity he felt clear to his bones. She wouldn't appreciate it—her dignity sustained her.

Fingering the few coins in his pouch, he re-calculated start-up expenses for his ranch. If he scrimped, he could barely buy food for himself for a couple of seasons. If the weather turned bad and he resorted to purchasing grain for Midnight and a new mare, plus a possible foal, he wouldn't have sufficient funds.

Not a penny extra to spare for a mount for Kit. So, instead of buying her one, he'd have to borrow one. From Diego.

He strangled the violent curse forming in his throat at the certain risk and kicked Midnight into a full gallop, heading to his old home, now Diego's ranch.

CHAPTER 10

Rounding the base of the bay waters, Kit shivered in the breeze cooled by northern fog, and gazed at the eastern hills reflecting the setting sun's golden light. She re-buttoned her jacket, glancing behind at the bewildering man who hadn't spoken for hours. Based on his scowl, the respite didn't help. Something gnawed at his gut, and gnawed good. She shrugged. If he wanted her to know, he'd reveal it to her.

What was it about Michael that compelled her to trust him? Despite his brooding aloofness, Michael treated her as a peer. That was a first. Kit almost believed his compliments were sincere.

If only he would drop his guard and start believing in her as well. Was it because she was half-Chinese? Or a woman? Pride stiffened her resolve to earn his elusive trust.

Because, my, Michael was unlike any other. Tall and courteous, he put to shame the unfocused drifters and treacherous speculators who frequented Bonita's. Ranch work tightened his muscles to a sinewy vigor. His piercing eyes became formidable with each scowl, yet teasing laughter transformed him every time into an approachable gentleman.

He'd put her at ease taking charge of that ghastly situation last night, despite her bluster. She endured many nights in San Francisco by not giving in to overwhelming fear. Last night, she couldn't. His aid and natural strength helped her re-establish her usual emotional equilibrium.

And he was so sweet earlier, soothing her when she disclosed the story of that nasty Father Angelo. After the attack, she considered men animals and evaded them as much as possible. Once she told Michael her secret, though, he understood, without demanding the details. His impatience to move forward called to an echoing restlessness in her, taunting her.

Why not grab this chance for a different existence? Michael would protect her.

She took her first relaxed breath in a year, exhilarating in the freedom from perpetual caution.

The last sunbeam disappeared behind the coastal hills, washing them indigo blue. A pink-fingered sky beckoned rest. Michael halted under a grove of gnarly oak trees and slipped from the saddle.

"You must be stiff from perching up front," he said.

He lifted her onto the ground. Cramps shot through her legs and they buckled. Kit gripped his forearms. Finally regaining her balance, she straightened, releasing him.

Michael's hands slid from her waist. "We'll camp here for the night."

"It's beautiful." She studied the knobby limbs of the spreading oaks and smiled. "Is this your ranch?"

"No, it's the neighboring property. They won't care if we sleep here. I used to all the time as a kid." He led Midnight to the stream and patted his withers, letting the horse slurp his fill.

She trailed after him, her curiosity aroused. "Running away?"

"How did you know?" Chagrin etched his face.

"Because when I got angry at my parents I ran off, too," she said. "I brooded...and they worried." She covered her giggle with her fingertips. "They always found me and brought me home. What about you?"

"Not a single person came looking." His jaw clenched, and a flush crept up his throat. "I went home once I could tolerate my stepfather again, not because anyone fretted." Tethering Midnight to the nearest tree, he removed the saddle, pulled a comb from the bag, and groomed the horse with slow, methodical strokes.

Kit scanned the area. "Can we build a fire here?"

"Keep it small. The winds kick up quick, and this grass is dry." He chucked the saddlebag toward her. "Food's inside."

She extracted flour, coffee, and bacon, plus rudimentary cooking utensils, and calculated how to turn the sparse food into a meal. She spotted a dip in the flat area, ideal to sit and eat. Gathering twigs and slender branches, she stacked them in a mound, lit the match, and blew the embers, feeding twigs into the sparks. Soon she had a fine cook fire dancing in the pit.

An even hotter warmth at her back infused her whole body. She braced at Michael's unnerving presence.

"Here's water to begin." The canteen brushed her cheek. "Give me that pot and I'll fill it from the creek." She caught the canteen with one hand and hefted the pot over her shoulder with the other, keeping her attention latched onto the flames. Michael's footsteps faded in the direction of the gurgling stream.

She spotted a cluster of shoots overrun by a creeping rosemary bush, yet flanked by what looked suspiciously like poison oak. Too bad— flavorful dandelion leaves would enhance their basic meal, but not if she ended up with an itching rash. Stepping into the chaparral, she assessed the situation. Maybe she could harvest what she needed if she bent double over the rosemary bush and avoided the nasty leaves on the sides. Her target was just out of reach.

Balancing on one foot, she lifted the other leg parallel to the ground. She wobbled, flailing, and toppled straight into the foliage, twisting as she fell to avoid the oak.

Dazed and lying flat, she heard Michael approach. His head materialized above her, his thumbs hooked into his belt.

"Want help?" he drawled.

Aware of her feet pointing skyward and her jacket tangled around her ribs, she clutched the cluster of plants and blew hair from her face.

"Thank you, no. I'm doing fine by myself."

She wrestled the fragrant twigs poking her shoulders and sat up. Leaning forward, he lifted her onto her feet, and with the back of his hand brushed dead leaves off her arms. She skittered aside at his touch.

"I hope whatever you found was worth it," Michael said, his eyes gleaming with mirth.

"Our stew will be more appetizing with fresh leaves." She waved her green treasure. "You'll have to tell me afterward if you like it."

"I like it already." Angling close, he sniffed behind her ears and winked. "New perfume?"

"Rosemary is an old favorite," she said with a rueful smile. "Supper won't be ready for a few minutes."

"I'll try shooting some meat for breakfast. We have a long road ahead, and we'll tire of bacon and biscuits soon." He picked up his shirt and rifle and sauntered toward the ravine, disappearing among its low hanging branches.

Kit set about finishing the rest of the meal. Working over the hot flames, she felt flushed and uncomfortable in the cumbersome jacket. Michael would be gone hunting for quite a while, she concluded. She removed it and tossed it aside, concentrating on adding the ingredients at the perfect time. With a final stir, she lifted the spoon and tasted the result of her efforts.

A disemboweled jackrabbit landed on the flat rock next to her, its raw skin pink and shiny in the amber moonlight.

"Breakfast," Michael said.

CHAPTER 11

Delighted with fresh meat, Kit peeked up at Michael. Her smile faded at his intense perusal. The spoon clattered into the pot from mid-air. She grasped for his unspoken message in the dim light. Goosebumps rose on her arms. Rubbing them, Kit uttered a hushed cry. She only wore her skimpy camisole!

Reaching a hand out in the direction of the adjacent rocks, she patted for her jacket and met earth.

"Looking for this?" Her jacket dangled from Michael's finger.

Donning the garment in haste, she buttoned it in haphazard fashion over her chest, ignoring his roguish smile. She portioned food onto the tin plate and held it out to him.

"Thank you kindly," he said. His polite words carried a hint of laughter. "Aren't you eating?"

"There's a single plate. I'll eat from the pot."

"No." He thrust the dish in her direction. "I'll not have you as a serving lady"

"And I'll not have you kowtowing to me simply because of my gender."

Michael dumped the contents into the pot. "Simple solution. We'll share without a plate." He stuck his spoon into the food and shoveled it into his mouth. "Hey, this is good. You can cook anytime. I'll trade you for hunting duties." He dipped his spoon again.

"I never mind the hunting. It's preferable to cleaning." Kit wrinkled her nose at the carcass, took a bite of stew, and grinned. "Not bad. And worth diving into a bush."

Michael chuckled, reached for the canteen, and drank a long gulp. He dropped his spoon into the pot. "We're less than an hour's ride from my stepfather's ranch. If we rise early, we'll get what we need and cross over the first range of eastern hills before tomorrow night."

Kit suspected worries concerning his stepfather contributed to the strain in his voice and his introspection this afternoon. "Will asking him a favor create a problem?"

He flung a pebble into the trees. Quails exploded skyward from the undergrowth, squeaking their protest.

"I raised and trained all the horses on the ranch," he said. "My parents owned the original stock, not Diego. Any horse is as much mine as his. I only took Midnight when I left, no mares. Diego should be willing to loan me another horse."

"Why do you believe that?"

"Because it's part of our Mexican heritage. The original rancheros swapped tired horses for fresh, no matter on whose property they grazed, no questions asked. Why wouldn't he?"

"Well, will he?" she asked.

"He'll want me groveling and begging for a favor first, so he can feel I'm at his mercy." He raked his hair with both hands.

"Your self-respect is worth more than that. There must be another means."

"Have you any idea what a pound of good horseflesh costs?"

Kit flushed with guilt, heedful of her pitiful resources. Unless—or until—it became crucial, she would keep her limited nest egg intact.

"I gather you and Diego don't get along," she said.

"We've fought since the day Mother first employed him to defend her land in court, just weeks after Father died." He cleared his throat. "It's been twelve years, and I still miss him."

Kit stared into the flames illuminating their campsite, sensing his sorrow. An owl hooted, and the nighttime rustle of squirrels faded.

"If you and Diego fight, why did your mother marry him?"

"The ranch was already too much for her to oversee alone. The new law went into effect requiring proof of title to her land, and she didn't know what else to do." Resentment colored his low voice.

"Which law?" she asked. "The California Land Act?"

"Yes, that was the one." Surprise crossed his features. He couldn't know her parents often discussed the complexities of that and other detestable laws over their campfire.

Michael continued. "Mother inherited her grandparents' ranch. You see, the government in Spain gave it to them before Mexico declared its independence. The Mexican government never questioned her ownership. But when California became an American state, Mother had to prove she owned the land legally. It got complicated because she was considered Spanish, not Mexican."

"What difference did that make? I thought America accepted everyone. Well, everyone except Chinese."

"Oh, we were accepted as American citizens, just not landowners. Easterners settled on their pick of land, and demanded official deeds and documents. Mother didn't have formal records, though her family lived on our ranch for decades. She hired a lawyer—Diego—and eventually won. Afterward, she owed him a fortune in legal fees. She married him to keep a roof over my head." His eyelids drooped. "No better than a whore."

Kit darted a glance at him and wished she hadn't. His tortured face matched his voice.

Michael sifted dirt between his fingers. "When I turned eighteen, Mother gave me my father's land in Gold Country, which had a clear title to him from the Mexican government. Diego was furious. He treats land as currency to trade favors, and wants Father's land to barter with some fancy Sacramento politicians."

"For what?" she asked, puzzled.

"I'm not sure," he said. "But it can't be good. I've spent six years battling him to get the property legally titled to me so I could leave San Jose and start out on my own."

"Won't your mother help smooth things over?"

"Mother finally gave up and died two years ago."

"I'm sorry for your loss." Painful memories of Mama's death stabbed her.

"Last week I got word I won," Michael said. "I packed up, went to San Francisco for the official deed, and started living without Diego's meddling."

"And now you're back in order to help me."

"I hate asking Diego for a horse, but I will," he said. "I don't promise getting one, though. Diego only cares who he knows and what he knows about them. He misrepresents the truth for his benefit—his way of thinking, his way of life. Then he ditches the rotting corpse of what was once good and moves on to loot the next victim." His fist clenched in the soil. "That's what destroyed my mother. I'll never forgive him."

Kit stared at him, taken aback by the powerful anger resonating in his voice. "I've heard of such unscrupulous men. After being pushed out of their mines in Gold Country, many Chinese cleared remote land so they could farm, instead. Then the government seized it, saying the public needed it. The land ended up in the possession of a bunch of rich lawmakers who sold it for their personal gain, not the public good."

"That describes Diego, for certain."

She twirled the ends of her hair. Every detail of that last conversation, when Papa eventually admitted defeat and went to work for the railroad, echoed in her mind.

"My Papa worked day and night to create a home for us," she said. "As soon as he succeeded, the government confiscated everything, merely because he was Chinese. He couldn't legally own property like everyone else moving into California, so he couldn't protect what he worked for."

Kit swallowed the lump forming in her throat. Papa struggled for so long, and kept his dreams alive instead of escaping into expedient opium dens.

"It isn't fair," she whispered.

"No, it's not," Michael said. "On the other hand, I don't think it's honorable to break even a bad law. I'll succeed if I don't spend all my years battling these atrocious looters. It's why I fought for title to this land—it's mine, and nobody can take it from me. I'm seizing this opportunity. My land's yield will reflect my efforts, decisions, and choices—not Diego's."

He scrambled to his feet, muttered under his breath he would see to Midnight, and strode into the darkness.

CHAPTER 12

Kit re-packed the food into the saddlebag, pondering Michael's outrage. She hadn't understood his deep-rooted ambition to succeed. Or how it connected to his self-esteem. Her respect for him increased tenfold.

Gathering the cooking tools in her arms, she wandered to the stream and relaxed into the velvety breeze. Her problems trickled away into the mud along with the dried gravy. Rolling up her sleeves, she knelt and splashed cool drops on her nape, entranced by the moonbeam's reflection on the burbling water.

A rustling beyond her shoulder caught her attention.

"I'm done here, if you'd like to wash up." She collected the utensils. Michael might enjoy this bit of peace before his confrontation tomorrow. "It feels wonderful."

She turned, expecting to see Michael's boots planted on the ground next to her. Nothing but clay and leaves. She frowned, certain of a presence nearby. The tree limb creaked above. A twig snapped. Of course—probably squirrels chasing each other. Rotating her head, she squinted against the glittering moonlight into the tree branches.

A mountain lion stared at her. Perched on the limb, the cat's black-rimmed, predatory eyes glinted, hungry and intent. Taut muscles rippled from its crouched legs to its solid body. Its golden tail swished in hypnotic rhythm.

Kit gulped. She racked her memory for stories about anyone getting into this predicament—and escaping safely. All used a knife or pistol. She had an empty pot and spoons. Palms sweating, she clutched the insubstantial missiles. Her harsh, shallow gasps broke the stillness.

She inched vertical, her concentration fixed on the lion. Taking one tiny step after another, she aimed downstream. Vicious-looking claws gripped the tree branch as it stalked her, its compact body in easy balance. Kit tiptoed from directly underneath the cat. Unblinking, a warning yowl rumbled from its chest. She froze. Her heartbeat thundered in her ears. Still too close!

Flashing her gaze to and from the animal for brief instants, she sought a refuge. Any protection from attack.

Not a thing. Not even a single large rock.

She drew a long, silent breath, and crossed her fingers.

"Michael! Help!"

The lion snarled. Hot breath washed over her. Bunching its muscles in a flowing surge, the cat lunged, teeth bared. Its front paws extended right toward her neck.

She screamed and wheeled, plunging into the woods. Her shriek ricocheted a mocking reply.

A bullet whizzed over her head. The shot's report deafened her. Heavy paws raked across her shoulders, and sharp claws penetrated her jacket. The beast hurtled into her. She tripped under its weight and fell, breathless. Tucking her chin, she froze, awaiting excruciating pain. Praying for a swift end.

Hands grabbed her armpits, hauling her from underneath the creature. Gasping for breath, she witnessed Michael slitting the lion's throat. He shoved it aside, cleaned the bloody knife on his pants, and sheathed it in his boot in a clean, precise movement.

On her knees, she stared at the dead animal just inches from where she collapsed. Waves of convulsions pelted her.

Michael lifted her upright and pivoted her around toward the moonlight. Fingertips prodded through the shredded jacket to her bare skin. Kit flinched in apprehension. Instead of anguish, she felt gentle pats along her spine. She sent a prayer of thanks heavenward for the tough cloth.

Keeping an arm snug around her waist, he turned her, his arm across her back as unyielding as a railroad iron.

"Kit! Are you hurt anywhere?" His shaky question echoed the aftermath of her panic.

She wavered, legs wobbly, arms quivering, and neck limp. Leaning into his warm strength, her heart beat an erratic rat-a-tat tempo. She inventoried every bit of threatened flesh. No pain. Her wild imaginings in those terrified seconds weren't real.

"Good as new." Dismayed by her assertion's betraying tremor, she forced herself erect and looked up.

Into a distraught, angry face.

Her words of thanks died unspoken. The mountain lion attacked her, not the reverse. She tried every conceivable action, and called for help. And his swift response was impressive. The cat hadn't even scratched her. Yet Michael's golden-flecked eyes, blackened to mere slits, scrutinized her with piercing relentlessness. His gaze flickered to the tawny carcass and back.

The acrid stench of gunpowder drifted into her nostrils. Michael still gripped the rifle that saved her. Rigid fingers stroked her hair from her jaw and smoothed her arms.

Kit's cheeks warmed at the comfort of his rough palms. Her legs buckled, and he steadied her. Alarmed by her continuing weakness, she pulled away.

"Thank you for rescuing me again." She tapped his hand resting on her wrist. "The Chinese believe if someone saves your life, it is no longer your own. It belongs to your savior, instead. By now I must owe you more than a guided trip through Gold Country."

"I shouldn't have left you alone. I know big cats hunt this time of day. You had no protection without me." Michael's grip tightened to a bruising strength. "I didn't hold up my end of our bargain. There's no need to thank me."

"Do you really think I should berate you for not taking better care of me?" she asked, relieved. He was angry with himself, not her. "For not safeguarding me?"

"Isn't that our agreement?"

"Yes, to a point. I meant protection from the two-legged predators we're bound to meet along the way. I'm perfectly capable of dealing with wild animals." Kit brushed the dust off her clothes in brisk sweeps.

"You didn't seem that capable five minutes ago." He gestured at the dead cat. "Or are you denying you were in danger?"

"That's because I don't have a gun. I'm able to take care of myself if I carry the same weapons as you."

"Can you really shoot, or are you too pigheaded to admit you need protection?" Michael waved his rifle in her face. "An animal doesn't scare from the sight of a gun. It waits until a bullet hits him to learn his lesson. By then, if you're lucky, it's dead."

"As soon as I get a gun, I'll challenge you to a shooting contest and we'll see who does a better job of protection." Catching a glimpse of the dead animal's blank stare, she sobered. "Until then, I could use your extra vigilance, if you're willing. Deal?"

"Deal." He brushed a quick kiss along her knuckles. "I'm still sorry I left you alone. You shouldn't be in danger a stone's throw from where I grew up."

His imperceptible caress sent shimmering tingles along her arm.

"This isn't your home anymore," she said. "Besides, I'm sure your new spread will have its dangers, too. We'll just handle those a day at a time."

His quizzical look became assessing. "Let's head to camp. It's been a long day and a worse evening. We need to rest."

She clung to him up the steep incline, aware of other dangers lurking among the shadows. And attuned to the man walking at her side, shielding her from them.

CHAPTER 13

Michael packed the gear while watching the sky turn from gray to pale blue. He dreaded Diego's predictable manipulations, and girded himself for the worst. One way or another, he would survive.

He left this once before. This time it would be easier. Now he knew how it felt to live free from a spider web of deceit, to unload the repugnant burden of his stepfather. Tomorrow, he would be far, far away again.

The sun burst from behind the eastern hills, a golden shout of promised heat and intensity. Full daylight tiptocd from west to east in a backward dance, leaving him shadowed in his dark thoughts, the new day still out of reach.

Kit stepped from the bushes. The jacket hung askew in half-tatters, secured by the front buttons. Her straw hat tilted forward, shielding her face from the morning glare. Shiny black tresses cascaded in a neat tail over her back, and covered most of the jacket's rips. She hurried toward him, her steps full of energy.

Proud of her resilience, he lifted her onto Midnight's withers. Except for her clothes, she seemed unaffected by last night's danger.

He couldn't say the same about himself.

Mounting, he relived the attack one more time. His silent bellow as he grasped the danger. His speedy prayer. Raising his rifle and firing. Her haunting scream echoed in his mind, swirling in an ominous vortex.

In his nightmares, she didn't survive. He failed as her guardian. As a man.

He'd shuddered awake in a cold sweat, shaken she disappeared from his life in an instant. And wondering at the alarm seeping through him.

Being her protector came easily to him—too easily. Unexpected urges provoked him to keep her safe, tucked safely next to his side. At least for the journey. Beyond that, he had no expectations or plans—except possibly she did.

Her presumptuous comment last night regarding facing dangers together unnerved him. It was almost as if she intended on living with him on his property. Why else would she say that? She understood him at the most basic level, true. But who was the real Kit Lee? And why did he care so much?

He didn't dare analyze his feelings in the cold light of day. Not with a confrontation with Diego looming.

Perched in front of him, Kit smiled over her shoulder. "I'm eager to see the horses you raised. Will you pick a match for Midnight?"

Michael hated ruining her good mood, but she should know the odds against them. "Don't get your hopes up. Diego won't feel obliged to me. Not after I rubbed his nose in winning the land claim." And especially not after taking Midnight without his explicit permission."

"Really?"

"It stuck in his craw that the court decided in my favor." If that weren't an understatement of Diego's reaction, he'd eat his hat.

"If there were another option..." Doubt colored her voice.

"I haven't figured out how to tell him about you," he admitted. The morning breeze flapped torn strips from her jacket, catching them against his belt buckle. He tugged the strands free, imagining Diego's critical perusal and guaranteed obnoxious remarks on her appearance.

"Why would you disclose anything? I'll gladly disappear until you talk to him."

Relief blew through him. "I'll meet you outside the barn. We'll pick a saddle for you then."

They passed an ornate wooden cross hanging over a driveway. "Was your family friendly with that neighbor?" Kit indicated the etched words 'Rancho de La Cruz'.

"You might say that." He slapped the reins onto Midnight's neck, hastening them past the ranch. "After Mother died, my stepfather attempted to betroth me to de La Cruz's daughter in order to annex their land to ours. I wouldn't marry Isabel."

"Why not? Is she ugly?" Michael swore a jealous note crept into Kit's voice. "Old?"

"No, young and beautiful, actually," he said. "Also mean and manipulating, just like Diego. How her father raised such a daughter, I don't know."

As a raw youth, besotted by Isabel's beauty and elusiveness, he contemplated staying on as a plain ranch laborer, confident he would win her. What a laugh. She directed her choosy attentions to a rich old man, leaving Michael picking up the rubble of a shattered heart and battered ego. He learned that lesson perfectly—don't give up your dreams for a woman, no matter her charms. Women betrayed everyone.

Michael settled his hat snug against his forehead. Hostility plagued his soul for so long he couldn't trust. Or laugh. Or love. Now this young woman enticed him to forget the bad memories. Unlike Isabel, she encouraged dedication to his values. She gave as much as she took, acting as a true partner on this trek instead of expecting him to handle every chore, exactly as promised.

And what had he done in return? Failed her trust by not protecting her last night. Was he treating Kit better than Isabel treated him?

"I'm glad," she said. "Otherwise you wouldn't be the least bit interested in living on your father's property, and I wouldn't have the opportunity to prove my guiding skills."

He steered Midnight through an ornate iron gate. "This is the ranch. I'll drop you off first and go up to the house. You vanish somewhere until I come find you."

Her uncharacteristic quietness up the long entrance road bothered him. They reached the barn, and she hopped off Midnight unassisted, her belongings clutched under her arm.

"Good luck," Kit said with a fleeting smile. "And you might lose that scowl before you scare off everyone in sight."

Amused, Michael relaxed. "After the horse, the next item I'll see to is your traveling clothes."

"Please don't concern yourself. I'll get by. I always have." She flushed red and traced her wooden soles in the loose soil. Powdery dust swirled around her ankles. "Unless you're ashamed of being seen with me, dressed as I am."

"No, not ashamed. Merely aware of extra danger by being out of the ordinary. People are funny that way. They're scared of differences. Where we're going, fear may cause people to act crazy. I'm just planning for the worst."

"I'll hope for the best." She waved overlapped fingers and stepped into the long shadows thrown by the barn.

Ragged strips hung down her retreating form. He would procure a dress, he vowed, no matter what she said.

CHAPTER 14

Michael dawdled approaching the sprawling ranch house, easing back on the reins. His stomach was as queasy as when he slaughtered his first cow.

Morning sun highlighted three steps of the shaded veranda facing the expansive valley below. The dwelling's two wings reached toward the surrounding hills in a loving embrace. Thick ivy climbed white adobe plaster alongside his childhood bedroom window to the red tile roof, the long, sturdy vine a reminder of periodic escapes from Diego's torment.

An unfamiliar cabriolet graced the circular drive, in spite of the early hour. Two harnessed mares gnawed their bits, their hides glistening in the rising heat.

Acorns from the old oak tree crunched under Midnight's hooves. Michael dismounted and tied the horse in its welcome shade. Ascending the stairs into the house, he followed a woman's voice down the corridor to the rear parlor.

"Can you believe they lived with these primitive Spanish relics?" A mocking tone snapped like a whip through the cool air. "I am going to convert this into California's most fashionable home and ship in furnishings from New York. Time to clean house. My goodness, he still has his wife's clothes stored upstairs. I will have Maria burn them, and begin re-decorating next week." Her waspish timbre set his nerves jangling.

"Are…are you…you certain Señor Salazar will allow you to do that?" This female's voice trembled. "Surely he…he has particular ideas. M-m-maybe you…you should wait until he returns to m-m-make changes to his house."

"When Diego marries me, he will keep me happy. I do not need his permission to prepare our home for prominent guests." Her grating pitch pierced the thick walls and echoed in the wide hallway without losing its supercilious cadence.

In mounting disbelief, Michael crossed the threshold into the airy room. Its double doors opened onto the walled-in courtyard, where the fountain burbled the household's morning greeting, and benches shaded by overhanging balconies and flowering shrubs promised respite.

His booted footfall thudded against the red pavers. Two women turned and faced him—Isabel and her younger sister Dora. Isabel's glance skimmed his trail-worn clothes with condescending superiority. Dora imitated her precisely.

"Ah, Miguel," said Isabel. "You decided to atone and return for your father's wedding. He will be pleased." She presented her hand with a cunning smile. Lustrous sable hair flowed in perfect curls beyond her shoulders. Her rich yellow dress enhanced the chestnut tones of her skin and complemented the showy gold jewelry decorating her ears. Yet neither brightened her calculating eyes. She was as cold as the large diamond winking on her finger.

Michael snubbed her gesture. "Am I to understand this time your fickle heart has been won by Diego, and you will be marrying him instead of me?"

"Your father is a better man than you will ever be. He will care for me in the manner I am accustomed, not expect me to forsake society to become the wife of a common ranchero." A smirk settled on Isabel's full lips. "If you are not here for the wedding, why did you come? I thought Diego kicked you out."

Vivid memories of last week's shouting match with Diego invaded his mind...

Once Michael received notice declaring him rightful owner of Father's land, he'd stormed into Diego's study, gloating over his imperious stepfather, the hot thrill of victory running through his veins.

"You good for nothing bastard." Spittle accompanied Diego's venomous words. He stomped around the leather chairs stained from decades of use, his round belly jiggling. "Your father was a no-good miner. You don't know if that land is even suitable for ranching, Miguel. You're behaving no better than an obsessive puppy trailing after your father's pointless dream."

"You'll never understand Father!" Michael's years of curbed temper finally erupted. "His loyalty and honor were dearer to Mother than riches, or his profession, or his land. Thank God he wasn't like you, trapping her into marriage for political power." That old feeling of helplessness to protect Mother from Diego's schemes surged to the fore.

Diego straightened to his full height, falling short of meeting Michael's gaze squarely by three inches. "You young whelp, you don't understand anything, do you?" His calculating stare chilled Michael. "California gold funded the Union's victory over the Southern rebels. This entire country owes its future to our large miners and landowners. My peers and I, who know in what manner to leverage our state's riches, will wield power in both Sacramento and Washington D.C. The best you ideal, small-scale ranchers can hope for by the end of your days is that you still have food on your table."

"I own that property, and I have the power of the law to enforce my rights!"

"Didn't you know the law is a living, breathing entity, Miguel? Whether it is Spanish, Mexican, American, or Californian law, it devises exceptions for astute men, and leaves you fools chasing mirages. Don't say I didn't warn you."

Battling a surge of rage, Michael lifted his fists, impervious to the consequence.

Diego narrowed his eyes. "You are no longer welcome in my home. Leave here at once, or I'll have the sheriff throw you out."

"With pleasure." Michael stormed from the room. He packed the essential belongings for his promising venture before saddling Midnight and riding north to San Francisco, swearing he would never return...

Yet here he was at the ranch again, hoping Diego wouldn't claim Midnight as his own, and near begging for another horse for Kit. It will cost him in pride instead of coin. He'd thrown aside more than that already. One new accommodation won't hurt him.

Michael stared at Isabel, contemplating the ugly spirit emanating from beneath the thin veneer of her physical beauty. He uttered a silent prayer of thanks that he escaped her mean clutches. "Where is Diego?"

"You fool!" Isabel scoffed. "You didn't understand what you were doing, angering such a powerful man as your father."

"Step-father." Michael enunciated the word with precision and heartfelt contempt.

"Whatever you call him, he will not accept a challenge by a weakling such as you. Of course Diego will restrict you to teach you a lesson."

"Where is he?" He wasn't interested in playing her petty games. Not with Diego on her side. They deserved each other.

"He is on his way to Sacramento to claim that land. Your mother was not thinking straight when she promised it to you." Spite coarsened Isabel's features. "His friends at the capital will help him, not you. The land is due him as her bereaved husband. And is soon mine, too."

Michael's stomach roiled at her unadulterated greed. He glimpsed familiar gilt lettering on the bookshelf—Mother's leather-bound novel,

The Ingenious Gentleman Don Quixote of La Mancha, carried by her grandparents from Spain. Its principled message certainly would be lost on Isabel.

He had more pressing worries than this bitch. Like fighting Diego once more.

"When did Diego leave?" he asked.

"What does it matter? You lost, and you have nothing left. If you think I will let Diego associate with a horse thief, you do not know me."

"I know you too well, Isabel." Michael strove for deliberate calm. "You better tell me, or I will—"

"You will what?" She tilted her jaw at an arrogant angle.

Michael bit back his reply. He jammed his hands into his pockets instead of wringing her throat, and strode from the room.

"I have accomplished sufficient housecleaning for today, Dora." Isabel's scornful laughter followed him into the corridor. "Let us call on my future neighbors instead of staying in this dreary old house."

Wishing Isabel straight to damnation, Michael walked to the kitchen garden, seeking Maria. A constant presence during his upbringing, the cook scolded and loved him as much as any family member. However, Isabel and Diego would be a ruthless team. He hoped they wouldn't trouble Maria. She didn't deserve their ire.

Michael found her watering strong, leafy sprouts pushing through the clay soil. He slowed his gait, removed his hat, and let the summer sun melt away his tension.

"Maria." Careful not to startle her, he kept his voice low and reverted to her native Spanish tongue. "How are you?"

"Miguelito!" Maria's bulk jiggled and swayed with each rapid step in his direction. Throwing her sun-darkened arms around his back, she gave him a hearty hug. "I thought you left forever. Why are you here?"

"I must talk with Diego." Michael inhaled the everyday cooking aromas captured in her coarse gray hair. "I understand from Isabel he is not home."

"That bitch would lie if it was in her favor, but on this she is speaking facts. Your stepfather is not here."

"When did he leave?"

"He received a telegram yesterday morning, and rushed out in one of his fine carriages, wearing his newest clothes. I overheard him tell Señorita Isabel he was taking the steamboat from Alviso to San Francisco, and then on to Sacramento. He had that look he gets the minute he's up to no good."

Maria spat in the freshly turned loam. "I don't know his business. He said he would not be gone long. His wedding is scheduled four weeks from tomorrow."

Diego had a full day head start and the advantage of the ferry's direct route to Sacramento, while they were stuck going overland. Michael wouldn't underestimate his cunning—or Isabel's. An arrogant proclamation of rightful ownership of Michael's land might be enough for Diego to bargain it away for a future favor. He could sell the property to the highest bidder for another supposed railroad spur, or for government-sponsored roads and dams. Then Michael would have to start over proving his legal title.

He scowled, sifting his mind for fresh strategies. He couldn't let Diego beat him.

"Miguelito, why are you here?" Maria asked. "You must be in trouble to return after that terrible fight you had with Señor Diego."

Michael raked his fingers through his hair, kicking himself for his rude musing. Diego was a curse on his existence. "I came to borrow a horse."

"I don't think Señor Diego is of the mind to lend you one," she warned. "He disowned you in front of the neighbors for taking your Midnight without his approval first. His pride would not let him bend on this matter, even to his stepson."

Maria spoke the truth. He shouldn't borrow a horse without asking. Taking Midnight was different—all the ranch hands knew that horse belonged to Michael. Yet his dear, vicious stepfather already set the stage to label him a horse thief and send a posse after him if he took another…assuming Diego hadn't already. He paced the warming ground, searching for another solution.

He was out of ideas—and time.

Kit's ragamuffin image danced in Michael's mind, reminding him of Isabel's caustic words. "Maria, is it correct that Mother's belongings will be destroyed?"

"It is natural for a new bride to rid the house of memories of the first wife." She cleared her throat. "I overheard Señor Diego say to change whatever she wished, because he would be wealthier on his return. If Señorita Isabel discards your dear mother's clothes and such, she has his permission."

"Then she won't mind if I rescue a few itcms." Renewed anger swept through him.

"That bitch won't notice anything missing. What's left is junk to her. She already ransacked the chests for jewelry, including that old emerald ring your mother prized."

"Why am I not shocked?" Now selling Mother's trinkets in return for another run-down mule wasn't an option.

Maria's sympathetic eyes filled with wile. "Go ahead, take what you want. I won't tell anyone. Señor Diego asked me to store the chests in your old room. Are you hungry?" She patted his cheek. "I will put fresh food in your saddlebags."

"Thanks, Maria." Michael swept her into a strong clasp and bestowed an affectionate kiss. Spinning on his heel, he re-entered the house. Getting Kit appropriate clothes was secondary, yet all he could provide. He failed at his end of the bargain—again.

Perhaps Diego was right. Maybe he was a loser.

Because instead of Diego deferring to the courts and loaning him a horse, as ordinary courtesy and long decades of tradition dictated, he still fought Michael for the land. How stupid was he for coming here in the first place? He should be at his ranch already, working it before Diego arrived. Wouldn't the document given to Michael by the San Francisco court be enough to halt whatever plans Diego had for the land? Perhaps it was not as clear-cut as the judge indicated.

Michael walked into the empty parlor and rescued the heavy *Don Quixote* from the bookshelf. His children, if he ever had any, would enjoy its story, too. Tucking it under his arm, he ascended the stairs two at a time and entered his childhood room. He threw open the lids of his mother's red leather trunks and dug into the finery. Essence of camphor wood wafted through the room.

His palms brushed the luxuriant cloth of his mother's riding outfit. He tugged, spilling clothes onto the floor, choosing black suede gaucho pants with bolero-style jacket, ruffled blouse for underneath, and a pair of sturdy gloves. Another trunk yielded a pair of heeled boots and a suitable black hat, studded with silver buttons and a snug leather tie for the fastest runs. He scrunched his brow and considered his mother's body height and weight to Kit's. They should fit.

Stuffing the tumbled clothes into the trunks, a scrap of green the exact shade of Kit's eyes caught his attention. He unearthed a dress from the surrounding finery. Cream-colored silk trimmed in emerald, he recalled Mother wearing it while sewing in late afternoons as Father schooled him. Given Kit's measly possessions and upcoming birthday, he could offer this as consolation if he left her in pursuit of Diego. He scrounged among the pile of lingerie for an appropriate set of undergarments—he hoped. Bundling the clothes and book into a discarded blanket and fashioning a tight knot, he walked from the house, swearing never to return.

CHAPTER 15

Kit slanted her hat against the morning glare and stepped into the barn from the dusty lane leading to the house. She wished she could be at Michael's side while he humbled himself to his despicable stepfather on her behalf, not simply count the passing minutes. Twice now, he saved her life. Or was it three times?

She hated being helpless. It was her problem, not Michael's to solve. Protecting her on the trail was one deal. Finding her a mount to get to her destination—something entirely different. If only Father Angelo's stubborn mule hadn't gotten away. She had starved many a night in order to keep him fed and ready to take her to Gold Country. To have him run from her when she needed him most—well, this might be Father Angelo's vengeance from his grave. Shivering at the thought, she sent a silent prayer heavenward to Mama.

Amid the nickering of horses, male jeers drifted from a distant stall. Curious, she slid her hat off and crept near, keeping to the shadows. Straw motes danced in the air, and she tucked her lips inward, repressing a sneeze.

"We'll be lucky to keep our jobs once these Señor Diego combines our ranch with the de La Cruz's ranch." The rough male grumble was in Spanish. "That new lady will run affairs her way because she owns lots more land than the boss."

Thankful for Papa's tutoring and insistence she become fluent in Spanish to fit in with the native Californios, too, Kit followed the fast-paced speech patterns.

Other voices muttered agreement. Peeking over the stall barrier, she found three men wearing wicked-looking spurs sitting on hay bales, huddled over fisted cards in the dim light. A heap of silver coins sparkled on another bale set between them.

"Hey, Pedro, how about betting that speedy mustang you won last Saturday against what I just got dealt? You haven't even ridden her yet." Kit's pulse quickened at the old man's goad. They might bet horseflesh. Dare she join in? Or would they refuse her as a woman?

"I rode her this morning, and she's fine. Shut up for once and let me think, Benito." The young speaker must be Pedro, Kit concluded. She shifted to her right and raised her head.

The players slouched along the walls, legs crossed identically at the ankles. Based on the puny stack of coins in front of Pedro, he was having a run of bad luck. Old Benito watched Pedro like a hawk eying its next meal, waiting for the precise second to attack. The other kept his back to her.

"I'll call with my horse." Pedro fanned his cards face open on the hay. "Let's see who has the better hand, you or Carlos or me."

Benito tossed his cards into the pile. "I thought you were bluffing. Too bad. I was looking forward to mounting that fine mare as much as that latest gal at the cantina."

Chuckling, Carlos gathered the cards and shuffled them. Benito fingered his remaining coins, and a gloating Pedro raked the winnings from the center.

Could she buy it from Pedro? Doubtful. She didn't have enough money to match the amount in the pot, nor his inflated opinion of himself. She had experience with boastful young men at Bonita's. He'd probably demand a too-high price to justify his pride in winning the mustang last week.

Kit dropped into the straw and scowled at the black grime coating her barely protruding nails. Who could even liken her to a woman in these clothes, anyway?

Maybe no one.

With a grimace and a prayer, she scooped up a fistful of dried muck and scrubbed it over her face and neck. She sprinkled gray powder over her braid, and massaged dirt over her hands up to her wrists. Flicking off the excess, she stared at the false wrinkles, wondering if they would fool these men.

She had nothing to lose by trying.

Kit tilted the cone hat over her nose. Slumping forward to minimize her breasts in the boxy clothes, she shuffled with an old man's gait into the light streaming through the barn door.

"Hello." She pitched her voice low and hoarse, and interjected a Chinese accent into her English words. "Play poker, yes?"

Surprise flickered over the rancheros' features.

"Where did you come from?" Pedro asked in English. His companions mumbled to each other in unintelligible Spanish.

"San Francisco, with young master." Kit maintained her subservient posture.

"What's Miguel doing here?" Benito asked. "Señor Diego kicked him out on his ass last week, and sure was pissed he took that fine stallion with him."

Kit jammed her fists into the wide jacket sleeves and crossed her fingers, pretending not to understand Benito's comments.

"Let's see your money, old timer." Pedro lifted his hand. A fountain of coins trickled to the floor into a heap.

She dug out her pouch containing her few gold and silver pieces, and held it waist high. "Enough?" Thank goodness these rancheros couldn't see her face. Without a doubt, they'd detect her uneasiness of losing all she owned. If Papa didn't meet her at the mine, she would have no choice except surviving as a penniless whore. But if she didn't get a mount, she'd miss her rendezvous with Papa. Michael's uncertainty of his chance of success hadn't been lost on her this morning. This could be her only way.

The men scooted apart, metal spurs rattling. Kit dragged another hay bale near the circle and sat in the shadows, tucking her coin bag between her legs. Benito flicked cards to each of them in turn. Tucking her chin, Kit picked hers up. She inhaled deeply in order to settle her nerves, and fought the urge to cough. These rancheros needed a bath—and soon.

She studied her cards, recollecting nights outwitting bored Chinese railroad workers gambling away their pitiful earnings. Never had she played for stakes this high.

Kit pitched in coins, matching the gamblers to prove she knew the game, while disguising the full extent of her skill. They seemed content to take her wagers and ignore her otherwise. Her losses deepened, her savings split between the other three players. She fought the growing knot in her stomach and kept betting. She had to create the illusion she was easy prey.

The distracting noise of a carriage rattling down the lane joined the warm breeze floating into the barn. Kit caught a glimpse of two young women dressed in colorful finery, one holding the reins of trotting horses.

"He is quite impudent if he thinks merely by showing up I will reconsider marrying him." The woman's haughty voice grated on Kit's nerves. "He barely restrained from kissing me. Fortunately, my good breeding kept him from taking advantage of me in his father's house."

Carlos snickered. "That so-called lady Isabel wouldn't know good breeding if it bit her in the ass."

Kit suppressed a giggle. She couldn't let on she understood Spanish—yet.

"Yeah," Pedro said. "I've seen her throw a temper tantrum that would shame a shrew, and she thinks it's a sign of good breeding."

"All Señor Salazar cares about is that Señorita Isabel acts the part for the fancy politicos from Sacramento." Benito ruffled his cards and chucked them into the center. "He cussed and swore when they moved the state capital from San Jose. He had set up his old Mexican government friends to help him here, like they used to before the war."

"It'll cost him his weight in gold to keep her in the style she fancies. Good thing he's rich." Carlos dealt the next set of cards.

"Rich in greed, not gold," Benito said. "Those new politicians pay him for delivering money or power. Why, I heard he switched overnight from being against slavery to backing it because some rich landowner traded him a favor."

Kit sobered up fast. What kind of man was Michael opposing on her behalf? She prayed his conversation went easily, because if she lost here—

"He's a fair man, Benito," Pedro said.

"Only if he gets the best of the deal, you young fool," Benito said. "You'd better remember that if you want to keep your job. Let's play."

Looking daggers at Benito, Pedro threw his cards into the center facedown. "I'll quit while I'm ahead."

Kit panicked. She had to keep Pedro in the game—he owned the horse.

"Not good enough, eh?" She injected as much ridicule as she could muster through her dry mouth.

"Guess not," Carlos agreed, and Benito chuckled.

"I'm the cleverest poker player this side of San Jose." Pedro picked up his cards and flipped his ante into the pot.

Each round netted an increasing pile of coins in front of Kit. Her chance will come when she had a winning hand and Pedro sweated a poor one.

In turn, she doled out fresh cards and picked hers up. Her heart beat faster.

Now.

She glanced under her lashes at Pedro. He glowered at his deal.

"Bet big, huh?" Kit pushed her entire amount into the pot. Benito and Carlos threw in their cards. She hoped she read Pedro correctly, and he would bluff to justify his boast.

"I'll throw in a purty mustang that might fit your skinny old body." Pedro shoved his few coins into the center.

"Saddle, too?" she asked.

"Yeah, all in. Let's see those cards of yours, Chinaman." With a flourish, Pedro cast a pair of aces on top of the coins.

Relieved, she laid down each card. Four nines. Benito and Carlos howled and clapped their hands.

"Dammit!" Pedro leapt to his feet. "I think you cheated when you dealt."

"No cheat. Won fair." Rising, Kit kept her head and voice low. "Where is horse, please?" She didn't dare gloat. Not yet. Nor will she let this bully intimidate her, not after winning precisely what she needed without Michael compromising his integrity.

"You cheated." Pedro took a menacing step toward her. His glance lingered on the piled coins.

Kit lifted her chin and frowned at him. Pushing the hat to her shoulders, she stood ramrod straight, and raised her voice to her normal modulations.

"I never cheated at cards, and I never will," she said in easy Spanish. "And it is certain this woman never dishonors a bet, unlike some men. I won playing a fair game."

"Fair? You're a lying, cheating girl!" Pedro yelled.

She swept the coins into her bag. "Where is my horse?"

"Tied up over there." Benito pointed his thumb to the left, grinning from ear to ear. "You're right. You won. Pedro's just embarrassed a gal beat him, and a smart Chinese one at that. He'll be the butt of jokes at the cantina tonight—I sure won't keep this game a secret."

Pedro glared at Benito. He advanced on Kit, a growl rumbling in his chest. He shot out his rough hand, grasped the bulging coin bag, and tugged.

"I wouldn't do that if I were you." Silhouetted in golden light pouring through the open barn door, Michael held his rifle at the ready. His cold tone removed any doubt he was dead serious.

Pedro withdrew his empty fingers in exaggerated motion, spreading his arms wide. "Hey, Miguel, mi amigo. Everything is fine here. If this female belongs to you, no problem. You should know she cheats."

Michael cocked his rifle. The snap interrupted the horses' munching and scattered chickens. "That's not what I heard, and I think your fellow poker players will agree. Isn't that true, amigos?"

Smirking, they nodded and elbowed Pedro's ribs from each side.

"Kit, let's go," Michael said, his manner unfathomable.

She tucked the money into her bundle and smiled sweetly at the rancheros. "It was an entertaining poker game. Maybe we'll have a re-match someday." She scurried from the barn and rounded the corner. Spying the mustang tied to the fence, Kit stopped short. What a beauty!

Michael backed through the barn door and joined her, his rifle still targeted at the men. "Admire her later. Let's ride out before they change their minds and decide that a girl who deceives them into playing poker really is a cheater." Tucking his rifle under his arm, he boosted her into the tooled saddle and adjusted the stirrup with efficient motions.

Pedro, red-faced and cursing, broke free of Benito's hold and charged. Michael swung his rifle up and pointed it directly at the ranchero's chest. Pedro halted mid-stride.

Michael leapt on Midnight and kicked the horse into a full gallop. Kit followed, enjoying the feel of a horse obeying her commands again. They thundered down the lane and onto the road, turning north toward a notch in the eastern foothills and Gold Country…at last.

CHAPTER 16

Feeling like outracing the devil himself, Michael urged Midnight into the gap. His horse soon tired climbing even the easier slope at such high speed. Michael pressed on, slowing to a trot only after Midnight's sides heaved with labored breaths. Glancing over his shoulder, he noted Kit's mount kept up despite the pace. He would rather not answer tough questions about why he was in such a blessed hurry. Her poker skills unsettled him in ways he couldn't yet name.

Michael squinted in the noonday sun, and spotted a running creek edged with lush grass. An eagle's cry taunted him with its magnificent freedom. He wished he had its ability simply to fly over the hills and beat Diego to Gold Country in a few hours, not days. Unfortunately, he had no wings, and they needed rest.

Removing Midnight's saddle, he wiped sweaty foam from the stallion's neck and turned him loose at the stream. He flapped open the blanket and dumped Maria's packages onto it.

Kit pulled up short, dismounted, and ran to the bushes. Michael led the mare next to Midnight and rubbed down the compact mustang, smoothing her sturdy legs and mottled coat with approval.

Returning to the clearing, Kit's eyes rounded at the piles of food. "Where did you get this?" She picked up a fragrant tortilla, tore a piece off and stuffed it into her mouth.

"I have a few friends left at the ranch." Michael smiled at the crumbs clinging to her lips. "Maria, the cook, prepared this food."

"Is she the only friend you saw?"

His guard flew up at the too-innocent question. "Yes."

"What did your stepfather say?"

He ripped off a hunk of cheese with his teeth, feeling downright savage. The less he told her, the better.

"Diego wasn't home. I discovered he is marrying my ex-fiancée in a month. Guess she'll marry whoever owned the ranch. Good riddance." He tamped down haunting feelings of betrayal. Isabel belonged to his wretched past, not his bright future. Forget her.

"It's fortunate I stumbled onto that poker game," Kit said, her expression full of pride.

"What on earth were you thinking? You might have gotten yourself killed, or worse." His raised voice matched his growing irritation.

"I thought if I won a horse, you wouldn't have to go begging to your stepfather on my behalf."

"Those were a bunch of tough rancheros you gambled your life on."

She flinched, but met his gaze head-on. "Guess they didn't know the Chinese love betting. I grew up playing poker and figured it was worth the risk. In fact, I think I'll name the mustang Lucky."

"What did you use as stakes?" Out of necessity, Kit might have taken matters into her hands by promising the use of her sole asset—her body. Identical to Mother.

She reached into her bundle and extracted a jumble of loose coins. "Everything I have. If gambling gets me to Papa without you having to compromise your values, it was worth the wager."

Michael stared at the money, impressed and bothered by her courage. She shouldered a great risk to protect his pride, while he avoided spending a single penny of his savings for her horse. He had earmarked that capital to develop his land and keep him fed. He wouldn't lay it down in winner-take-all poker if it jeopardized his dream. Was he spineless? Or no better than Pedro, begrudging a woman outdoing him because she dared?

Yet Kit more than dared. She won. Not as a careless girl, but as a driven young woman. Grudging respect warred with chafing at her myriad contradictions. Maybe her decisions would stop surprising him if he could just forget her time at the whorehouse.

"Let's add to your provisions." He reached into the blanket stuffed with his mother's clothes. Avoiding the dress and book, he untangled the riding outfit piece by piece and placed it next to Kit.

Her jaw dropped on a squeaky gasp. "Are these for me?"

"They'd be a mite snug on me, don't you think?"

She stroked the gaucho pants as if they were fashioned of the finest material. Lifting the fabric, she rubbed it along her cheek. "Thank you. I've never seen such beautiful clothes. Are these Maria's?"

Laughter burst free. "It would take at least four of these outfits to cover Maria's body," Michael said. "These belonged to my mother."

"Oh, then I'll return them to you once I meet up with Papa."

"No, these are for you. My mother has no use for them anymore. Nor do I."

"Not for a future wife?" She picked up the bolero hat and spun it. Silver studs reflected the brilliant sunshine.

"No wife in the future. No woman in her right mind would marry me until my ranch and livelihood are secure. That won't be for years to come." Isabel's callous rejection still rung in his ears.

Kit bit her lip. With a sigh, she scooped up the clothes and disappeared into the bushes. Michael stretched flat and tilted his hat against the mid-summer sun's daunting heat.

Sensing Kit return, Michael half-opened his eyes and ogled her transformation. His mother's clothes fit as if sewn for her by the world's most talented seamstress. Set at a rakish slant, the hat accentuated her high cheekbones and emerald irises. Its rough cord slithered along her throat like a gentle rein. She left the blouse unbuttoned to her collarbone, the ruffles emphasizing the small mounds of her breasts. The jacket dangled from her fingers.

She raised her arms and revolved in a slow circle. Unlike the baggy and shapeless coolie pants, these form-fitting trousers emphasized the smooth arc of her hips and thighs, flowing gracefully to below her knees. The riding boots cupped her calves' long, slender muscles.

"They're perfect. Thank you," Kit said with a happy smile.

"You'd pass for a Mexican señorita in that outfit. Tell me if you still like them after you've ridden for a day. That leather may take getting used to."

"Oh, no, I doubt it." Kit stroked the suede material encasing her legs.

Her graceful, lithe body moved with the unconsciousness of a kitten, and Michael imagined what it would be like petting that suppleness. Losing patience with his improper fancies, he eased to his feet.

"Let's saddle the horses and get going. We'll reach the main road to Gold Country by nightfall, and then you take the lead." He captured her gaze, alert for signs of hesitation. "You got additional surprises to spring on me? Details you've neglected to share regarding your supposed guiding talents?"

"I'm ready to lead," Kit said. "Let's stop before sundown so I can study your records and plot the safest route."

Michael tipped his hat up, measuring the confidence in her words. "I'll show you my papers tonight."

CHAPTER 17

By mid-afternoon sweat poured off her body. Kit rolled her shirtsleeves above her elbows and wove her hair into a knot under the perky hat. She heard a hawk's scream floating on the miles-away ocean breeze. Imitating his freedom, she stretched her arms wide and flapped as the hawk dove toward the fertile valley below.

"Seems hard to believe we were shivering two mornings ago, doesn't it?" Michael stripped off his shirt and stuffed it into his saddlebag.

"Leaving that cold fog is my favorite memory of San Francisco, and that's while we're baking in this heat. Come winter, those distant hills can be covered in snow."

"I'd try to imagine a touch of snow. It may be the only means to cool off for a few hours." He kicked Midnight into a gallop, controlling his brawny stallion with easy capability. Kit urged Lucky to match his pace, engrossed in turbulent thoughts.

What a perplexing man! She dismissed that woman's intimation that Michael swooned at her feet. He could never be interested in someone as self-centered as Isabel was—at least not the man he is currently. Maybe as a youth, with no better role model than his stepfather, Michael believed marrying an acceptable beauty was the correct step in becoming a man and entering San Jose's cliquish society. Now he seemed to prefer a no-nonsense wife working the land by his side, and certainly not being coddled.

She considered her upcoming future at Kit's Mine. She had vague recollections of a remote valley tucked between hills. Life will be hard and lonely, even with Papa. Before, other Chinese miners lived nearby, alleviating some of their isolation. Those men scattered throughout the West, unlikely to be mining while the current law taxed every penny they earned. And if there was no gold left in Kit's Mine, she needed to focus on frugality and survival, not illusions. The extra coins she won at poker wouldn't last forever.

Kit sighed. She didn't have any feasible prospects beyond tunneling for gold. Perhaps Michael had it right—grab opportunities when she could. She will guard her savings from here on out—she might need them for a very long time. No further gambling, she pledged, squeezing her eyelids shut and sealing that promise into her memory.

Lucky pulled up short, snorting. Kit fluttered her lids open.

"Kitten?" Michael had maneuvered Midnight directly into their path. He caught Lucky's halter and tugged her to his side. "Is something wrong?"

Confused by the endearing nickname, she gazed into his troubled eyes, framed by curly lashes.

"Wh-why do you think anything is wrong?" Warmth crept into her cheeks.

"Because you looked so pained, I figured either your new clothes rubbed you raw or you had to hustle to the bushes."

Embarrassed, Kit jutted her chin. He wasn't far from the truth in either case. Nonetheless, the sacred promise to herself couldn't possibly be of interest to him.

"Thank you for your concern. I'm fine." She spied a worn path cutting through the gap in the undulating terrain. "Is this the beginning of the trail to Gold Country? Are we there?"

"Yes, though I hope you know better than I exactly where it leads." He scanned their back trail and steered Midnight toward the stream. "The river bends here, and it's a good place to stop. Let's set up camp and go over our plans for tomorrow."

They entered a U-shaped glade, the riverbed snaking around low hanging willow trees. Dismounting, they removed the gear and cared for the horses, combing them to a shiny gloss. Once the horses ate and drank their fill, he tethered them, picked up his blanket, and snapped it open onto the flat ground.

Kit threw a longing glance at the tempting river. "Is any of Maria's food left?"

"Yes, plenty for dinner and then some, unless you're going to eat as much as those horses did."

"Since we don't have to cook, I'll bathe and wash my old clothes first. I won't be long." She grasped her bag and set off toward the riverbank.

CHAPTER 18

Michael hesitated, scratching the hair on his chest as Kit withdrew into the scrub lining the distinct game trail. The branches over the swift-moving river cast long shadows, the trees' wind-dance obscuring and revealing perilous whirlpools. She didn't expect his protection every minute, especially while bathing. Or did she?

He cursed under his breath. This time, he'd take his role as her defender for their journey seriously, and perform it thoroughly. Not like last night. Living through gut-wrenching terror once was quite enough. He grabbed his rifle and set off on a slight trajectory to her course, hiding behind a concealed line of bushes and veering toward the angled sun.

The noise of splashing water drifted toward him on warm air drafts. Peals of laughter and moans of contentment teased his senses, yet shadows from overhanging sycamores barred his view. He crept closer to the river, wondering how anyone got that much enjoyment from doing laundry.

Then he understood.

Kit had donned her old clothes and stepped into a protected cove. Her tattered blue jacket hung over her shoulders, gaping wide open. Golden light played over her features, setting her eyes ablaze and turning her flesh as bright as a polished nugget.

She lathered up the clothes. Bubbles ran down her length and she giggled. Her musical tones rang in harmonic counterpoint to the river's hisses and roars. She arched, dipping her hair into the pounding cascade.

A groan rumbled low in his chest, but he smothered it. He didn't dare alert her to his presence. Not yet.

She massaged soap into her heavy tresses, appearing blissful. Tilting sideways, she grasped an overhanging branch from a willow and hung fast, a picture of languid relaxation. The strong eddy bounced and parted her floating legs in a watery dance. Foam slid from her head, and gilded her torso and hips in an intimate caress.

Only strength of will kept him on dry land.

Gaze intent on her figure, he removed his boots and socks. In case she got into trouble, he convinced himself. He stashed his knife inside a boot and eased to the waterside.

She stood, and picked her way among the mossy rocks. Wet garments outlined every inch of her slim curves. Lucid thought fled Michael's mind.

Kit's foot skidded. Muscles clenching, he held his breath. She stretched for a nearby branch, inches from her reach. Teetering crazily on a stone, she wrung water from her clothes and jumped. Her fingers encircled the slender bough.

The brittle limb cracked and snapped off. She fell backward with a sharp cry, arms revolving like a windmill in splashing futility. The swift flow whisked her downstream.

Michael leapt from his hiding place and plunged into the river. She bobbed up for air and her feet swept past him. He captured her wrist. She jerked, flailing her arm, pounding at his shoulders.

"Stop hitting me or you'll drown both of us!" he shouted.

She went limp in immediate obedience. Caught unaware, he staggered and lost his precarious balance. Careening to the side, they sunk underwater. He snaked his arm around her waist and held her fast against the relentless current, bare toes searching for purchase among sharp rocks. Pushing upward, he gulped a lungful of air and scrabbled toward the bank.

Kit coughed and wheezed, bent double. She stumbled, tangling his legs. Smothering curses, he picked her up and held her high on his chest above the lapping rush. With slow, deliberate steps, he carried her to the dry embankment.

She stared into his face scant inches away, arms wrapped in a stranglehold around his neck. Michael didn't mind. Turning in the direction of camp, he repositioned his grip and tilted her body to avoid sharp branches tearing at their dripping clothes.

CHAPTER 19

Coordinating with each subtle shift of Michael's bulk through the undergrowth, Kit nestled her head on his shoulder and let her mind drift.

Obviously, she had underestimated the challenge of traveling alone to Gold Country. A mountain lion chose her for dinner, and she couldn't even take a bath or wash her clothes without facing danger. She thought her parents taught her a breadth of survival techniques. Their lessons only guarded her from civilization's menaces, not the rigors of the wild.

Michael had rescued her again without a thought to his peril, instead of letting her fend for herself. Such earnestness stupefied her. Especially since he'd wanted to shunt her off to a mission at the beginning of their trek. And seemed quite upset with her gambling streak.

For some reason, he hid his wide streak of gallantry from the world, especially after Isabel's callousness. Easier to retreat and become detached than risk a broken heart. Was she any better? She'd let Father Angelo's vulgar advances rule her choices for the past year. If fate threw Michael in her path in San Francisco and gave her a chance to rely on someone else for her welfare, she should cooperate without complaint. Especially with this man. He'd proven his trustworthiness many times over.

Kit peeked at his stern profile. Water rivulets trailed creases from his hairline along his lean cheeks. His jaw muscle ticked in quick rhythm. His full lips glistened, tempting her to run her thumb across them. Trailing fingers along his nape, she dared tugging the springy curls. His grip strengthened on her thighs, and an unexpected fever warmed her from her toes to her hairline.

They reached the campsite and he stopped, fading skylight hiding his expression. He dipped his head, one inch at a time. She smiled, meeting him halfway, happy to grace him with the thank you salute he earned. His mouth grazed hers. She absorbed his presence, craving more.

Michael separated, and lowered the arm holding her legs to his side. Her hips slid along his wet torso, and her feet touched earth.

"I know I'm supposed to protect you, but will you require rescuing every day, Kitten?" His voice was gentle, teasing. He stroked a tendril of damp hair from her cheek.

She blinked and met his gaze, mesmerized into muteness.

"If so, we may have to cut another deal for trading favors…and kisses." He rubbed his thumb across her lips.

Kit stiffened and pulled away. Will this thickheaded man ever believe her? "I told you—I'm not a prostitute, and you cannot trade for my favors! Keep any ideas of a new deal to yourself."

"That's not what I meant." Matching her voice in ferocity, Michael's hands clenched and unclenched at his sides. "You keep getting into trouble doing stupid things, and you know it."

"I was fine before you jumped in to rescue me. I was not stupid." Bewildered by his callous words, she already regretted her body's treachery.

"Oh, really? How far would you have drifted before you got ashore?"

"Not far, and I'm perfectly capable of walking to camp alone," she said.

"Barefoot? Looking no better than an abandoned Chinese camp whore in those clothes?"

"I'm not a whore! Don't you listen to me?" She was a fool for expecting anything different from a man. "Besides, who's around to see?"

"Besides me, you mean?" Michael ran a sardonic gaze the entire length of her body.

Too late, Kit noticed the clinging clothes outlining her form. Maybe she did resemble a whore. And just behaved like one with her ardent kiss.

CHAPTER 20

Michael allowed his anger free rein.

"Who's around to see you?" he asked. "Let's see. Disillusioned miners who lost everything or angry squatters kicked off their claims. Not to mention run-of-the-mill no-goods inventing trouble." His gut churned at her inexperience. "We're on a major trail, leading into a wilderness that attracts all kinds of troublemakers. I guarantee it."

"They'd ignore me," Kit said. "Everyone else does."

"How can you be that stupid? Any other man will use your body until he gets to San Francisco. He'll sell you for a quick dollar at the auction to Bonita or her kind, and then congratulate himself on a profitable and enjoyable few days."

"You said I looked identical to a señorita, not a Chinese slave girl." Her voice quavered, belying her mulish protest.

Michael flicked her tattered jacket. "Not in these coolie garments. Whether you're an escaped Chinese slave or a woman unescorted, you're victim to whatever man fancies you. You think you're in control of the situation, but you're not. Don't you remember Pedro turned on you when he thought he could grab your winnings? The world is full of Father Angelos. Do you think you'll keep a single-minded man off you because you're a year older?"

Kit tossed soggy hair over her shoulder and remained silent. Uncertainty flickered across her face.

Disgusted, he retraced his steps for their clothes. She didn't realize the significance of being a young woman alone without the protection of her family. They flaunted society's conventions by journeying unchaperoned. He needed better tactics to protect her from fellow travelers. She was oblivious to danger until it was too late.

And he was the most dangerous man to her now.

He hadn't anticipated this much difficulty keeping his attraction in check. His chivalry wasn't as ingrained as he credited. And she might be speaking the truth about her innocence. In which case he owed her protection, not seduction.

Reaching his socks and boots, he jammed them on, ignoring the sharp pains from multiple cuts on his soles. He planned going without a woman for years anyway, might as well grow used to it.

Shouldering his rifle, he marched into camp, ready for verbal sparring.

Lavender-hued twilight backlit Kit, her face buried in her palms. Michael swore and dashed into the clearing. Drawing closer, he spotted tears slipping between her fingers. He squatted by her crumpled form and tilted her head up with his thumb. Red, swollen eyes met his. Her thick lashes clumped together, and her usually firm chin trembled.

Queasiness knotted Michael's empty stomach. He didn't mean to upset her, merely teach her reality. She scared him to death. Except she was right—it was her decision when or if she required assistance. He should protect her simply when she asked, despite the limitations of her womanhood.

He clasped his hands between his knees, confused by this latest vulnerability. Whatever he said obviously broke her indomitable spirit.

Probably likening her to a whore.

He had to let that go. She cooperated every time, at his every request. And more. She even got a mount by herself.

Disgusted with his pigheadedness, he sat cross-legged and leaned his elbows on his knees. If she needed bolstering, he'd provide it.

"I'm sorry," she said in a broken whisper. "I didn't mean to cry. It's just once I left San Francisco and its prejudices, I thought I could be a person—not only a Chinese, not only a woman. Simply a person with the same rights as anyone else in America to travel to and live free on land I possess. I guess I was foolish to believe that outside San Francisco I would be safe."

Cursing under his breath for losing control, he caressed away her tear. "I'm sorry I forced myself on you. I acted no better than that priest who raped you, didn't I?"

CHAPTER 21

Rape? Kit popped her eyes open.

"No, you don't understand. That's not what happened," she said. He thought Father Angelo had taken her virginity! No wonder Michael believed she became a whore. Few other choices existed for young women, especially Undesirables.

"Besides, you didn't force yourself," she added. A flood of remembered sensations washed away the rest of her explanation—his arms secure around her, his lips beguiling, touching hers.

"That's still no excuse." Remorse crinkled his forehead. "If it helps, I've never known anyone who sought land ownership as much as you who didn't succeed."

"You really think so?"

"I learned a bit about the law fighting for my land. Let's see. You're a natural born American. Therefore, although you're a woman, in California you're allowed to own property."

"Supposedly," Kit muttered.

"As long as you follow the guidelines regarding settling on your property, work it, pay the taxes and file the claim on time, it's yours."

A tiny bit of hope took root at his encouragement.

"Why does this mean so much to you?" Michael asked.

"Since I was a child, I never had a place to call home," she said. "A place to return to, where I kept my personal belongings safe and secure. Where I had a predictable roof over my head, where I felt I belonged. Where my family had roots."

Kit gazed at the darkening hills, blended stripes of blue to violet coloring the sky above the lingering golden rays. "I guess I'm more like Papa than Mama," she said. "No one figured she would stowaway on the last voyage her father captained to China. A young woman with wanderlust? Unthinkable, is how Mama described it."

"You seem to have inherited her daring, at least."

"Yes, I guess I have," Kit said with a wistful smile. "When she met Papa in Hong Kong at the Jesuit church, they fell in love, and asked my grandfather to marry him. That was the first time they encountered such deep prejudice," she added. "Mama saw beyond Papa's features to the intelligent, caring man he is. Her father couldn't."

"Why did they choose to come to California?"

"Papa knew many ambitious Chinese had already come here, seeking to make their fortune." She shrugged, remembering the light in Papa's eyes when he recounted his past dreams, so many years ago. "It seemed like a perfect solution—bountiful land, a mountain of gold, a society forming of newcomers like them. So they found a sympathetic ship captain who agreed to marry them immediately, and headed for San Francisco."

"I guess that they didn't quite find the utopia they expected," Michael commented.

"Sadly, no one would help them. Mama was shocked at the discrimination she faced for marrying Papa. After all, California was part of America, and she'd been raised on the promise of equality for all."

"So was I, as were other young Californios," Michael said.

Kit tilted her head, considering the bigotry he faced. "Perhaps they were biased because so many didn't speak English?"

"A lot of miners arrived from all over the world, and were accepted," Michael said, bitterness coloring his tones. "No, it was because of the color of our skin—and the fact that Easterners couldn't just claim the best land, like they did in other territories. That rankled them, and they retaliated."

"Well, the way Mama and Papa were treated in San Francisco early on destroyed their aspirations." She sighed. "Since they didn't have family or friends to rely on, they created their home in a tent, on the move, always alert for danger."

He frowned. "Yet somehow they ended up with Kit's Mine, correct?"

"Yes, we lived there for a few years." That swathe of solitary land was an ideal they clung to during their later privation. A fairytale place they recounted to their daughter as a life they could have led, but never did.

"You told me earlier your father couldn't claim it," he reminded her. "So you want to lay title to it now as his American daughter? Dig it out as a miner? That's a lot of hard work for a woman, even one as strong-minded as you are! Why would you pursue such a goal?"

She felt odd sharing her most secret dream with Michael. Not a soul knew. Not one person ever cared. "You cannot relate—you always had the ranch."

"Try me." Michael picked up her right hand and stroked the palm, his easygoing touch reassuring. He warmed it between his, searching her face with intentness.

"I want a chance—just a single chance—to work for myself and succeed by doing my best. I have to own my property, so a landlord or employer or the government cannot take it from me by force, or by edict, or by an awful law targeting me or my family." She paused, searching for the precise words.

"There was a book Papa read every day for inspiration. There was one line it he loved, and I memorized it. *'I was born free, and that I might live in freedom I chose the solitude of the fields.'*"

"That's from *Don Quixote*! How did your father know of a book written by a Spaniard?"

"I guess because Spanish missionaries educated him. I'm glad you know it in such detail, too." Kit recalled her whispered response to Mama on her deathbed, her promise to resurrect Mama's dream of a home, and the addition of her private quest.

"I crave true freedom and working among people I respect," she said. "I thought the modern laws of California and America would protect me and give me that opportunity. Is that such a far-fetched possibility, or must I choose solitude, too?"

Her somber question drifted into the night.

"No matter the good intentions, the laws in this state don't work," he said. "They've created a lot of chaos and grabbing, with the strongest man winning."

"And what happens to women?"

He interlinked her fingers with his. "Usually women win less than men. I've seen it work through marriage, though Mother's experience was horrendous."

Tears welled up. She brushed them aside with a quaking breath. "There's a first time for everything. I'm willing to fight for it."

"I'm counting on that, because I'm fighting for my dreams, too. We'll be partners in this crusade for freedom. New deal?"

"All right, partner. Deal." Kit returned the hearty shake, ignoring the spark in his eyes.

He winked. "Hungry yet?"

"Starving. I guess my short bath took longer than I expected."

"You're never boring, that's for sure, Kitten. It's too dark to study the map tonight. Let's enjoy a relaxing meal." He unearthed the remaining food and Kit spread it in neat piles between them.

Stretching back, he eased his boots off. Michael's wince and bloody socks captured Kit's attention. She stifled her offer of help, uncertain if he would consider that yet another stupid action, and unwilling to jeopardize their truce.

CHAPTER 22

Uncomfortable under her scrutiny, Michael shifted upright. He tore his gaze from her still-damp top, filched the last piece of meat, and bit off a plug.

Her poignant words and wistful demeanor haunted him. Her dilemma wedged his heart into a tight ball, demanding he remedy her plight. She expressed his own desires so succinctly, almost as if her deepest thoughts melded with his.

Michael remembered the rest of the novel's passage. *'My taste is for freedom...'* Father had drilled Michael in detail on that fundamental reason behind Mexico's declaration of independence from Spain, and lauded America's Constitution as the noblest framework to ensure freedom for all its citizens. Undoubtedly, Father would be outraged at the poor treatment of the Spanish and Mexicans, as well as Chinese.

He ignored his strangled emotions clawing for liberty. "Do you think fighting your whole lifetime is worth it? What about your father, or babies?"

"Life isn't only parents or children. There is satisfaction in achievement. Papa will surely understand."

Michael considered Kit's perspective. "After Father died, my family essentially perished. I can't think of anything more beneficial than creating a large one of my own eventually."

"Then why are you going to the middle of nowhere without such a prospect?" Kit asked. "Why didn't you marry Isabel?"

"Because Isabel doesn't know beans about creating a real family." He didn't dare confess the truth. Isabel's harsh rejection drove him into self-imposed seclusion where he licked his wounds. Once there, he couldn't pull himself free from that rut.

"If I ever marry, we'll plant joint roots from scratch," he continued. "I'll find a strong woman who has no family, either. No one to rely on or to run to once it gets tough. Someone who'll protect our youngsters, not surrender. That won't be for years to come. And I have to resolve that far, far away from my stepfather."

"I used to think the safest method to win was to gather a lot of people and stand up in a group, like a big family," she said.

"Does that work?" Besides the fellowship of working alongside the rancheros in the dust and mud, Michael had minimal experience with the positive aspects of a large group. No brothers to tussle with, no sisters to tease. Only books and studies to comply with his parents' wishes.

She cupped her cheeks in her hands. "Not really. The more the Chinese banded together, the larger a target they became. Honestly, I think the way to succeed is without being noticed—at least for people like me."

"You're not so very different," he said. "Each of us comes from a unique background. Our values conflict at times. It's simply a matter of who's writing the rules today."

"It certainly isn't the Chinese!"

"It's not the Californios, either. When my parents married, being a Californio was a matter of pride, combining the finest of Spanish and Mexican. After thousands of white people settled from the East, our heritage became a matter of shame. My parents didn't change—the social norm did. And it will change again, I'm sure."

"For us?" Kit's tone was pensive.

"Perhaps not. Certainly, we don't have to blame ourselves for not being good enough for society. Just be good enough for yourself and whoever else you care for."

"Maybe." She sighed. The rising moonlight transformed her black hair into a sheening cascade of quicksilver. Stretching her arms, she yawned and smiled at him. "I'll stow the food if you see to the horses. I'm beat after all the riding today."

Michael scrambled up, relieved for the convenient excuse. Sharing his inner thoughts forged an emotional intimacy both tempting and foreign to him.

"Don't wait up," he said. "I'll check to see if we have neighbors for the night before turning in."

He hastened toward the horses and stalled by inspecting the reins and straps for weakness. Kit was incredibly smart. And profound. If she were a man, he would seek her counsel on a whole range of ideas. But she was a woman! He already compromised his leadership role, turning guidance over to her. No need to swallow additional pride.

He circled their camp several times, cursing and muttering. Exhausted, he approached from the woods and dropped to his knees beside Kit. She was sound asleep. He braced an arm on the blanket, leaning close, and frowned. Her clothing still felt damp, just the thing to catch a chill from the night air. He secured her in the blanket from top to bottom and laid beside her on his poncho. Turning onto his side, he tucked her into the curve of his body and relaxed more than he had in ages.

CHAPTER 23

The lonesome call of a mockingbird roused Kit. She disregarded the faint light, snuggling into the warmth behind her. She didn't remember falling asleep, only sitting on the blanket, waiting for Michael.

Fresh, cool air wafted against her cheeks. She parted her lips and inhaled. A heavy object weighed down her lungs. Startled fully awake, she realized Michael's arm encased her over the blanket, pinning her to his chest. His other arm served as her pillow.

Reassured by the rumbling cadence of his snores, she cataloged the novel sensations, breathing in shallow, imperceptible movements. Not budging an inch, she listened to the racket of the bird's urgent call for an answer, and contemplated what Michael divulged last night, whether he meant to or not.

He certainly was a confusing man—sweet one minute, evasive the next. He acted tough and uncaring, yet she saw his approachable side. Despite touting the virtues of bachelorhood, her intuition told her he craved a lifelong mate sooner rather than later. She was sure that greedy Isabel had convoluted his heart and mind.

Reluctantly, Kit acknowledged her surprising eagerness to uncoil them, to resurrect his demolished ego, to keep his fear of intimacy from dooming him to loneliness. He hadn't shared his goals, true. She suspected they would be ambitious, and ones he would achieve. Michael didn't do anything halfway.

Of course, she owed him the whole truth concerning what Father Angelo had and hadn't done to her. She never meant to suggest he raped her. If pity drove Michael's helpfulness, she would have none of it. Did she dare bring that topic up again? She still experienced recurrent nightmares, still recoiled from unexpected touches.

Except Michael's.

She hadn't asked for his comfort in the cool air. Yet even in sleep, her body recognized what he afforded, and rested beside his with easiness. She yearned to help him start his next life as unafraid.

Michael tightened his arm around her waist. He rolled onto his back, kicking his legs free from the tangled poncho. A peaceful sigh escaped him. He shifted Kit so her head rested on his broad shoulder and his arm encircled her. The heavy blanket wrapped her from neck to toe.

Lying motionless, she surveyed his outstretched body. One palm rested on his flat stomach. Calloused fingers twitched in his dreams, turning to strokes in perfect, sensuous rhythm.

Confused by a prickling, inner rush, Kit wiggled snake-like against his embrace. His arm constricted further. She glanced up, suspicious. Wide-open eyes and a mischievous smile greeted her.

"You scoundrel! Let me go." She tugged harder, panting, her lips curving up.

"Why? You seemed comfortable last night." His easy tone belied the intensity of his gaze. Their coziness promised simple pleasures, if she had the audacity to sample them.

"That may be. Nevertheless, we have a lot to do this morning." She injected efficiency into her voice, hoping it would dispel her feeling of awkwardness over last night's intimate sleeping position. That was not appropriate guide behavior.

Abandoning subtlety, she fought the covering and pulled it fully off. She scrambled to her feet and twisted in search of the saddlebags.

His swift intake of breath halted her. Kit followed the direction of his rapt stare, and her cheeks flamed at the loosened buttons. She snatched closed the wide-open edges of her camisole, seized the blanket, and wrapped it around her shoulders.

Michael frowned, a betraying smile pulling at his lips. "Why did you do that? I was admiring the scenery."

"Ha, ha. This scenery is not on the itinerary."

"Since we didn't set our route last night, I was simply taking a side excursion. Feel free to include more in your plan, Miss Guide." Michael winked.

"We have better paths to travel, Mr. Protector. And we better move if we intend on getting to them any time soon."

"Oh, all right. I'll leave you my map to decipher while I fish for breakfast." Michael sat up and jammed on his boots. Rummaging in his saddlebag, he produced well-worn pages and lobbed them in her direction. He got to his feet and winced. "Get dressed, would you?"

Once he was out of sight, Kit donned her riding clothes, gathered wood, and built a fire. Perhaps that spark burning inside her would subside as soon as they mounted up. But was that what she truly wanted?

Sitting cross-legged on the blanket, she nestled the coffee pot into the flames and studied Michael's papers. Her stomach clenched.

Kit's Mine could be on his property.

With rising anxiety, she perused the diagram. No indication of a gold mine anywhere on his land. Perhaps her mine was a few yards over his property boundary. She re-checked the landmarks, dearly hoping it might be that straightforward. No, the markings looked too familiar.

Groaning, she gnawed her lip. Maybe she should conceal the possibility of Kit's Mine being on his land. Sharing an unsubstantiated hunch wouldn't serve her purpose whatsoever. If true, he'd ultimately learn of her falsehood once they arrived, and be furious. Their friendship of this morning would surely disappear.

Yet if she told him now, he might abandon her, suspicious of her motives. Certain she tagged along for his gold. Any respect destroyed. No better than Isabel behaved.

She needed better options.

Kit inspected the drawing once more, turning it upside down and sideways. Perhaps he was unaware his home site included a gold mine. Conversely, simply because he hadn't told her didn't mean he was ignorant of its existence. His pretense was perfectly understandable. He didn't trust her enough.

She pounded her thighs in anger and glared at the betraying papers, hating her skills. If only she wasn't positive she was right.

He kept his secrets. That allowed hers. Studying the map again, she ignored her twinge of conscience.

Papa will be waiting for her there. She couldn't fail him.

Unfortunately, the rest of their expedition will be tricky. She never fibbed convincingly.

Michael walked into the clearing with an awkward gait, sniffing the air. "Is that coffee already? You're a real honey." He grinned like a proud boy. Three gutted trout hung from his fingers. "Look what I caught."

Kit's appetite fled. She poured coffee into the cup and shoved it into his free hand, taking the line of fish. "Let me start these." She skewered the catch and balanced the stick high above the fire to prevent charring.

She didn't dare say a word.

CHAPTER 24

The sizzle of their cooking breakfast interrupted the awkward silence. Michael studied Kit's averted face, disoriented by her strange behavior. What was wrong with her?

The truth hit him. Her sudden aloofness coincided with her study of his papers. Suspicion crawled like an insistent spider along his nerves.

"Did you learn the information you need?" He kept his voice level. Nowhere on his diagram indicated gold. She might cancel their deal real quick. And he wouldn't allow himself to be disappointed if she left. Not one bit. Not this time. Certainly not with a conniving woman. Living alone was fine by him.

"If you mean, did I figure out where your property is, then yes. From the landmarks and the description, I have a good idea of which trails to take. It's in the heart of Gold Country, northwest of Angels Camp, near the American River." Kit flipped two cooked fish onto a plate and handed it to him. She sat opposite, balancing the hot skillet on a rock between her feet.

Kit picked at her food. Michael shoved his entire meal past a dry, tight throat. Finished, he wiped his dish clean with dried grass and studied her drawn features. She chewed on her bottom lip so hard he swore she would draw blood. Something on his map worried her.

He captured her jaw and rotated her face up to his, refusing to succumb to a crafty female's capricious words again.

Her cheeks reddened. She shifted from his grip.

Kit hid something. He must discover what, despite his unrelenting attraction. Ignoring the inner voice alerting him it already was too late, he knelt beside her.

"What's wrong?" He framed her cheeks with his palms.

"N-N-Nothing." She met his gaze for the briefest of seconds, pleating the blanket between her fingers.

"Tell me the truth, because our lives depend on it. Are you able to guide me to my property, or should I return and engage someone else? I don't relish dying before I arrive."

"I can absolutely guide you. I recognize the surrounding area, and I know the various trails in between." She jutted her chin up. "Besides, it's your responsibility to keep us alive, not mine."

"I will, if you don't lead me on a reckless chase through backwoods country. I'm on a schedule, so don't get yourself into further scrapes." He pushed away, incensed at her defensiveness. If she wouldn't share her thoughts, he sure wouldn't share details on Diego's tactics and trip north.

"We should be able to arrive and meet Papa on my birthday—midsummer eve," she said. "What's your timetable?"

"I aim to start my horse ranch operation as soon as possible, that's all. Calculate how far we had better go today, and I'll pace us." He gathered up the gear and rose. Pain shot through his feet. Staggering, Michael swore under his breath.

"What's wrong?" she asked.

"Nothing that concerns you." Liar! His pain started with her. The last thing on his mind during that rescue had been sharp river stones. Limping across the clearing, he threw the saddlebags over their mounts.

He led the horses over and threw Lucky's reins to her. "Better get used to clambering up by yourself if you're going to live alone."

Maybe he should take his own advice and adjust to life without her, too—without her compassion, without her laughter, without her guts.

His choice from long ago. So why did he feel deserted?

Michael set a fast pace over flat terrain. Raw effort spawned development, wrested from the acres of land. Farms marked their boundaries with fallen tree limbs. Crude irrigation troughs crisscrossed the properties delivering vital water to young plants in neat rows of maturity. Scattered trees cooled inconsequential shacks, proof the settlers' first priority was improving their land to validate their claim, not worrying about comfort. Establishing legal ownership seemed to be everyone's problem.

They approached the Sierra Madre mountain range on a steady upward trail. Dense pockets of trees framed the yellowing grasses, creating a muted kaleidoscope of verdant hues contrasting with the cloud-free, azure sky.

Kit pulled alongside Michael. "This land looks good for crops. Is that what you're planning for your property, too?"

Michael tensed, shooting her a quick glance under his hat brim. "I've never farmed, though many people do near San Jose. It's a tough life, subject to the whims of nature, and takes years to pay off. Of course, it feeds you. That's key when you're living a ways from town."

"Why did you choose ranching?"

"I enjoy working with horses—breaking them and training them." Michael patted Midnight's neck. "This boy will be a fine stud if I add a few breeding mares. Cattle are stupid animals, and a good workhorse is worth its weight in gold to corral them. Ranching is not a lot of fun, but it's predictable—if you have money to start a herd." He frowned and rubbed his neck. It would be a whole lot easier without Diego breathing down his back.

"Do you have the necessary funds for a herd?" she asked.

He tilted his hat up and stared at her, amazed at her snooping.

"I'm sorry," she said. Pink color bloomed on her cheeks. "I didn't mean to pry."

"Yes, you did, like every other female. You measure men by their wealth." He resettled his hat against his brow. "Well, you won't learn that about me."

He dug his heels into Midnight's flanks. The stallion's hooves clobbered the hard dirt, mirroring his runaway fury at letting her worm his dreams from him last night. Her true interest seemed to be his money, just like Isabel. Her supposed ambition of living independent of a man? A pretense. He didn't trust her as far as he could throw her, and he could throw her tempting body pretty far.

Worse, since she saw his map, she might intend to claim his land as hers. By sweet-talking Diego, his stepfather might grant Kit ill-begotten land in return for her favors. He released a long string of oaths.

Taking a calming breath, he directed his attention to fixing the aftereffect of his idiocy. His legal title might require verification in Sacramento's court, if his stepfather's undoubted bribes were well-enough placed. Diego always sought to sell his land to the highest bidder, no better than other land speculators infesting California like locusts. However, a crude structure and fencing should keep the sheriff from evicting him from Father's land. He could build them in a week. In San Francisco, judges sympathized with the landowner's plight if they settled and worked the land.

A fleck of lather spattered him from Midnight's heaving chest. Michael pulled up on the reins and slowed to a trot. A shady glen materialized ahead, welcome relief from the midday sun. He brought Midnight to a cooling walk. Kit caught up to him, slumped and wilted in her saddle. Dismounting, he cared for both horses without saying a word, and kept a sharp lookout as she laid out food from the saddlebags.

Michael shuffled toward the blanket. His lacerated soles stung more than he expected. He sank next to her and eased off his boots.

Concern wreathed Kit's face. She dug into her bundle, retrieving a miniature tin. "Let me put this ointment on your feet. Otherwise you risk infection."

Michael hesitated, his feelings still raw. Was she trying to apologize? Perhaps he'd overreacted to her nosiness. She might be sincerely interested in his plans, even if she wouldn't disclose what was going on behind those pretty, imploring eyes. He would bet his last penny she hid something from him. Of course, if she were interested in gold, after seeing his property record she would have skedaddled out of here. She repeatedly trumpeted her claim that she could survive on her own very nicely, thank you.

At least while she was still here, she could be useful—his feet smarted. With a grunt, he removed his sock, uncovering the raw wounds. Kit sucked in her breath. Her fingers skimmed his red, angry flesh. She reached into her bundle another time and unearthed her tattered jacket, ripping lengths of worn cloth without hesitation.

Her destruction of clothes on his behalf smarted more than his feet. He started to protest, but her beseeching expression stopped him. Well, all right. If mending fences was her intent, he should cooperate.

Placing his foot across her lap, Kit poured cool water from the canteen over it, patted it dry, and massaged salve into the wounds. He sighed at the unexpected relief—and pleasure.

This attraction was bound to cause him trouble. At least she wasn't a whore. To the contrary, she was a lady who deserved his respect. Just not his trust. For sure, she didn't deserve his poor manners anymore.

Kit wrapped the cotton strips snug around his foot and eased it onto the blanket. Feeling bereft, he extended his other leg. Wearing a half-smile, she repeated the gentle ministrations, oblivious to the affect she had on him.

"Does that feel better?" She placed his foot down and gave it a little squeeze.

"So far, so good. Whatever's in that ointment sure works fast."

"Papa put this tincture together. It's made up of a bit of butcher's broom, olive leaf, and bayberry," she said. "Chinese herbal medicines work better than the methods American doctors use. I hear they prefer amputating young men's festered limbs to saving them."

"My feet aren't that bad!"

"Not yet. However, if you don't take care of them they might gangrene. Then the only option left is cutting them off."

"Are you joking?" A slight frisson of fear ran up his spine.

"I daresay you might have a better use for them than the doctor." Kit's expressive eyes twinkled up at him.

God help him, he already forgave her prying. It was just his luck her plans didn't include a man. In any capacity.

"Let's ride." He drew on his socks and boots and rose. "My feet feel better already. Thanks for taking care of me, Kitten." He pulled her to her feet. "Point out our direction so we can make tracks."

Kit peered northeast. "We take a diagonal shortcut toward the bottom of that tall hill."

Michael drank in the unconscious beauty in her confident posture, tempted to wrap her in his arms. He shook his head and left to saddle the horses. He didn't dare be near for another minute.

CHAPTER 25

Navigating a cottonwood-lined ravine, Michael forged their trail on foot. Thick bushes drinking the last drops of winter's heavy snow caught at his pants and boots. The steep canyon blocked the mid-afternoon sun and cast welcome shadow for ground-hugging wildflowers. A falcon screeched overhead protecting its isolated nest, interrupting the sultry quietness.

Kit stumbled over a gnarled tree root. "Ouch!"

He caught her waist, barely preventing her knees from smacking into the muddy earth. "Are you all right?"

She nodded, regaining her balance.

A shot rang out.

"Look sharp!" Michael grabbed his rifle. He dove for a crevice in the hillside and searched the slit of sky. Kit threw herself next to him.

"Who's there?" A stern, heavy-accented male voice drifted to his ears from above.

Michael lifted his gun to his shoulder. "Just travelers passing through, destination Gold Country," he called. "Don't mean you no harm."

A rifle barrel aimed down the gully's walls. "Prove it."

Michael hesitated, searching the gorge for an escape route. None. Stashing his weapon, he took hold of Midnight's line.

"Stay behind me, and if anything happens, run like the dickens." Michael pointed at Lucky's loose reins.

Kit tightened them in her fist. He leaned forward in the dim light and raised his brows, praying she understood. She nodded.

He scrambled up the gulch, Kit crowding his heels. Breathless, they halted at the top, awash in dappled sunlight. Michael maneuvered Kit to the rear, and scrutinized the man training his sight on them.

Under a drab hat brim, white hair tangled past narrow shoulders and framed sharp blue eyes. A scraggly beard with faint tinges of auburn covered his throat. He looked years past his prime yet still fit and robust. And, despite ragged clothes, his rifle was clean and shiny.

"What are you and your wife doin' on my land?" The stranger lowered his firearm a notch.

"I'm not his wife." Kit held onto Michael's belt and poked her head around him.

Michael grimaced. The unwritten rules in the wilderness dictated that a woman traveling alone with a man was either his spouse, or loose and available. Kit's impulsive words confirmed the latter.

The stranger grinned. "Then, mister, I see why you ain't stickin' to the trail. If it's privacy you're after, I'd appreciate it if you'd carry on with your woman on someone else's property. That way I won't be jealous, seein' it's been a while since I enjoyed a female." He guffawed, slapping his thigh.

"It's not like that." Despite Kit's imprudence, Michael half-raised his fists in defense of Kit's honor. "She's my guide."

"Huh. She's right pretty, too, and I won't be the last to think so." The stranger perused Kit's face for long moments. "Mosey along. And if I were you, I'd watch fer a gang of ruffians who passed through here last night. They were bent on kickin' up trouble."

"Thanks for the tip. I'm sorry we bothered you." No longer on guard for danger, Michael examined his unusual surroundings. Trees of varying size grew in neat rows. The afternoon breeze rustled their leaves, exposing ripe fruit weighing down the branches.

"You a farmer?" Michael asked, injecting a note of friendliness into his voice.

The man lowered his rifle to his side. "In a fashion. I planted fruit trees. They're a lot easier to tend than stoopin' over the soil, and they grow pretty darn well here. It's ten years 'til the first harvest, so they're not fer everyone startin' out."

Kit stepped from the protection of Michael's bulk wearing a polite smile. "What kind of fruit?"

"Peaches, apricots, plums, apples—I plant whatever I fancy. The newcomers to California favor variety, and they pay fine fer a good crop." He pointed his rifle at the orchard. "Pick some fer tonight's meal if you have the time."

Kit turned toward Michael, looking hopeful.

"Oh, go ahead." He couldn't stop her even if he wanted to, Michael thought with chagrin. She dashed off into the orchard.

"Much obliged." Michael resettled his hat. "Now that the lady is gone, I'd appreciate it if you could fill me in on these troublemakers. My name is Michael Rivers, by the way."

"I'm Ivan Sankovitch." The old man grasped his palm in a firm grip and studied Michael's features. Releasing his hand, Ivan scratched his nose. "You hail from around these parts? You look kinda familiar."

"From near San Jose. I'm headed to land I inherited from my father in Gold Country. And you?"

"I came to California from Russia when I was your age and land was still up fer grabs. No better home than this." Ivan's gaze roamed over his grove, contentment permeating his relaxed stance. "Only missin' a wife."

At the yearning shading Ivan's voice, Michael swallowed hard. He had many lonely nights in front of him. "Did you learn where the troublemakers came from?"

"Recently from San Jose, like you. The four varmints traveled together from the Carolinas. Confederate soldiers all, bitter as heck they lost the war. They're bustin' to take it out on someone, I figger."

"Soldiers?" Michael gulped. "How did you get the jump on them?"

"They were plumb drunk and lookin' fer a place to lay their heads, so I managed the lot, even though they appeared right skilled with their pistols. I moved them along this mornin', but they seemed itchin' fer a fight to feel like men again." He shot Michael a warning glance. "I have a notion a woman might do the trick, if you catch my meanin'."

Michael's worry ratcheted up. "Did you see their heading as they left?"

"Up that-a-way." Ivan gestured at the hill on a direct line along their intended route. "From there, I don't know. Best steer clear of them."

Kit ran into the clearing, huffing. Bright apricots and reddish plums filled her hat, and her hair swung free from its ribbon.

"These had fallen onto the ground," she said. "Since you don't like to stoop, I figured these would rot." She winked at Ivan and grinned. "I'm too short to reach the fruit in the branches anyway."

Ivan burst out laughing and took her hat. "Yeah, I wouldn't bother pickin' them up. You're welcome to these, miss. I hope you enjoy them."

Kit began plaiting her hair into its usual braid, and Ivan's cheeriness evaporated.

"Let's get you up, miss." Ivan boosted Kit onto Lucky and helped Michael stuff the fruit into Midnight's saddlebags.

Ivan kept his back to Kit. "You'd sure better dodge those no-account scalawags," he said in a low voice. "They got to quarrelin' about searchin' fer some Chinese whore from San Francisco. I bet they wouldn't mind usin' her."

Grim, Michael nodded his understanding and vaulted into the saddle.

"Thanks for the fruit, mister." Kit smiled at Ivan. "I won't forget your kindness."

Watching, Michael was flustered. Kit was sweet to a grumpy old man, beyond what good manners dictated for the gathered fruit. He should follow his instincts, not wallow in frustration over Kit's changeability."

Ivan returned her smile and hat. "You're welcome, miss, and I hope we meet again. I surely do." Hoisting his rifle over his shoulder, he sauntered off into the orchard, whistling.

Michael turned Midnight from their original track and urged him into a full gallop.

"You're going the wrong direction." Kit's yell topped the din of thundering hooves.

He slowed until she drew near. "Search for an alternative path. We're taking a detour north."

She studied the hills and gestured at a secondary gap between them. "That way is probably steeper, but should get us near Angels Camp. After that, we angle north anyway. It won't be much of a detour."

"It'll have to do." They were losing daylight fast—too fast. They needed a safe location for the night. No footloose drunkards will turn into her worst nightmare while she was his responsibility. He steered toward the gap, hoping they reached cover before midsummer's blessedly late sundown.

CHAPTER 26

Kit flapped the open collar of her blouse and rolled her sleeves over her wrists. Sweating from the fast pace Michael set, she struggled keeping him in view.

For the life of her, she couldn't figure him out. His temperament changed every few minutes. Was his reaction now due to something she did? Or said? She truly had no idea how to flirt. Or if she should. She simply knew Michael's essence called to her in a mysterious, fascinating manner.

He led them into a narrow valley cutting between forbidding slopes. Shadows blended into rapid darkness. No other hoof marks or footprints scuffed the dirt. Michael reined Midnight in and dismounted in a single move, approaching Lucky before her legs stopped.

"We'll keep them saddled tonight," he said, and hoisted Kit onto her feet with a grunt.

"But—"

"Stay here."

Michael's harshness kept Kit rooted where she stood, wagging her head at his abrupt change in behavior—one more time. He tethered the horses to an ancient oak near the trickling stream. Lifting the rifle free, he tucked it under one arm and set their belongings adjacent to the massive outcropping. His jaw twitched as he stared at each section of rock above. An ominous scowl descended on his features. He paced by and scanned their back trail.

"May I have your permission to visit the bushes before morning?" she asked, irritated.

"Stay close, and put your riding clothes on afterward," he said, his expression implacable. "I mean it. If I can't hear you, I'm coming after you."

Kit suppressed an angry retort. Two could play his silence game. She scooted to dense bushes she assumed met his approval, and finished her business in record time. Returning to camp, she gathered twigs for a fire. Michael snatched them from her and threw them aside.

"No fire. Eat," he said.

She counted to ten under her breath. He stalked the camp's perimeter, checked behind every nearby tree and gazed up the canyon. Pausing, he stared into the moonlight-stippled blackness. He finally reclined next to her, and inspected his rifle with thorough, precise movements. Sliding his boot knife from its scabbard, he ran his thumb along its lethal blade. He scrounged in the saddlebag, pulled out fistfuls of cartridges, and crammed them into his pockets. Continuously searching their environs, he picked up an apricot and bit into it. Juices ran unnoticed down his chin.

"What's going on?" she asked, bewildered and disturbed by his intensity.

"The next time someone assumes you're my wife, don't correct him. Just say we haven't stood up yet in front of a priest or a judge. Or say nothing. It may sting your pride pretending you're married to this poor Californio, but it may save your hide."

"Surely you don't think that nice orchard farmer will harm us? Why, we're eating his fruit!"

"We're in no danger from him." Michael contemplated his half-devoured apricot. "The troublemakers he mentioned are going the same route, and I prefer by-passing them."

"You're afraid for my sake, aren't you?"

"Yes. Follow my orders until I'm sure we're out of danger."

A warm tremor rippled through her at his fierce protectiveness. Only Papa and Mama ever cared for her in this manner. She laid her hand on his arm and gave a gentle squeeze. "I promise."

"Good. Try to sleep. If we're lucky, we'll be uncomfortable only for tonight."

Kit settled under the overhanging boulder, fastened the jacket up to her chin, and shut her eyes against the black sky and unseen danger. It was sweet comfort Michael guarded her.

CHAPTER 27

Pulled from a dreamless sleep by a continuous slither of pebbles spattering her cheeks. Kit swiped her lids and batted her eyes open.

Boots thumped the ground to her left. Startled, she lifted her head from Michael's shoulder. A looming shadow fell over them. She sat up and peered at the man's obscured face.

The stranger tripped over Michael's bulky saddlebag. Lurching in their direction, he fumbled with a pistol dangling from his belt.

One of the troublemakers! She stifled a gasp and cowered against the rock.

The sharp report from Michael's rifle blasted her ears. The bullet slammed into the man's thigh and catapulted him backward. He collapsed to the ground, writhing, and blood oozed from the wound. Michael scrambled to his feet.

Three more men converged on them in a silent rush. Her heart skittered a beat.

Michael jerked her up and shoved her straight into the yawning darkness. "Run!"

Kit stumbled to her knees from the force of his thrust. She dared a peek behind. One attacker knocked Michael's rifle from his grip. A second man tackled him around the knees and pinned him to the earth. Pushing up from the ground, she gathered herself. The third man stepped into the path, blocking her.

Veering to the right, she dodged his outstretched arms and prayed for speed. She angled her waist and tried racing by. With a snigger, he grabbed her unbound tresses and dragged her behind him toward the thicket.

Kit winced. She scratched his hand and clobbered his shoulder. Timing their strides, she kicked high between his legs, and hit her target with perfect accuracy. He doubled over. His loud, ugly curses echoed off the canyon walls.

Straightening, he yanked her around by her hair. She cried out in pain, tears flooding her eyes. He swung his arm, and slapped her cheek with a wallop. He backhanded her on the other. Again. Her ears rang. Overwhelmed by dizziness, she weaved, and fought for distance from the hurtful blows.

He skated his touch along her front and parted the heavy riding jacket. Groping one breast, he pinched deep. She squirmed, whimpering. His cruel grip increased. Tears spilled down her cheeks.

The assailant pulled her close. His fetid odor and liquor-saturated breath assaulted her nostrils. She recoiled, and strained against his iron arm locked around her waist. His palm slid to her backside, clutching, probing. He pushed his fingers between her legs, and tugged at the fabric.

Vivid memories of Father Angelo engulfed her. Kit froze, lost in the past. A sharp bite on her earlobe dragged her into the present. She snatched her arm free and clawed at his leering face.

He wrenched away. With a grunt, he carried her back to the clearing and heaved her atop the bleeding man. Her breath flew from her and she collapsed, wheezing, as limp as the body beneath her.

"You coolie bitch!" Her attacker spat on her face. "I'll get you for kicking me. We're going to take turns with you all night long. But keep that spirit in you handy—I'm hankering for it rough. And don't you run...if you do, I'll catch you again, and then take my sweet time killing you." He booted her buttocks and joined his two accomplices taming Michael.

CHAPTER 28

Muscles straining, Michael fought his opponents. He kicked and thrashed, gouging and punching their flesh. Their alcohol-laden breaths hinted at impeded efforts, and the two men struggled keeping him pinned.

He glimpsed the third man dragging Kit into the gloom.

No!

He freed an arm with brute strength fueled by dread. For a few seconds he won the brawl. But the third man joined in, cruelly screwing Michael's fist along his upper spine and overpowering him.

"You nancy-boy, did you think no one would notice you with a coolie slave girl?" The burly man's taunt assailed Michael, captive between the other two. "I bet she warms your blanket real nice. Only from what I hear, she cheats at cards. Pedro wants his horse back. And the money she robbed from him."

"Pedro says your father will pay big for proof you're an illegal slave owner and horse thief." A second man poked Michael in the chest. "After we've had our fun with your whore, we'll drag your ass to Sacramento for payment. Your father will see what a sorry son he's raised."

Cold fright shot through Michael. These weren't random drunk soldiers. They were hunters, and he and Kit their prey.

The beefy soldier grinned in depraved amusement and slugged Michael. Pain exploded from his nose. The next one delivered a series of relentless punches to his stomach. Michael grunted, struggling to remain erect. His knees gave way. As he toppled to the ground, they took repeated turns kicking his back and stomach. Michael lay still, eyes shut, hoping his possum ruse would catch them off-guard.

Yelling drunken boasts, the attackers hoisted him onto his feet and started over. Michael's ribs throbbed with every blow. Blood oozed down his throat. He choked, fighting for breath. Fighting for survival.

"Let him go." Kit's harsh command, threaded with trembles, was unmistakable in its resoluteness.

Michael lifted his chin. Sweat blurred his vision. He shook his head, and blood flew around him.

"Can't wait to get me between your legs, bitch?" The large attacker reeled toward her, fist raised high.

"Leave her alone!" Michael heaved against his restraints.

Unblinking, Kit leveled the glinting pistol at the drunkard's chest and fired. A gush of red spurted into the air, and he collapsed at her feet.

The other two whirled toward her. Michael twisted an arm loose. Pulling the knife from his boot, he plunged it into the neck of one attacker, pivoting the blade in the exposed flesh with a final, ruthless wrench. Eyes wide in impotent disbelief, the thug clawed at his lifeblood draining away. Michael slid the weapon free and readied for another strike.

Kit swung her pistol toward the last man and shot pointblank. His face exploded. She flinched as his body crashed to the ground.

Michael jammed his knife into his boot and stumbled to Kit. He lifted the pistol from her shaking hands and wiped her spattered face, seeking fresh wounds. Besides extreme pallor, she seemed unharmed.

He scanned the surrounding bushes and rocks for additional threats, grimacing from even those trivial movements. Bending at the waist, he prayed for relief.

"How badly are you hurt?" Kit clutched his arm, her eyes round and anxious.

"Not so bad that I'll stick around here."

Taking a steadying breath, he picked up his rifle and blew gritty particles from its sight. He gave her the pistol, weak and ashamed of his performance. "Catch the horses. Don't hesitate to shoot if you meet someone."

He failed her protection one more time—in fact, she saved him. Despite Ivan's warning and his precautions, those thugs got the jump on them. He spat blood, disgusted at himself. Forget worrying whether he should trust her. He didn't deserve her trust at all.

How he wished she would turn to him for comfort, though. He longed to erase any trace of cruel brutality, to wash away the blood, to kiss away memories of the thugs' lives she ended in his defense with such admirable valor.

A wave of gratitude and forgiveness washed away his doubts.

Kit arrived at his side, horses in tow. She tossed him Midnight's reins. He reached for the saddle horn and fiery talons of agony shot up his side. He doubled over, gasping.

"Here, step on my leg and boost yourself up," she said.

Michael complied, in too much torment to protest. Escaping the deadly chasm and its unpleasant surprises was paramount. He sagged over the horse's neck, and fought a spell of vertigo. With a tap of his heels, he led them into the pitch-black valley, giving Midnight his head through the dense forest. Kit followed, for once silent.

At the first bend in the trail, they discovered four tethered horses. Strangling a moan, Michael reached forward and untied three of them. He hesitated at the reins of the fourth.

"Is the first man I shot dead?" he asked.

"He was bleeding a lot when I took his gun, and still conscious."

"Better leave a single mount in case he survives. A dead man's horse is up for grabs, but I don't want extra accusations of thievery."

"Murder is permitted, though?" Her mouth puckered into a bleak frown.

"Self-defense is. Jumping two people by four men is considered unfair by everyone." The attack's nightmarish images filled his mind. His first kill. Until tonight, he never harmed a man beyond the damage of fists. Now, he couldn't forget the thug's dying eyes.

He guessed Kit grappled with the same haunting problem. Michael wanted to lessen her horror. He didn't have the strength. Yet.

"Tie those three together, and hitch the front pony to your saddle." He mumbled the curt order through painful lips. "I'd help, except I don't think I could re-mount."

CHAPTER 29

Frightened by Michael's admission of helplessness, Kit jumped onto shaky legs and cobbled together the horses in a line. She remounted and indicated a path barely visible by the wan moonlight.

"I bet this takes us up and over these hills," she said. "By morning we'll be near the river running toward Angels Camp."

He nodded and urged Midnight forward, collapsing against the stallion's withers.

She bit her tongue, thwarting the welling tears. Her old fear of rape at the whim of a bully hadn't compared to her terror once she realized Michael's danger. Witnessing his pitiless beating sickened her. She prayed her pistol hand wouldn't tremble and betray her repulsion of killing. Thank goodness, desperation overcame her weakness. She just aimed and pulled the trigger, choosing Michael over the thug's life.

Vivid images of gushing blood and splattered brains hammered at her. She breathed deep, battling nausea. They might still be in danger.

If only Michael would hold her close in his arms, as he held her after the lion attack and her near drowning. No harm ever came to her when surrounded by his concern. Sizing up his awkward posture, she drew a steadying breath. This time, she would supply comfort, not take it. She sniffed, jammed her hat across her face to hide an errant tear, and snapped her reins across Lucky's neck.

Michael pressed his mount up the steep, rough path through the long night. As dawn lightened the eastern sky, they crested above Angels Camp. The prosperous mining town sat at the junction of three paths snaking down from the Sierra Madre Mountains.

"Look, there's a stream where we can rest for a bit," she said, waving at a close by glade.

He bared gritted teeth and nodded. With a click of his tongue, he urged his weary horse along the path. Midnight stumbled over loose pebbles, and Michael's groan drifted to her ears. She couldn't wait for this harsh night to end—for all their sakes.

At the lush clearing, Michael somehow dragged his leg over the horse's rump and landed on his feet. He swayed. Kit jumped off Lucky and ran to him.

"Lean on me," she ordered. Lifting his arm to her shoulders, she slipped the poncho off Midnight and took a tentative step. She staggered under Michael's heaviness. They tottered to the shade of a spreading oak tree and she threw the cover down, helping him drop flat onto it. His pitiful moans flayed her emotions.

"I'll be right back. I have to see to the horses." Five mounts to care for, not two. She tied them to trees on long ropes within reach of the stream and its proximate grass, unsaddled each in rapid succession, and left the saddles where they fell. Juggling her bundle, the blanket, and the canteen, she hurried to Michael's side.

Kit bit her lip, and winced at the stinging reminder. She couldn't concern herself with her own aches and bruises yet. Ripping strips from her old jacket, she dampened them, and lifted Michael's head. He sipped from the canteen and lolled to the side.

Swiping off the worst of the dried blood, she studied his injuries. Blackening eyes, puffy nose, and swollen mouth. Bruises covered his cheeks and jaw—fortunately mere surface gashes. The men's drunkenness kept them from exerting their full strength. She smoothed ointment over every bit. Michael sighed, his lids drifting closed.

She unbuttoned his shirt and froze, aghast. Welts decorated his ribs and stomach. Prodding with gentle fingers, she searched for broken bones but found no sharp edges. Worried about hidden injuries, she reached behind him, cautiously hovering over his tender flesh. With a swift movement, his hands encircled her waist and he set her onto her heels.

CHAPTER 30

"That's enough." Michael summoned his waning reserves. Tugging his shirtfronts together and holding his breath to avoid stabbing pain, he struggled erect.

The morning sun's rays gilded Kit's swollen face.

His breath caught. "What did that skunk do to you?"

Using the mildest of touches, he tilted her chin side to side. He seized wet strips of cloth and cleaned away dried blood. Luckily, none was hers. His vicious anger dissipated slightly. Large handprints marked her cheeks, framing broken and bruised lips. He dabbed at her skin, swearing under his breath. Hating himself for not protecting her. She remained silent under his attentions.

He paused. "Are you hurt anywhere else, Kitten?"

"Only my backside, and that's gotten a lot tougher from riding." Her puffy mouth stretched into a grimaced smile. "I'm fine except my face. And I've ruined your mother's beautiful clothes." Tears gathered and wobbled on her bottom lids. A rogue droplet left a trail on her bruised cheek.

"Clothes are replaceable, Kitten." You aren't, he barely stopped himself from adding. Or confessing his absolute fear those brutes would rape and murder her. "You're covered in blood," he said. "Are you positive you're not hurt?"

"The blood isn't mine." Erratic tremors shook her body in lessening spasms.

"We'll rest the day here." He scanned the distance for riders. None. "I'll go to the river for water and to clean up, and then it's your turn. You should be able to remove the blood from your clothes if you wash them this morning. We'll let them dry in the sun while we rest."

She didn't answer.

"Kit?" He examined her for new signs of distress, but couldn't detect any. Maybe the thought of cleansing the thugs' blood bothered her more than she let on.

She finally nodded and rose in a smooth movement. "I'll see to the horses while you're gone."

Michael watched her leave, admiring her resilient toughness. He rolled to his knees and clambered to his feet, strangling an expletive. Hoisting the blanket and canteen, he lurched to the river.

Painful minutes later, the blanket wrapped tight around his waist, Michael limped toward a flat, open space. He spread his clothes on the grass to dry, ignoring twinging muscles. Straightening, he assessed the bruises mottling his battered torso.

Kit approached. "Does it hurt much?" She pressed light fingertips to his back ribs. Flinching, he clenched his teeth and stayed still, focusing on the pain. Otherwise, he'll be mightily embarrassed wearing a gaping blanket. She touched his lower spine where he withstood the worst pounding. He winced and shifted aside.

"Poking sure doesn't improve it," he said. "However, that ointment you used on my face seems to help. I thank you for that."

She smiled, curtseying. "Why you are quite welcome, my kind sir, especially since it seems once again you rescued me." Her light-heartedness faltered, replaced by grimness. "It wasn't just me they were after, was it?"

She earned the truth after saving his hide, that's for sure. He searched for the appropriate words.

"Tell me, Michael. What's really going on? How is your stepfather involved?"

"Go clean up," he said. "That cool water will help your bruises. When you're done, we'll have a nice, long chat. You'll learn what a fine gentleman my stepfather is. I promise." He sagged to his knees, the hard thump jarring his injuries.

Kit scanned the trees, and her gaze halted at a stand of willows. "Start a fire before you get comfortable, and boil some water. I'll brew a tonic that will help us feel better."

She was gone a long time. Loud splashes provided welcome reassurance of her safety. He followed her instructions and finally relaxed, tending the pot. The sun's balmy warmth eased his aches. Soon he heard her in the adjoining grove, presumably stretching her clothes next to his.

A bare arm appeared over his shoulder, and Kit scattered large flakes into the bubbling water.

"Willow bark tea," she said. "Tastes awful, but works every time." Kit walked to his side and settled onto the poncho. She sat cross-legged with dainty grace, and flicked soppy hair over her shoulders.

Michael sucked in his breath. The provocative black dress sloped low in front. Her short skirt rose high, exposing her legs. Ugly bruises scattered across her arms destroyed her skin's purity, and the welts on her cheeks served as a glaring reminder of their ordeal. Furious, he clenched his jaw.

"Let me put that ointment on you," he said.

She tilted her face toward him. He concentrated on being gentle in spite of swollen fingers, awkwardly feathering the balm over her cheeks and mouth.

"You know, I found the girl who wore that dress at Bonita's incredibly attractive." He hoped playful banter would lighten the mood.

"Yes, Penny is very pretty."

"That's not what I meant." He shook his head, frustrated he was unable to muster a smile. Nor convincingly demonstrate he found Kit irresistible, not some girl named Penny.

Nonetheless, he could confess another truth. "I'm glad you're my guide," he said. "You've done an excellent job."

"Thanks. Now how about being honest with me?" Guilt shadowed her eyes, followed by her usual confrontational glare. He paused, curiosity roused. What was she thinking? No, he wouldn't challenge her in return. He didn't have any fight left in him.

"Diego headed out for Sacramento one day before us to try to snatch my property again." He massaged the recurring tension in his neck, tamping down his kneejerk anger at his stepfather's devious antics.

"Can he do that? I thought the court in San Francisco gave you legal right to the land."

"So did I. However, there's nothing that motivates Diego more than taking property that doesn't belong to him in a dirty contest."

"I still don't understand," she said. "What might he do?"

"Bribe someone to reverse the ownership of the deed to suit his purposes. I'm positive he intends to hammer at me until I come crawling to him a total failure, even if it means cashing in favors. He doesn't want my land for practical reasons. He only cares to take it so he owns me, too." Michael tightened his bloated fingers into half-fists.

She paled. "And he could destroy your chances to hold onto the title of your land if you've done something illegal? Say, stealing Lucky? Or owning a slave girl? That's why those men jumped us?"

"Yes." Despair flooded him. "I didn't exactly advise Diego I was taking Midnight when I left. I raised him from a colt, I rode him—everyone knew he was mine. Still, Diego might alter those facts and claim

I'm a horse thief. Plus, since I haven't had a chance to improve my land yet, Diego may assert I don't warrant it based on my moral character. A sympathetic judge might rule the additional information is adequate to invalidate my claim."

"That's not fair. He cannot invent lies about you and expect a court of law to believe him," she protested. "Did Maria warn you he thought you stole Midnight?"

"She told me that Diego condemned me publicly for not first asking his permission." Michael hesitated, hating what he had to divulge, knowing it might cut her self-confidence into ribbons. "He's willing to pay witnesses to substantiate his cause—like a poker player convinced my Chinese slave girl cheated him out of a favorite horse. If a judge believes I own you, which would be damaging, I'd be responsible for your actions. That would brand me a horse thief, no matter what."

"That's ridiculous." She snorted. "You're not answerable for my actions."

"How old are you?"

"I'll be eighteen in two days. Oh! Any way you consider it, they'll think you're responsible. He must have a weakness. You know him, Michael. Think of how to beat him at his own game."

CHAPTER 31

Michael's land ownership was in serious jeopardy—likely hers as well. Self-reproach plucked at her. It wasn't fair to press him for his full story while she withheld her secret. As soon as she confirmed the specific position of Kit's Mine relative to his property's boundaries, she would disclose it to him. Worrying him over what might or might not be could wait.

He stared into the flames. "If only Father made improvements after the Mexican government paid him with the land!"

"Why is that significant?"

"Then it could stay a simple matter of a hereditary dispute," he said. "The San Francisco court sided with me completely. However, if Diego puts it into the realm of every other settler's land claim, requiring tangible proof of development, I don't stand a chance."

"And the charge that I'm your slave?" Kit asked, incensed at that mischaracterization.

His heavy exhalation created a fire dance. Sparks drifted upward. "Like I said last night, let's keep speculation to a minimum by letting everyone think we're married. At least then, we won't be the subject of gossip that might reach Diego. That's part of what attracted those hoodlums last night."

"Didn't seem as if gossip was on their minds."

"The orchard farmer cautioned me they seemed enthusiastic to find a Chinese slave girl for their own," he said. "You simply provided them an extra incentive to track me fast."

"I haven't thanked you properly for saving me." Life had become infinitely precious since she left San Francisco. She had her freedom once more—and Michael at her side.

Through puffy eyelids, his embarrassed regard locked onto hers. "If I recall correctly, it's me who should be thanking you. They were trouncing me before you shot two of them dead. No man could have done better."

Kit curled her lip at his grudging compliment. "They discounted any threat from me because I'm a woman. Worse, I guess, because in their minds I was just a subservient coolie slave." She sniffed. "Guess I showed them not to underestimate me."

"I won't either, partner."

She recalled the gruesome end to the men, and swallowed rising bile. Cleaning the blood, flesh, and skull fragments from her jacket earlier had made her gag into the stream. She dreaded facing that kind of danger once more. Especially alone. Without Michael's protection, those brutes would have raped her—or worse.

The water in the pot hissed. "Whatever you have cooking is steaming like sulfur springs—and smells as bad," he said.

"Good." She poured hot liquid into the cup, added cool water from the canteen, and handed it to Michael. "You get the first dose, I'll take the second, and between us we'll down the whole batch."

"Must I drink this?" He sounded like a youngster begging out of a licking.

"Every bit." She chuckled. "Remember, I have to swallow it too. I swear it will ease our body aches. We don't have recovery time to spare if we have to improve your home site fast."

"We?"

"Of course I'll help you defend your property. It's in jeopardy because of me." She hoped her face didn't reveal her second motivation—to shield Kit's Mine from unjustified seizure.

"Diego would concoct some other trick to grab my land if it hadn't been for you."

"We'll never be sure, will we?" Crossing her arms over her chest, she glared at him. "I got you into this mess by delaying you and winning Lucky. It's the least I can do to help you out of it."

Michael blinked twice, staring at her with the oddest air. He opened his mouth and closed it. His forehead crinkled, and he appeared as if waking from a trance.

Draining the liquid, he grimaced. "Your turn, and then we should sleep. As soon as the clothes are dry we'll mount up and ride through the night."

"Not around here. Caves open up directly under the ground, big enough to trap an entire horse. We have to be careful with our footing, or stick to the trails." She poured her tea and downed it at once.

"We'll ride until dark then, and skirt around Angels Camp," he said. "How long until we arrive at my property?"

She visualized Papa's diagram. "If we're lucky we should arrive by tomorrow night."

With a nod, Michael struggled to his feet. The blanket loosened as he walked to the clearing, slipping lower on his muscled hips.

He felt each of the garments in turn, and squinted at the morning sun. "I think the clothes will dry by early afternoon at the latest." He walked to her and extended a hand. "Let's move into the shade, otherwise that beautiful skin of yours will burn to a crisp in that tiny dress."

Kit's cheeks heated at the realization that Michael ogled her in return. She picked up the poncho and stretched it under the wide branches of an oak tree. Coiling into a ball, she fell fast asleep.

CHAPTER 32

Michael winced against the scorching noonday rays, keeping his breathing regular. Lying on his side, his ribs throbbed touching the hard ground.

He sensed Kit stir behind him, then felt her fingers stroke in delicate sweeps from his shoulders to his beltline. Shocked, he didn't dare move. She traced back up again. Her lips brushed across his flesh, accompanied by a warm, moist exhalation.

With a sharp, painful intake of air, he rolled over and arched one of his brows. Her ivory skin reddened to her ear tips.

"I'm sorry I woke you," she said, her eyes bright with a mixture of curiosity and desire.

He licked his mouth, grimacing from even that slight pressure. No kissing her until her head spun. Nevertheless, he could give her a bit of her own medicine.

"I'm not sorry. Do I deserve a bit of playtime now?" Plenty of such ideas occupied his thoughts every night—and day.

Kit nodded, breathing in short pants.

"Lie on your stomach." He eased her flat onto the poncho.

Her exposed spine curved in sweet temptation from the low-cut dress. He traced a finger along the flouncy edge, crossed the small of her back with his palm, and drew a single nail tip along the other side. Reaching the sleeves, he pushed her heavy tresses aside. He caressed her nape in infinitesimal circles, toying with the fine hairs curling alongside her neck.

She sighed and visibly relaxed into his touch. Keen to see her expression, he lifted her by the waist and eased her around into a loose embrace.

"Playtime over, Kitten," he said with regret. Recovering his physical strength took precedence. "Did you enjoy it?"

"Let's just say I should be creative when it's my turn next, don't you think?" Her drollness didn't fool him a bit. She liked every second of their play.

Michael snickered, hugging her tight despite the pain. "I think you're dangerous to my sanity." He stood and lifted her onto her feet, securing the blanket around his waist. "And I think we better take advantage of the rest of the daylight to travel. Are the clothes dry yet?"

She tested the assortment of garments and scowled. "I'll never be rid of the blood."

"Better theirs than ours."

"You're right. I'm being a child about dirtying my pretty clothes." She peeped at him. "Will you turn aside, or should I hide in the trees to dress?"

Michael grabbed his clothes and trotted into the bushes. Kit's bubbly laugh followed him.

Concentrating on the remainder of their journey, he circled the new horses. Three quality mares, still in their prime, with minimal damage from abusive spurs marking their sides. Good additions to his future stable.

He saddled Midnight and Lucky, whistling a jubilant tune. He was so close to his dream—once he got rid of Diego's interference. After a dozen years of postponement, the time had come. Only he wasn't sure celebrating alone was what he wanted.

Kit's offer to help improve his land blew his previous opinions of her to smithereens. Nothing had prepared him for her pure, unselfish generosity.

They should start a new deal. It seemed a no-risk proposition. She got Lucky on her own, told him the truth about her navigation skills, and acted as a full-fledged partner on this trip, not once shying from what was required. Including calling on steely nerves in a deadly battle.

She was unlike any woman he ever met. How long before he tired of her?

Never.

How senseless to tolerate a bachelor existence simply to prove Diego and Isabel wrong. His ideal life included Kit. At present, not sometime vaguely in the future.

He leaned against Midnight's withers, considering her declared independence from men. Might she expand her dream, or compromise it, to include him? Not the kind of unappealing compromise Diego mandated to Mother. Something better.

His parents achieved marital happiness—by what means? He should have asked Father their secret before he died, except that topic hadn't crossed his young mind. He knew Father stopped traveling, discontinued his career as a well-respected geologist, and became a rancher after they married, all for Mother's sake. Michael ruminated over the Lees' considerable sacrifices with a newfound respect for beginning a loving, vulnerable family in the wilderness.

His usual brash confidence wouldn't be worth a penny tackling the eventual challenge—protecting a Chinese-Irish wife for a lifetime.

CHAPTER 33

Saddlebags and blankets stacked across her arms, Kit approached, and helped fasten them in place on the extra horses.

"Ready?" she asked.

"Ready to follow my guide." He hoisted her onto Lucky. Crossing to Midnight, he awkwardly swung his leg over the saddle, unable to prevent a wince.

"I think we should cut across here and join the trail leading north from beyond Angels Camp after nightfall." She tugged the hatstrings snug under her chin. "These mining towns get rowdy, and we'd be wise to avoid them."

Nudging Midnight into step, Michael frowned. "I planned on riding into town to see if I might uncover information on the thugs."

"No. You'll draw attention with those bruises. It's obvious you've been in a fight. If Diego's bounty is common knowledge, someone else will come after us."

"That bad, huh?" He fingered his bristly jaw and attempted a grin. "I figured it may be an improvement—adds some maturity."

Kit's somber gaze skittered across his injuries. "Trust me, Michael. You'd be asking for trouble."

"How do you know about rowdy towns, anyway?"

"My parents traded mining supplies for a while. Saloons and brothels usually sprang up first. They must be quite profitable. I wonder why?" Irony laced her tone.

"Did your parents actually bring you into the brothels as a kid?" he asked, shocked.

"Don't worry," she laughed. "All I glimpsed were pretty ladies dressed in fancy clothes and loud, eager men. I certainly wasn't let upstairs in any of them—not until I worked at Bonita's."

Finally, a chance to determine the truth regarding her experience with men. "Just what did you do at Bonita's?"

"I trust you understand I never worked as a prostitute," Kit said, thrusting her chin high in that style he'd come to admire.

He nodded.

"Otherwise, I performed every chore—changing beds, cleaning rooms, bandaging the beaten girls, helping the cook, and serving drinks."

She shrugged. "Essentially, Bonita worked me as a slave—except I never entertained men."

"Are you certain you really understand what she expected from you?" Michael asked. Kit may have had her virtue taken by that old priest, yet she seemed untouched in the ways of men and women. If she didn't pursue further intimacies, he would cease his advances. Otherwise, he was no better than that lecher.

"Of course. Bonita's girls talk on and on about their evenings." Kit giggled. "What I learned from Penny would probably cause Papa to blush, let alone Mama. The girls treat most men as simply customers, although they each have favorites." She wagged her head. "Can you believe they fight over those worthless men because of jealousy?"

"Thanks." Michael held on to his temper but couldn't prevent his sarcasm. "I was at Bonita's, remember?"

Her dismayed gaze shot up to his. "I'm sorry. I didn't mean to insult you. One-timers pay for a girl's company and gratification, and that's fine. Most of the regulars are married and living in San Francisco. A few have mistresses on the side, too. I just don't think any of them will sweep a girl into improved surroundings because he shares her bed once in a while."

"Is that why you're so fired up to live independently? Because you don't trust a man could give up other women?" She had good reason for her poor opinion of men, no different than he had of women. Nevertheless, he must convince her to respect him, despite his failures to keep her safe.

"No, it's not that. The girls at Bonita's will go with anyone to escape, regardless of the conditions."

"Isn't anything else better?"

"Not necessarily. Not if it isn't a life of her choosing." She stared off toward the far horizon. "I swore I'd direct the course of my years, not float along counting on fate's intervention."

He followed her westward focus, envisioning the turbulent San Francisco Bay meeting the calm Pacific Ocean. "Have you ever been sailing?"

"No. Mama told me stories of her adventures, that's all."

"Then you must know that on the water, the wind often changes suddenly, or the current is stronger than you planned when you charted your course," he said. "You adjust according to conditions. That's what living is about."

"Are you saying I'm being pigheaded regarding my choices? You're just as bad!"

"Fair enough." Michael scratched the back of his neck, scowling. "I've focused on my goal so much I didn't always heed good advice. Yet I'm learning real fast that my notions regarding getting to my land, or the specifics of my property, or the method by which I'll earn my livelihood, may be wrong."

He captured her recalcitrant gaze. "I'll only survive if I change my preconceptions of how to accomplish my dream. I refuse to fixate on living in a certain manner, and risk pursuing a literal dead-end."

Kit gnawed on her bottom lip for long moments. "Mama said all beings must flourish, or they die too early. Maybe I've only planned to grow, and forgot to act." She shared an apologetic smile and threw her arms wide. "To life!"

At least Kit might consider other courses now. Perhaps he could convince her to stay and devise a future together.

A feeling of contentment and rightness crept through him, not his usual panic. Her exuberance was uplifting. Her passion enthralling. Her zest motivating, as she carved a place for herself in this tough world. She definitely supplied what was missing in his days.

If only she would include him in hers.

Considering she initiated the caresses this morning, it might not be as difficult as he feared.

CHAPTER 34

A diffused, violet sky embraced them as they reached the trail junction a mile north of Angels Camp. In silence, they hugged the row of pines lining the faint road, keeping within their pungent shadows. Kit detected excited hoots and hollers of men dashing into town, and drunken songs of those leaving. After days of isolation, even this negligible bit of civilization intruded.

Full dark came over them, and Michael reined in. "You were right about the danger. We'll take turns standing watch for anyone coming near, in case we need to leave in a hurry."

In unison, they unloaded the mounts. A sense of pride descended over Kit, despite her fatigue. Michael considered her an equal partner, not a helpless female.

"I'll take the first shift," Kit said. Sleep will elude her for hours yet. Her nerves still jangled. Plus, she needed time to think before they went their separate ways. A chill ran the length of her spine, and she rubbed her arms briskly. "May we boil coffee at least?"

"Yes, but only build a small fire. I won't be long." He collected the reins and led the horses toward a sheltered area. Kit ignited convenient kindling, satisfied. Coffee will calm her and keep her awake.

Fragrant hisses soon filled the night air. She poured the draught and enfolded cold fingers around the dented cup. Sniffing the vapor, hypnotized by the embers, she sorted jumbled thoughts.

Waking up this morning and facing Michael's back had been awful. Colorful welts and bruises arced in uneven rainbows across his flesh. They served as a terrible reminder of her raw fear that the men would kill him.

When had his existence become as cherished as her own? With a languid sigh, she faced the truth—she loved him. She recalled his mesmerizing, poignant focus. How his gentle fingers trembled as he tended her minor wounds. His earlier sweet, tantalizing kiss.

Awe and bittersweet cynicism seeped through her, nestling into every pore. She was certain of his attraction, but love? She doubted it. He still believed she was barely one step better than a prostitute. Besides, men always preferred a buxom physique. Her stick figure will never round out the top of that lacy dress Penny gave her.

Of course, Michael did treat her with respect. He may not approve of her playing poker and winning Lucky, yet he defended her in front of those rancheros, and accepted the result. Most men would have smacked her and left her behind.

He was a kind man. Given a chance, he would thrive away from the confines of other people's dictates. His new land should provide that environment.

Yes, he was impatient at times, mistrustful most days. His temper got the best of him. Then again, Kit understood his hatred of women. Her adult encounters with men certainly left her jaded. First Father Angelo, then Bonita's patrons, now last night's hoodlums. Yet Michael's fundamental nobility proved good men existed.

Given time, he might see good women existed as well. Women worth a kind word.

A woman worth loving.

Finally relaxed, she sipped the last of her coffee and grimaced at its cold temperature. Kit jolted to full alertness. What was keeping Michael? Memories of the attack jittered through her mind, worries of danger quickening her pulse.

She berated herself for such foolishness. Blocking the glow from the fire with her hand, she peered into the dark, finally spying a figure limping toward camp. Her heart panged in remorse. Caring for five horses must have pained him something fierce. She should have helped him, or at least offered.

Michael squatted next to her with a muffled grunt. He cupped her jaw with chilly fingers, his demeanor serious. "I'm happy you dropped into my arms, Kitten. No guide would be more accurate. Nobody could save my hide better than you did. And no one else could furnish as many pleasant diversions these last few days, either."

She captured his palm against her cheek. "Thank you. I cannot believe my luck you were at Bonita's to help me. If it hadn't been for you, I would be her slave. You gave me my liberty." She gazed into his eyes, seeking a glimmer of caring. The firelight was too dim for other than hope.

Michael nodded and stood up. He staggered, and threw her a sheepish grin. "I'm tempted to keep you company, except we need our sleep for tomorrow. I'm sure looking forward to the end of our journey."

"Yes," she said guardedly. "Good night."

Stepping across the clearing, he dropped to the ground, pulled his hat low, and wrapped the blanket around his shoulders. Fitful snores quickly emanated from his direction.

Kit's thoughts careened this way and that, synchronized in erratic rhythm to her churning emotions. His compliments sounded too like a farewell to a favorite bedmate. Playing with her might be the most he ever intended.

His earlier advice to identify further options haunted her. Was she chasing an impossible dream instead of coping with reality? He no longer asked mean-spirited questions, or made sneering comments. Given their new rapport, he deserved truthful answers.

Then again, maybe love blinded her.

If Kit's Mine fell within the boundaries of his property, his wonderful considerations would disappear in the wind because she lied to him. Well, not lied exactly. More an omission of the whole truth. Of course, he probably wouldn't see it that way.

She propped her chin in her hands. Why didn't she trust him?

The answer whispered from her heart. Because she couldn't bear his rejection. And he wouldn't reject her if she were wrong about the exact location of her mine. There was no advantage to risking hurt in advance.

Besides, she wouldn't ever dispute the claim to his property. She prayed Papa wasn't already trying. Michael had fought hard and long. He oughtn't to have a new adversary blocking his dreams.

Kit's Mine would be his if it were on his land.

If...

Tears welled, blurring her view of the smoldering ashes. Most of her dreams had evaporated when she examined Michael's map. Without Kit's Mine to support her, she couldn't be truly independent. Nor could Papa.

Kit wondered again what kind of existence Papa led today. Could it include her? Or would she spend her years roaming the wilderness again with Papa, unable to create a home? Chinatown abounded with tales of random aggression targeting Chinese men throughout California. With the railroad complete and Papa's respected job finished, he will face the same prejudice no matter where they live. Without Mama to stand at his side, witness to his worth as a man, he may crumble and wither, or turn violent himself to protect his daughter.

The hated deadline of their arrival at Michael's property bore down on her. She slammed her fist onto the dirt. There must be a good answer somewhere.

In San Francisco, she lived one day at a time—crises befell her with too much frequency. She will deal with reality once, and not fret each moment over possibilities. It was an acceptable gamble. Otherwise, she'll go crazy.

The stakes were higher than risking her savings for Lucky.

Now, she bet her heart.

CHAPTER 35

The celestial hunter Orion drifted above Michael, the constellation's winking stars a haunting reminder someone had tracked them, putting their lives in danger. He scanned the shadows. Nothing extraordinary. No movement, simply frogs croaking their nightly courtship and an intermittent yip from a lonely coyote.

He reconsidered the papers in his grasp, unearthed from the thugs' saddlebags. Tilting the sheets, he squinted at the indistinguishable words in the fading moonlight. He tossed the papers aside and stretched his legs. The embers had shriveled to ash hours ago. No fire meant he waited, counting the minutes until daybreak. Spending half the night gnawing over what motivated their four pursuers had gotten him nothing. He suspected these papers could give him a clue.

Finally, the sky lightened. He picked up the scattered sheets and perused the text.

The first document was a land warrant for 160 acres, granted to a veteran named MacInnes for service during the War of 1812. Its yellowed pages and creased, precise folds testified to the value generations had placed on it. Diego once boasted that land warrants are as good as cash—whoever holds the document can sell or give it outright, transferring ownership as the paper exchanges hands. Ivan said the thugs were ex-soldiers. Military service could be a family tradition for one of them. Michael didn't recognize the name, so had no clue to his cruel behavior.

His stepfather's name at the top of the next document startled him. This contract retained Diego Salazar for representation in Sacramento of Abigail Jenkins' legal interests regarding squatters on land southwest of Angels Camp. No surprise, a clause at the very bottom promised Diego land in lieu of payment for his legal expertise. That identical clause trapped his mother when she hired Diego. Who was this Jenkins woman? And why did a thug carry her contract? Had Diego traded this contract as payment to those bastards for attacking them? Or the land warrant? Baffled, he set the contract aside.

Scrawled on a scrap of telegraph paper were Pedro's name and the words *"Capital Hotel $100 gold."* The telegram came from Diego. Michael's jaw clenched. He remembered the mocking threats of their attackers, their taunts that Diego will pay good money for slanderous information about Michael—and pay in gold.

Some common purpose linked those men. What could it be? Diego reserved land as payment for politicians, not thugs. Then how was Jenkins' land involved?

Michael re-read the papers but didn't uncover answers. He tucked them into his saddlebag and sorted the dead men's belongings into uniform piles, setting aside a battered plate and tin mug. Shaking out a second blanket, he rolled it up with a tarpaulin and secured the lot across the five horses. Chores done, he returned to camp. Kit still slept as peacefully as a newborn foal.

"Kitten, wake up." He tapped her shoulder.

She rolled toward him and yawned. Sorely tempted by her allure even at this early hour, he resisted kissing her fully awake.

Tomorrow, he promised himself. Nothing would hinder him then.

"Good morning," she said with a drowsy smile. "Do we get coffee?"

"No, you got your treat last night. Water and jerky for you."

Kit beamed. "We also have that nice man's fruit. I see why he started an orchard. Every meal is delicious."

Michael grinned in reply. "Fruit it is." He pulled her upright. She grimaced, rubbing her backside. His smile collapsed.

"I'm sorry I didn't protect you better, Kitten." He feathered his thumb over her battered lip. Her bruises had faded and the swelling lessened, yet he wished he'd beat those thugs to a bloody pulp before they died.

Kit nudged him into the sunlight and scowled. He bet his injuries looked worse than they felt.

"How is the rest of your body?" She scanned his entire length, fortunately keeping her hands to herself.

"On fire..." Did she understand his cryptic answer? Exerting faltering willpower, he resisted pulling her into his arms and giving her a complete demonstration. He wouldn't stop at light touches. And they simply couldn't carve out time for games this morning.

Blushing, she removed two pieces of fruit, passed him one, and headed for her mount.

The long day's ride carried them over ever-steeper hills and yawning valleys. The vista of distant mountain ranges grew into distinct snow-covered peaks rising above forested hillsides. Their mounts' chests heaved in uneven rhythm in the thinning air, so they followed tributaries carving the land into easier terrain, lessening the horses' burden.

Michael pulled up next to Kit, frowning at the late afternoon sun. "Isn't today the day you're supposed to meet your father?" Disgust warred with a guilty conscience at his forgetfulness.

"Today or tomorrow." She fiddled with her reins. "I'm sure he'll wait an extra day for me. The mine isn't far from your property, a couple hours ride at most."

"Good! After we take a quick tour of my land we'll go meet him." His false bravado covered galling uncertainty. Lee might react negatively to a Californio escorting his daughter, and rightfully demand a marriage proposal, given the circumstances. And that Michael would happily grant.

Of course, Kit might not accept. Michael would hate it if her father pushed social conventions and forced her hand. They hadn't done anything requiring an apology. Yet. It was still her choice. But he couldn't imagine a future without her.

"Don't waste time on me," she said. "You have work to finish on your property. I'll see Papa first, then come and help you. Please."

Her obvious unease discomfited him. She was keeping significant information from him, he was certain. Perhaps her father embarrassed her somehow. No matter what, pushing wasn't fair, nor would it change her mind. This was her dream, to pursue as she felt best.

"Then please inform your father I look forward to meeting him. He's welcome to return with you. Or, if he'd rather, I'll ride to his property."

"Why is it important to meet Papa? It's not necessary."

Michael's skin prickled. Unease crept up his spine. Maybe she didn't consider him worthy for her father, no better than a cad.

He chose his words with extreme care. "Because I admire and respect you, and from what you've told me I'll admire and respect him. I think it's polite to meet the father of the woman I've been escorting this week. Remember the rumor flying about us? I'd rather set him straight."

"Which rumor?" Disdain colored Kit's intonation. "That I'm your Chinese slave or that we're married?"

"Hopefully he'd never believe you were anyone's slave." He wished she didn't ridicule passing as his wife. Then he'd be sure of her answer to his proposal of a real union, not this pretend arrangement.

"Everyone else does," she mumbled.

"Stop thinking like that!" The vein in his neck twitched.

"Why? It's the truth. Not a single person wants a Chinese here, man or woman."

He curbed his anger and lowered his voice. "You're an American citizen, remember? Your mixed background is no different from most people's in this country, including mine. So what if you're a mongrel? That's a badge of honor in this tough wilderness."

"You're right." She ran her fingers along her hat brim. "I've gotten used to other people labeling me, and forgot who I really am. Besides, you said I could pass for a señorita." She batted her eyes.

Thrown by her sudden change in mood, Michael floundered for an answer. "Yes, you can, especially since you speak Spanish fluently."

"Gracias, señor." Kit sent her horse galloping off.

After a half hour's swift ride in the dying sunlight, she pulled up at the bottom of a steep incline.

"Your land begins on the other side of this hill," she said.

His heartbeat accelerated. "If we give it one hard push, we should get there before full dark, don't you think?"

She kicked Lucky's flanks, her lyrical voice cajoling the tired mustang forward. Michael followed on a struggling Midnight, pressing him over this last difficult hurdle. The three mares lagged, digging their hooves into the rocky soil and stumbling repeatedly.

They crested the hill and reined to a halt. The last rays of sunshine crowned Kit's hat with a halo, resembling the Mission's painting of the Blessed Virgin Mary. His gaze followed her finger to the protected valley below.

My land. All mine.

CHAPTER 36

Kit stared into the shadows. Hauntingly recognizable landmarks conjured up memories of playing in these fields as a girl, splashing in that stream, climbing the far hills holding Mama and Papa's hands.

Kit's Mine was close.

Tomorrow morning she would finally determine whether her mine was within Michael's boundaries. If it weren't, then she'd travel to meet Papa farther north. Would he be there? Of course, that land might have a titled owner, too.

And if she found Papa awaiting her on Michael's claim, what would she tell Michael? Or Papa? And if Papa weren't there but the mine was, her next step would be to search for Papa—if he were still alive.

She sighed. It seemed hopeless.

"Let's walk, shall we, and let the horses cool down," Kit said. Dismounting, she led their silent march over a faint trail zigzagging into Michael's land. They reached a level grassy area, and a bubbling creek gurgled its welcome.

Michael jogged to her side. "Don't you think we should stop here for the night?"

Kit nodded and averted her face. Unshed tears threatened at bursting point. A single drop moistened her cheek. She shoved the betraying mark away, stepping into shadows.

If Michael noticed her strange behavior, he was sensitive enough not to say a word. Instead, he led the horses to a thicket of trees near the stream, unsaddled them, and set to brushing sweat from their flanks.

She strolled along the meadow's edge and contemplated the silhouetted shapes along the horizon. Was this her old home? Her next one? Or would Michael dismiss her without a thought, now that he attained his dream? She throttled her emotions as he approached with the saddlebags hoisted over his shoulders.

"You've got a magnificent piece of property here, Michael." She cleared her throat and forced a congratulatory smile. "Whatever you decide should make you proud—and wealthy."

"If it's as good as it looks in the dark, you may be right. I can't wait to ride it tomorrow morning." He grinned, every inch a satisfied owner.

Kit's spirits sank further. Tomorrow would be too late. If she found her mine on his property, he would harden his heart, considering her another Isabel. He might give her a second chance. However, she couldn't count on it.

She loved him, but didn't dare say the sentiment aloud. He didn't feel the same in return. Not yet.

Her best hope was tying him to her through a physical bonding. And, she prayed, an emotional one. If not, any dream she harbored for a better life that included him would be gone forever. She had to secure the tenuous strands weaving around them. Maybe then, no matter what happened, he would believe her. If she trusted him first with her body, wouldn't he listen to her explanations?

"I cannot wait, either, Michael. Why don't you set up camp? I'll be back in a moment." She seized her bag and set off into the bushes.

CHAPTER 37

Michael busied himself starting a fire, arranging food, and laying the blankets side-by-side. Despite his forced concentration on mundane tasks, an image of them lying together kept rising up unbidden.

He peered through the dim light. No sight or sound of Kit. He started in her last direction. Taking a large breath to holler, he spotted her emerging from the underbrush. He halted mid-stride, his breath whooshing from his lungs.

The rising moon tinted her skin with a golden-hued glow. That skimpy black dress fluttered with each hesitant step forward. She drew nearer, crossing her arms across her breasts, and the moon lit her face. A crooked smile didn't quite reach her eyes. Her fingertips pressed into her arms, forming dimpled craters. Each dainty foot scuffed the dirt.

Nervous innocence rolled off her in waves, calling to him, yet reminding him of her painful past. Keeping his pace to a stroll, he met her halfway across the open meadow and snaked the bag off her arm, avoiding her tempting flesh.

"I worried you took so long," he said.

Kit stared up at him. Dried tears crisscrossed her cheeks. He let the bag fall and cupped her jaw, sketching the telltale marks with the gentlest of touches. Fresh drops formed on her bottom lids. He gathered her into his arms and rocked her.

"Ah, Kitten. Whatever it is, I'll fix it. Remember, my job is to protect you. After such dependable guidance, I have a lot to repay."

"You don't owe me." She sniffed and wound her arms around his waist. "We struck a deal, and the deal is over."

"Not until we reach your mine and find your father." Fondling the hair cascading down her length in silky waves, he prayed for her father's delay in order to prolong their time alone.

Kit offered up a timid smile. "You said you wanted Penny after seeing her in this dress, and you liked me wearing this before. I'm not as pretty as Penny, but maybe I'm adequate to please you tonight."

Michael shot his brows high, speechless. She still didn't understand the power of his attraction to her. Or how breathtaking her beauty.

Kit's quivering fingers toyed with his shirtfront. Stretching up, she planted a light kiss on his lips and twitched away like a frightened deer.

He expelled a heavy breath. "I don't remember which one was Penny. I watched you, not Penny, dancing in the mirror before the fire. I longed for you that night…and every night since."

Her eyes rounded. She clutched her skirt.

"Kitten, you always please me, whether in that dress or not." He lowered his voice, caressing her arms. "Don't you realize that?"

She trembled. "No, I-I didn't. I've never spent time with a man. How could I know what pleases you?"

"I thought my kisses made it clear." He positioned his mouth under her jaw and nipped her flesh. "I'll try harder."

Lifting his head, he brushed his lips along hers. Her arms stretched across his shoulders and she molded her body to his.

Heat flamed through his blood. He stroked her bodice's lacy edges, reveling in her responsive twitches and shivers. Dancing a light touch over her back, he was alert to signs of distress, silently cursing that priest for stealing her innocence.

Patience.

"Isn't it my turn to play?" Kit's breathless voice carried a coy lilt.

Michael hesitated, tamping down excitement urging him to greater haste. He tucked her fragile hand into his and led her to the fire's warm glow. Stretching out on the blanket, he smiled up at her.

"What kind of game did you have in mind?" His gruff question suspended in the still night air.

Her lids drifted half-closed. Kneeling beside him, she unbuttoned his shirt. Her nails tickled his chest as it gaped open, and he caught his breath. Leaning forward, she slid her mouth along his collarbone in smooth rhythm.

Michael squeezed his eyes tight and let her play. A smothered groan escaped.

She broke free. Missing her contact, he raised his lids and encountered her confused gaze.

"Did I hurt you?" she asked.

"Not in the least, Kitten. I enjoy your game too much. Should we keep going, or stop?"

"Oh, keep going. Please."

He sat up and gripped her wrists, giving them a little shake. "Are you sure? We might make a baby."

"Yes, I'm sure." Her confident smile entranced him. "I want you…this." Kit waved in vague circles encompassing their cozy nest.

"This isn't because of some form of payback, is it? That's not what it is for me. I mean, you shouldn't be thinking that because I first met you at Bonita's, I consider this a...business transaction."

He watched her gnaw on her bottom lip, a sure sign she felt uneasy.

"Meaning what?" she asked. "That you won't owe me anything afterward?"

"No! That I owe you everything right now." He searched her features, seeking her reciprocal commitment to a future together.

"You won't owe me for this. I want you because you are who you are. Not anything else." Placing her hands on his shoulders, she pressed her open mouth onto his. He slid his arms across her back and worked the dress buttons free.

Michael paused for breath, gazing at her dishevelment. He shifted them both and slid on top, nuzzling her neck and ears. She shivered at his slightest touch. He tangled her tongue in provocative strokes, acquainting her with passion's tempo.

He lifted a scant inch. "More?"

"Oh, yes. Please."

Michael couldn't resist her sweet begging. In any case, she wasn't a virgin. She'd even worked at a brothel. She understood exactly what she asked for.

He pulled off his boots and kicked free of his pants. Leaning on an elbow, he inched the lacy dress to her hips, eased her weight up, and slid the garment over her slender legs.

Moonbeams caressed her nakedness, and spotlighted her reaching for him.

He exulted in his fortune at her wordless invitation—Kit matched his every desire. An alien sensation washed over him, indescribable and unstoppable, outside the realm of any of his experiences.

She touched his soul.

Rising to his knees, he settled between her legs. "You vixen. Have you any idea what you do to me?"

"I can guess." Curving her arms around his neck, she kissed him thoroughly.

Michael groaned at her provocative caress and drove into her, barely registering her flinch. He halted, trembling, despite his ruthless hunger.

"Kit? Am I hurting you?"

"No more than any other woman her first time, I imagine." She nipped his sweaty chest like one of Bonita's sirens.

"Your first time? You told me that priest raped you." Doubt overwhelmed him. He fought it at the profoundest level, fearing her lies beyond what he'd ever feared at Isabel's deception.

"I said he attacked me. He couldn't…you know." Kit's fingers danced over his arms. Her caresses tempted, willing away her betrayal. "I wanted to forget the whole episode."

Should he believe her? His mind roared into focus, sifting through remnants of distant conversations, resurrecting his suspicions regarding her evasiveness.

"I'm sorry," she whispered. "I didn't mean to ruin this, or mislead you concerning my past."

Michael exhaled in a slow hiss, still doubtful, yet unable to pinpoint a lie. He had the crawling sensation he still didn't know vital information about Kit Lee.

She wrapped her legs around his hips and moved in silent invitation. He clung to the last fragment of control until her quickening gasps urged him into an overpowering, peaking rhythm.

His breath broken and uneven, he collapsed and pulled Kit into the shelter of his arms. Silky hands flitted over his body, no longer ones of an innocent. He ought to forget everything and relish the pleasures she bestowed, not hold the partial truth of her near-rape against her.

Because Lord knows, he couldn't fight his body's clamor. He was lost to her, no matter what.

CHAPTER 38

Michael arched his spine under the rough blanket as birds chirped their morning greetings. He and Kit had a few moments before practicalities interrupted their coziness. If he put off exploring his land for another hour...

A yawn cracked his jaw, a vestige of interrupted sleep and prolonged bouts of lovemaking. Not that he was complaining. No sir.

His physical satisfaction placed second to his emotional completeness. Finally, he could count on Kit staying with him. What they shared was too special. They would resolve the details, starting today.

He reached for Kit and encountered cool emptiness. Stunned, he shifted to his elbows, and listened for footsteps or rustling. He scanned for her shadow in the camp and nearby bushes.

Nothing.

His gaze fell on four grazing horses. Lucky was missing.

Piercing disillusionment replaced hot desire. After last night, he thought she would have faith in him and await his escort to her father. In the cold light of day, he wondered if she trusted him at all. Had he really jumped to the wrong conclusion regarding Father what's-his-name? He didn't remember that conversation in detail.

Except he was positive he referred to the incident once before. Didn't she realize he misunderstood? And if so, why would she keep the fact of her innocence from him? To entrap him? To control his life to suit her? To destroy his dreams?

No—Kit was different.

Wasn't she?

Rising, he pulled on dewy clothes, and shook off disgruntlement over Kit wrecking his admittedly trifling dream of a good morning kiss.

There would be other awakenings together. Any doubts were his problem, not hers. It was time he left them in the past. She had plenty of burdens without coping with his. They would untangle these missteps together.

He brewed coffee and dug for last night's forgotten jerky. His stomach rebelled after the first, tough bite. Instead, he studied the map of his claim, pairing each detailed symbol to the landmarks in front of him with awed gratitude. Kit hadn't exaggerated her unerring sense of direction.

Scolding himself for not believing in her, he savored the last sip of coffee. His land beckoned with exciting discoveries. He owned over 4,000 acres, and riding just the boundaries would take the full day. He'd follow his plan, just as she followed hers.

Last night they entered his property midway along the south side. He remembered Kit saying her mine lay a few hours distant to the north. He would swing southeast first, surveying the property line in a big circle. He would run into her if she returned midday from the north. No matter what she kept from him, he wanted her input while exploring his land and musing over possibilities.

Saddling Midnight and heading out, he skirted the forest belt tilting downward toward the expansive grassland. A burbling stream ran its entire length. Juniper trees stood in a row like sentinels, protection from storms barreling in from the Pacific Ocean. Turning east along the southern border, Midnight scrabbled on the rising terrain. Granite stones tumbled along a ravine, abandoned helter-skelter after melting snow fed the land.

Marking new features on his paper, an acute sense of contentment bathed him. Mine. To launch a future with Kit, to raise a family, to finally live free. He inhaled the pine scent and laughed aloud. Constructing quick improvements as a defense against his stepfather would be simple.

For once, his prospects were positive—in spite of Diego's trickeries!

He turned north along the hilly eastern border trail and urged Midnight forward at a canter. His map could wait. His life and Kit's wouldn't.

An odd cluster of boulders came into view. Slowing Midnight to a trot, Michael watched out for an entrance to the derelict mine Mother had mentioned purely as an afterthought. According to her, Father hadn't marked the chart, convinced there was no gold left, if there had been any to begin with. Michael sure hoped he would recognize it. He already may have passed it among craggy fields cut in half by the running stream.

Maybe Father was wrong. In a couple of weeks, he'd try his luck panning the multiple riverbeds for gold nuggets. Not now. Not when Kit might be nearby.

Rounding an outcropping, he hauled Midnight to a stop, astonished by the sprawl of a mature orchard to his left. Bright leaves protected spheres of ripening treasures. At least a hundred trimmed and pruned trees met his vision, covering acres of his land. Not a dead tree or branch in sight.

Squatters.

His excitement for the day vanished. He checked his rifle load. Another title dispute. Further confrontations.

Urging Midnight forward, he rode alongside the neat rows, marveling at the order wrested from his wild land. No human trail was visible, and strain as he might, he didn't hear voices. He pondered Ivan's wise choice of fruit as a money crop and grinned. Kit would throw herself into his arms and kiss him if he surprised her with thriving agriculture and a means to earn an initial living off his land. He kicked Midnight into a faster pace.

At the northeast corner, he checked his bearings. The boundary markings were vague, a scattering of lines indicating a generally westward bend. Turning Midnight's head, he guided the horse down a steep path, searching the ground for shrouded openings that might indicate a gold mine. Midnight slowed halfway and picked with mincing steps over the loose stones. His hooves skidded, and a hail of rocks slithered over the crest.

A loud whinny broke the late morning peacefulness. Michael dismounted. The squatters must live close—a family, an old miner, or young hoodlums. Any might resent the lawful owner's eviction. He retrieved his rifle. Better safe than sorry. He slunk to the bend and peeked around the rock.

"Kitten!" He ran toward the slumped figure. "Are you hurt?"

CHAPTER 39

Kit stared up at Michael, drained of energy. Ecstasy and grief from the last day scampered around in her brain, squelching a response.

Early this morning, she wanted to share every sentiment with Michael. His willingness to start a family had captivated her as proof he cared, even without the words. He must have wanted her for more than the night. He must want her for his wife.

She ached to kiss him awake, to see his eyes alight, and to reassure them both that the loving they shared was real...and lasting.

Kit never wanted to leave him again.

But she would have lost her courage to face his inevitable questions. She had to finish what she started. Her dreams had propelled her for too long to discard, regardless of the temptation of Michael's snug embrace.

She snuck from camp, ignoring dawn's light kissing her face instead. Disconcertingly well-known landscapes ushered her trek north. She didn't care what she found at the mine, only that she move beyond any hurt she caused if it were indeed on his land.

Too soon, she reached the mine entrance, for a minute uncertain if she was at the right place. Vegetation overgrew the stout wooden frame, reclaiming it inch by inch. Peeking inside, she stared into threatening murkiness. She ventured a half step forward and stubbed her toe on a weathered board. Stooping, she picked it up and tilted it toward the pearly morning sun, examining the faded scratches.

"Kit's Mine."

She hurled the signboard outside.

Her tear-blurred gaze caught the flutter of paper affixed to a tree guarding the mine entrance. She lifted it from the nail with utmost care, opened it, and recognized Papa's scholarly cursive.

"Kit, if you find this you are well, and for that I am grateful. I sent a message to the San Francisco Mission; however, they did not know who or where you were. Circumstances force me to return to Sacramento immediately. You cannot stay at the mine. It is not ours. Come to Sacramento by Independence Day, otherwise I will seek you in San Francisco. Ask for me at the county courthouse. Your loving father, Lee."

She clasped the letter to her chest and wept, smiling in relief through her tears. Papa was alive—yet clearly not able to fulfill his promise and claim their mine, nor remain even one additional day. Pity swept over her. She would do whatever it took so Papa could feel like a man again, not a failure—nor a slave.

For long hours, she paced to and from the mine, alternating between sobbing and shaking her fists at the sky. The likelihood of claiming the mine had sustained her family for years. Acknowledging its fruitlessness before confirmation would have betrayed Mama's loyalty, Papa's struggles, and her abiding faith in their love and hope. But now she knew.

She'd never be able to convince Michael that she had doubts, or that she prayed their properties were coincidentally tangential, not hopelessly intertwined. Would he have understood if she told him yesterday? Two days ago? This morning? No time seemed appropriate. Now, he might misinterpret last night as a ruthless seduction, not an honest demonstration of the depth of her feelings.

His powerful loving was more beautiful than she ever imagined. The bliss he gave her intensified their intimacy. She craved to become a part of his future, to incorporate him as a part of hers, fully and completely. She wanted her nights spent sheltered in his arms. It was how to spend the rest of her days that troubled her.

Pulling herself into the present, she stared at the furrows etched onto Michael's brow. Guilt sealed her throat, every silent second dooming her further.

"What are you doing here? Did you see your father? Are you lost?" Michael's rapid questions stung her like pellets from a shotgun. "Tell me what's going on, Kitten. Whatever it is, we'll work it out." Squatting in front of her, he rested his palms on her knees.

"You'll never forgive me." She forced the hoarse whisper through constricted neck muscles.

"Try me."

Tears streamed down her cheeks. She shook her head.

"Did you find your father this morning?" he asked.

"He left a note. He lives in Sacramento at present, and couldn't stay to meet me. We don't own the mine." Kit crumpled the note into a ball and clutched his left hand. She swiped her nose, willing the tears away.

He tilted his hat up. "Aren't you happy you know where your father is, even though someone else owns your mine?"

"You own the mine," she said. Feeling dull and listless, she kicked the signboard toward his feet.

"Your mine is on my land?"

"Yes."

"How long have you known?" he asked.

"I wasn't positive until this morning. I suspected it since I first read your map."

"And you didn't see fit to enlighten me?" His brittle voice vibrated in anger.

"You would have assumed I used you to get to my mine," she choked out.

"And didn't you?" He wrenched his fingers free.

Kit stiffened. "No! That wasn't the real reason. I was afraid you would leave me, and I had to meet Papa on time. Remember the dangers? I never would have arrived if it weren't for you." The depth of his mistrust pained her after their passionate interlude last night. Would she ever stop believing in foolish dreams?

"Besides, you kept a secret from me as well," she said. "You should have warned me of those ruffians before they attacked us."

Shame crossed his face. "That's different. It didn't affect you."

"Being almost raped and killed didn't affect me? Are you joking?" She raised her voice. "And in case you forgot, if I had told you and your stubborn male pride left me behind, you probably wouldn't be here, either."

"At least when I got here, I wouldn't worry some cheap coolie gal snagged me with her innocence!"

Kit reared back. Fury replaced despair. Her tears dried in an instant. Jutting her chin up, she rose and linked her arms against her chest, glowering.

"I guess now I know your true feelings. I won't stay and help since I'm less than muck beneath your feet." She battled for a cool tone. "I'll leave today for Sacramento. You'll never see me again." She spun on her heel and swung onto her horse.

"Wait a minute!" Michael's shout halted her.

She kept her face averted. "What?"

"I don't have much work to finish. Someone lived here in recent months. As a result, I hold improved land. That should cover the claim."

"Why should I care?"

Michael captured her stirrup and shook it. "Because I'm able to escort you to Sacramento."

"I'm perfectly able to ride to Sacramento without you." Kit reached for her remaining dignity. She flicked the ends of the reins into her palm.

"Our deal included escorting you to your father safely. My part of the bargain is unfinished. I keep my word. Besides, I have business in Sacramento with my stepfather that won't keep."

Kit tilted her head sideways and met his gaze. More secrets. What nerve, being angry at her for not notifying him about the mine. "What business?"

"Since you didn't share what you knew in advance, I don't think I owe you any courtesy, either. A partnership is only as good as the trust between two parties. So much for your handshakes—and your kisses." He snorted and released his hold on her mount.

Kit's anger deflated at his undisguised hurt. She still loved him, but what good would it do to profess her feelings? He'd never believe her.

"All right," she said. "After we're done here, we'll go to Sacramento and settle our respective family business. Funny, isn't it? Our fathers are keeping us together when they both drove us away." She kicked Lucky hard and galloped into the woods.

Arriving at the campsite, Kit sought distractions. She thoroughly groomed the four horses and tidied the gear. Still feeling troubled, she hunted for rabbit, planning a hearty stew. She transferred her aggravation onto the carcass, hacking the skin and meat off the bones and tossing the raggedy scraps into the pot. She searched for fresh greens, and added them to the stew. Settling next to the fire, she stared at the disappearing twilight, striving for her usual enjoyment of the night sky. No use. Instead, the pot's slow simmer matched her seething emotions.

Dreams for her future went up in smoke in a matter of hours—including the wisps of a life with Michael. She was past tears. Only heartache remained.

He didn't want to hear why she didn't disclose everything. He jumped to conclusions as usual. Worse, he didn't comprehend how much she respected his ownership of the mine. She would never take it from the rightful owner. She merely wished Papa were that person, someway. Foolish, childish dreams.

Now, her future appeared desolate and all too real. City living, probably in a slum full of Chinese men, saddled with a husband Papa would choose.

No freedom. No space to grow.

Nothing.

And no Michael—except perhaps his child to remember him by.

CHAPTER 40

Under the rising moon's amber rays, Michael approached the grassy meadow as weary as if he'd single-handedly lassoed an entire herd of cattle. After scouting for hours, he found no signs of recent habitation. Yet someone tended the orchard—who? He was stumped.

Too bad Father never spoke of this wonderful refuge. The orchard and pastures conformed to the lands' contours, and abundant fresh water irrigated them. Sunny and shady areas offered a choice of prime home sites framed by the far-off ranges. In a word, Paradise.

As long as Paradise included a certain woman.

Should he forgive Kit's lies? Her reddened eyes and tear tracks provided ample evidence of her sorrow. He'd deliberated their encounter all afternoon, and couldn't jettison his suspicions. He reached deep, for once not burying his feelings. Grown men acknowledged facts. And he knew without a doubt, he was in for a world of hurt.

For what? She pretended ignorance of the whereabouts of Kit's Mine. Her furtive departure this morning served as proof. Then, she remained silent and aloof even as he demanded the truth, while his gut screwed into knots over her betrayal.

Yesterday he would have scoffed at the idea that she would manipulate him for gold. He was convinced her feelings toward him ran as pure as her loving, despite her body's abused imperfection. Last night, he discovered otherwise. Her body was chaste, yet not her motivations.

He cursed his stupidity with a string of profanities.

Just this morning he planned building a life together, including the responsibility of raising an already-conceived child with her. When she threatened leaving for Sacramento alone, a knife blade of agony shot through him.

He still wanted her, no matter how terrible the cut. Kit burrowed under his skin to his heart. To his very soul.

Except...what other lies was she hiding? He prayed meeting up with her father would furnish the complete truth. Until he found out, further intimacies were unwise...assuming he wouldn't go crazy from not touching her. He groaned, the sloping valley echoing his dejection.

He was the biggest fool he knew.

Riding into a neatened camp, he spied Kit huddled near the cook fire looking as miserable as he felt. He sniffed in hungry anticipation and his mouth watered.

She rose and approached, grasping the halter. "I'll care for Midnight while you clean up. You've had a long day, while I rested this afternoon."

Michael started to protest, but his muscles voiced their complaint. He caved, too exhausted for a protracted argument, and dismounted. "Thanks. I'll help you."

She constantly stunned him—first lies, now kindheartedness. Despite their fight and his rebukes, she reverted to business as usual. Fine by him. They did better keeping their distance.

He pulled the saddle off and stacked it with the others. She led Midnight to the pasture, retrieved the comb and started grooming. In short order, they completed their routine and walked to the fire side by side.

"Would you like supper?" Kit dolloped food onto the plate and held it out to him. "I'll eat from the pot."

Ignoring her selfless offer, he ransacked the saddlebags, unearthing the spare plate, mug, and fork he uncovered yesterday morning when his spirits were high. He spooned up his portion and settled onto the ground, his rumbling stomach filling the gloomy hush.

She nibbled at her fare. "Did you discover squatters?"

"No, and it doesn't appear anyone has lived here for a long while." He didn't trust her enough to share the rest. He shoveled the remaining food into his mouth. "This is delicious. May I have more?"

"Of course." Kit refilled his dish and met his gaze. He sensed her reciprocal study—weighing facts and circumstances, seeking any fleeting confirmation an emotional tie survived.

"I have a couple of questions," he said. "Will you promise to speak the absolute truth?"

"Yes. You always deserved that." Her throat convulsed. "I-I'm sorry I didn't trust you before."

He managed a jerky nod, not yet ready for her apologies. "Do you think your father has been living here this past year?"

"No. If he had, he would have built a shelter near the mine to survive the winter cold." Melancholy settled on her features. "He traveled all those miles simply to leave me a note, and couldn't stay an extra day to meet me. Obviously he doesn't have the freedom to leave—not yet."

He hesitated. "Is he trying to claim the mine as his?"

"If he is, he will fail. You know a Chinese man cannot buy or claim land. Unless you or your father gave it to him, he has no right to this property."

"Father bequeathed this land to me," he reminded her, perturbed by the transparent hint for a gift of his future livelihood.

"Well, yes. Papa's already conceded the mine isn't ours."

"Will you try to claim the mine instead?"

She gaped at him. "Of course not. Why would you think that?"

"Because after our conversations, I'm well aware how keen you are to own land. You know your legal rights, and now have something to hang over my head for at least title to the mine."

"What on earth do I hold over you?"

He searched for signs of disingenuousness. "You naïve fool," he breathed, holding her gaze. "Don't you realize there are consequences for taking your innocence?"

"No! You didn't take it. I gave myself to you." She choked on her cry, her hand outstretched in mute appeal.

"Are you sure?" Michael couldn't stop the sarcastic remark, memories of his utter disillusionment washing over him once more. "It's a more sophisticated form of prostitution. Nonetheless, the end result is the same—payment for services rendered."

Kit flinched. "I've told you I'm not a whore many times. I'm tired of saying it. You don't owe me—especially for that." She wrapped her arms around her upraised knees. "It was priceless, anyway."

He hesitated at her last, whispered words. Venting his annoyance was pointless. Maybe he had been too quick to assume the worst.

Scrutinizing her, he swallowed the last bite and set aside his plate, debating if he should share his afternoon's strategizing. Which of the two plans had the greatest chance of success?

The one demanding his full trust—and her full cooperation.

"Tell me what you remember from your childhood here," he said, poking at the fire with a twig. If she released her anger, he would as well. He merely needed convincing to trust her another time.

"I don't remember much." Her head moved in a broad sweep, paralleling the dim landscape. "We lived adjacent to the mine. Mama kept my play far away from the entrance. Occasionally my parents would bring me on walks and we ended up in this field."

"Did your parents mine any gold?"

"I assume so, since they stayed for a few years. Obviously, they didn't dig up a fortune, or we would have led very different lives."

She paused. Apprehension replaced nostalgia on her features. Her chest rose and fell in uneven rhythm. "Will...will you demand payment for the gold we stole from you? I'll pay you back. It may take a while. I need a job first. I don't know what Papa's circumstances are. They're probably not very good."

The iciness sheathing his bruised heart thawed in degrees.

"I don't expect reimbursement," he said. "If not your family, it would be someone else who is long gone. Those are the risks Father took by not living here."

She dipped her head in quiet acquiescence. At least she didn't pile on with further criticisms. His self-recriminations stacked high enough already. However, she could shed light on what had bothered him since morning.

"Do you remember your parents planting trees while you were here?" he asked.

"Trees?"

"There's an orchard near the mine—dozens of trees. I can't figure out who planted them—or who's been tending them since Father died."

"I recall Mama saying she missed the orchards from her childhood home in Boston," Kit said. "All I remember is them working the mine."

Rolling that mystery over in his mind, he propped on his elbows and contemplated the dying fire. Exhaustion weighed at him. He wished this day would simply end. Tomorrow had to be better. Kit seemed to have told him what she knew. Her anguish, once she let her guard down, appeared genuine.

Why was trust difficult? Pain from a juvenile infatuation shouldn't hold sway over his interactions with women forever. Nor disappointment in Mother for weakening and marrying that bloodsucker Diego. None of his past related to Kit, here and now.

It was his own judgment he didn't trust, not Kit's. His inflexibility created this predicament, not hers. Diego's taunts calling him a fool preoccupied him too often. With luck, Diego would soon be a faint memory, not a persistent nuisance. It was past time he grew beyond a boy's hurt and into a man.

He roused himself from the reverie. "I'm building a sort of shelter— a shack at best. If you help, it shouldn't take more than a day. After that, we can leave for Sacramento."

Kit nodded, extinguished the fire, and covered the stew pot. She gathered up the utensils and turned aside, preventing further conversation.

He captured her wrist, pinning her in place. Touching her skin set his blood on fire. He clenched his jaw. He didn't dare lose control. His heart wasn't ready. A good rest and time should sort out his feelings. Loving her once more wouldn't.

"You keep surprising me," Michael admitted in a low growl. "Last night was bad enough, but then again this morning...I still don't trust you completely."

Kit knelt next to him. "I apologize. I didn't mean to deceive or hurt you. I wasn't sure where the mine was until this morning. I'm not hiding anything, truly." She grazed his knuckles with fingers that trembled.

"I want to believe you, Kit. I can't. Not yet. Perhaps it will seem clearer in the morning."

Her damp lashes lifted and fell in rapid succession. "Go to sleep. I'll clean up and turn in soon."

Michael succumbed to the wave of grogginess, rolling into the blanket and letting blissful stupor engulf him.

CHAPTER 41

"It'll have to do," Michael said, stepping back and surveying their day's handiwork.

They'd spent hours of hard effort dragging branches to the mine for a shelter and lashing them into three dividers, then balancing the makeshift structure alongside a vertical boulder functioning as the fourth wall. Kit gathered fir branches and strewed them atop the tarpaulin for a roof. She spread broken twigs and leaves onto the ground several inches high, creating a fragrant bed. He scattered the belongings from the dead men next to the walls as if someone lived there.

"It doesn't look lived in." Kit snapped her fingers. "I know what's missing. There's no fire pit."

He gouged his heel in the dirt, scraping loose soil to the edge of a growing circle near a fallen tree. "How's that?"

"It's still too pristine. There should be a worn path to the water." She kicked aside pebbles and trampled weeds leading from the mine.

"Let's spend the night inside the shack, and at least it will appear used," he suggested. "We'll leave for Sacramento straight from here tomorrow. I already hobbled the new horses near the stream, and they have plenty of fresh grass to hold them for several days."

"If you say so. What else still needs doing?"

Michael cocked his hip, inspecting Kit's drooping posture and grim mouth. She'd worked without complaint, pushing the limits of her physical strength.

He had one final test to overcome his misgivings. Why proof of her loyalty was essential, he wasn't certain. His calculating actions resembled Diego's—and against Kit! No, he wasn't that bad—or was he? He swallowed rising mortification.

"We'll finish in the morning. Let's rest." He tugged her next to him onto the inviting log. "I need to share information with you before we leave, and it may take a while for you to understand."

Her clinging fingers relaxed a bit. "What is it?"

"Based on what I learned from Maria and Isabel, I will have to fight my stepfather for this land another time. It's become quite complicated." Exasperation clouded his vision for a brief moment, and he pulled on fistfuls of hair to clear it. "I decided on a plan I think will work. I'll need your help to pull it off, and I'd like to strike a different agreement."

"I'll abide by whatever you say. Truly."

He extricated the fistful of papers from the saddlebag, and handed them to her.

Kit read the first page. Crossing her ankles, she skimmed the rest, her brow wrinkling. With a shake of her head, she gave them back. "I don't understand."

"I found these in the belongings of the men who jumped us." He lifted the scrap bearing Pedro's name in a messy scrawl. "It seems Pedro holds a grudge against you for whipping him at poker and winning Lucky."

"Her name says it all."

He managed a half-smile, relieved she could still joke. "My guess is Pedro spread the word we were horse thieves and you're my Chinese slave girl. He figured my stepfather would pay for proof."

"Is that what this telegram means?"

"Probably," he said. "Diego usually stays in that hotel in Sacramento. Those four men figured it was worth their while to stalk us and collect the reward."

"How is Diego linked into this?" she asked.

Michael drew a settling breath, mentally running over the precise order of his entire plan. With her intelligence, she could help remedy its flaws—it was in no respect foolproof.

"This next paper is a contract between my stepfather and a client named Jenkins, hiring Diego to defend her land claim in court," he said." I can't imagine Diego ever allowing this contract to see the light of day. My guess is one of the four men is her relation. He probably owes Diego a bundle of money for legal fees. Maybe he was interested in trading information about us to pay Diego."

Her alarmed gaze swung up to meet his. "Go on."

"What he probably doesn't know is Diego intends to seize the land in lieu of payment, which is the method he used to confiscate our San Jose ranch. By keeping the land title in dispute for months while his client lives on it, Diego bills the settler rent while he purposely delays it in court. Then no matter who wins the legal claim, Diego owns the land as payment for services rendered."

"That's plain theft!"

"I told you he's a wonderful person, didn't I?" He booted a stone clear across the stream. Too bad he couldn't kick Diego's contemptuous butt, instead.

"I had no idea he would go to these lengths on a routine basis," Kit said. "I thought it was just you he hated."

"And that makes him a better man?"

"I'm sorry, Michael. I don't mean to be hateful. I..." She nibbled at her lip. "I promised you last night I'd speak the truth. Honestly, I had no idea the courts legitimized false contracts and side deals to steal outright from lawful citizens. I thought it was only Chinese immigrants who were exploited."

"Oh, he'll go further if he thinks it's worth it. I think I can use this document to turn the tables on him and bring Diego's world of elaborate schemes crashing down. Which brings me to the final document. Do you understand its value?"

"No." She stared at her folded hands.

He cupped her jaw, lifting her face toward him. "It's basically a title to own any available 160 acres for whoever holds the paper."

"Who owns the paper?"

"You, if you consent to my plan."

"What do you mean?"

Michael released her and strove for neutral tones, keeping his emotions buried. In the end, she might still choose to pursue her dreams without him. "In return for pretending to be my wife in Sacramento to fool my stepfather, you collect on this land warrant. It will allow you to obtain acreage anywhere in the country, at no cost to you."

Silence met his recommendation. He clamped interlinked fingers around his knee.

"No," Kit said.

"No to the land or pretending to be my wife?"

"I won't accept land as payment. I already told you I would gladly help you for free—including pretending to be your wife." She folded her arms across her chest and scowled. "And if you don't understand that about me yet, you never will."

"Really?" Astonishment battled relief.

"Consider it another case where I surprised you and leave it at that. Though surely by now you should have gotten it through your thick skull that I am not for sale."

Irritation slithered through him. He drew a deep breath. She lifted a finger in warning, forestalling his argument.

"I told you I'd agree to whatever you asked," she said. "And that was before you advised me of the land warrant. Consider that when you decide what kind of person I am."

"Hmm. What kind of person do you think I am?" Instead of the careless inquiry he strove for, lurking insecurity laced the question.

She leaned her chin on clasped knees, her gaze unflinching. "I think you're a very caring man who grew up disappointed by people who claimed to love you. As a result, you have a difficult time trusting anyone, including yourself. Women close to you betrayed your faith in them. When I hid the whole truth from you, it added to your belief you shouldn't rely on any woman."

A tear glittered on her lashes. Using the heel of her palm, she brushed it aside.

Kit continued. "I think you are also a generous man, a good man, someone who is worth the effort to earn your trust. Once I had it, it was the most beautiful feeling in the world." Moisture brightened her gaze. "And I'd give my soul to have it again," she whispered.

His defenses melted a little further at her candor. He searched her jeweled eyes, seeing but not quite believing the depth of her emotions. His feelings had mirrored hers—until yesterday. Until he concluded that she had seduced and used him. Yet today, she'd—almost—re-earned his full trust.

Now here he was, plotting and scheming, using her in pursuit of his objective in the same manner he accused her of using him. He cursed silently. If this was Diego's style, why should she believe his word in return?

Michael bowed his head. "I'm sorry it seemed as if I was offering to pay you like a prostitute."

"Thank you for that, at least."

At her wounded tone, he glanced up, wanting to bore into her mind and read her thoughts. Disgrace pummeled him, yet he couldn't choke words past his knotted throat.

"It seems you've finally begun to accept the truth concerning who I am—and who I am not—despite your bad experiences," she said.

"I'm proposing a method for you to still live your dream, even though your old one isn't viable." He winced at the lame explanation, and forged ahead anyway. "You remember we discussed taking advantage of opportunities instead of fixating on a single goal?"

Kit nodded.

"That land warrant holds no value for me," he said. "Rather than sell it, I'll give it to you as thanks for helping my dream happen."

"I appreciate your consideration, but I meant it. I'll help you for no payment. It's the least I can do." Wistfulness colored her refusal.

Curiosity piqued, Michael nevertheless stopped further attempt at persuasion. From this point on, he would believe she wasn't hiding anything. "Agreed, then. Thanks."

He rose from the hard log and stretched his arms high, disgruntled at his role as favor seeker instead of as a fair trader. Perhaps this is how Kit felt at the start of their journey, beholden to him, a hindrance rather than a help. If using another tactic would thwart Diego, he sure didn't know it.

Rising to her feet in a graceful motion, Kit gestured to the lean-to. "Those pine needles are very soft, and I'm quite tired. Are you ready for bed?"

Longing tore at his last vestiges of disbelief. He stepped in her direction and halted, deliberating whom he trusted least. Her—or himself?

Her lips formed a crooked smile. "We'll sleep. I'm not expecting anything else." She ducked into the shelter.

He followed her inside, layering the blankets so they could lie on one and share the other. Snuggling her back against his, Kit fell asleep immediately. He lay wide-awake and stared into the darkness.

Half of him was ecstatic. She proved his suspicions wrong, and was as gallant as she claimed. The other half wished she would accept the cursed warrant. Then his sense of right and wrong would allow him to re-define their whole relationship as simply a business transaction. No deals. No obligations. No hurt.

No Kit.

Stay focused.

Diego was his problem, not Kit. His land battle started before he ever met her. He would win in Sacramento, no matter what.

Unfortunately, that left him scarce comfort. What good was life if no other person shared it?

A cascading swirl of emotions tormented him. Rage at Diego for his selfish greed. Belated terror from their near death at Diego's orders. Frustration he couldn't follow his simple plan. Confusion that Kit was in the middle of it. And he was no closer to discovering what she truly desired from him, or from herself.

CHAPTER 42

Kit shaded her eyes from the evening sun blazing sideways down O Street in Sacramento. Store banners shimmered like fool's gold above freshly hewn wood. Business buildings dotted the town, their flapping signs promoting flourishing endeavors. Emporiums, iron works, assayers, and taverns served this bustling crossroads of transportation, politics and miners.

Plodding through crowds, her skin crawled at the ever-increasing oppressiveness. They eluded fast-moving carriages and lumbering wagons full of newcomers. It reminded her of San Francisco—minus the cleansing fog to hide its warts. Sacramento seemed raw, crude, and proud of it.

She prayed Papa didn't enjoy his existence here. Living in the wilderness suited her far better. She would ask for him at the courthouse after Michael settled the pressing affairs with his stepfather. There was no rush. She still had two weeks to locate Papa —and maybe keep Michael at her side in the meantime.

They rode by the Capital Hotel, an imposing three-story structure split by an encircling balcony. Based on what Michael told her, Diego probably roomed on the top floor to feel powerful, above the hassles of politics. Better than everyone else.

Michael pointed the horses toward an unassuming inn on Front Street, set atop a row of busy eateries. Dismounting, he walked to Lucky's side and lifted her free, waiting until she caught her balance to release her waist. He pushed the door open and escorted her inside.

"I'll order a bath right away, and you can relax," he said. "It will take me a few minutes to arrange for the horses, and then I'm going to set up a meeting with Diego. Take a nap if you like."

Kit soon followed the proprietress up a steep flight of stairs, her weary legs faltering. They stopped inside the door of a spacious room. A high curved tub nestled in the far corner, adjacent to a wide bed with a pristine coverlet. At the opposite side stood a pine dresser, topped by a reflecting glass. The twilight's rays poked through lace curtains, patterning the mirror, and flooding the room with a peachy glow.

Incredulous at Michael's extravagance for their stay, Kit was also disconcerted. Apparently, he assumed they would share a bed.

A chambermaid younger than Kit elbowed past, a steaming bucket dripping watermarks onto the floorboards.

"We'll fill that tub for you in a minute, dearie, then we'll leave you be," the older woman said. "You poor thing. Your nice husband said you were real tired."

Of course. Their make-believe as a married couple started now.

The matron patted her arm. "A hot bath will set you straight. We won't empty it until morning, so enjoy your soak." She bustled from the room, shoving the chambermaid in front of her. The maid returned with two additional buckets of hot water, then closed the door with hardly a click.

Kit wasted no time stripping off her filthy clothes. She sank into steaming water up to her chin and pondered Michael's contradictions while sponging off the grime. True, he shared the blanket last night, but he didn't touch her once. Her heart ached at his cool distance. He barely said two words to her during the long hours, yet surprised her with this attentiveness.

She bemoaned her ability ever to get past his closed mind. Yes, she kept from him the possibility her mine was on his land. But she told him the truth as soon as she confirmed it, and was honest ever since. However, assurances wouldn't ease his wariness. She was one more in a string of people who lied to him.

He was living as he always had—uncompromisingly aloof, guarding his heart from emotional turmoil. She rested her head on the bathtub edge, remembering instead the warm, responsive man who came alive in her arms. If nothing else, she had the memories of their passion. And possibly a child. A son who might resemble him, helping her preserve these precious days.

Loud footsteps jostled her from a doze. A grim-faced Michael entered the room, slipped the saddlebags onto the floor, and approached. Gazing into the shimmering water, his eyes became half-slits. A blood vessel ticked in rapid beats alongside his throat.

"Rested?" He knelt facing her, and his finger traced the length of her arm.

Kit pulled herself from her sensuous dreams and bobbed assent, reaching for the towel hanging on the tub's far edge.

"Where are you going?" he asked.

"I-I was going to let you bathe while the water is still hot."

"Make room for two." He shed his grimy clothes in fluid motions, never taking his gaze from her body.

She pulled her legs up until her knees broke through the surface, uncertain, yet hopeful. He stepped into the tub, maneuvered into the remaining space, and tangled his legs with hers. Reaching for the soap, he scrubbed hard, ignoring her. She watched in fascination, and smiled in anticipation.

"I'll clean your back," she said. Clutching the slick bar, Kit lifted up and out of the water. Her thigh grazed his grizzled jaw. He froze, hissing, and gripped the rim with whitened knuckles. She knelt and washed him with a provocative touch.

"Am I getting the right place?" She craved to re-capture their laughing banter and easy friendliness, to lose herself in those wonderful sensations, if only for a brief moment of unreality. It might be her only experience of love.

"Apparently you learned seduction at Bonita's," he growled, creating a small wave as he twisted to face her. "Will any man satisfy you now?"

In silent denial of his accusation, Kit nonetheless tolerated his lurking doubt, his need to feel special. She ran trembling palms over his slick muscles. If this was all she got from him, she would take it. She might never change his prejudices. Maybe love wasn't enough. On the other hand, desire might vanquish that old, habitual distrust.

He gripped her jaw and kissed her with bruising force. "Let's see if you can really enjoy a man."

CHAPTER 43

Michael would give her exactly what she asked for—and what he coveted. His lust went beyond physical, beyond the present. Possessing her drove him. Branding her his and his alone. This would cost him, but he no longer fought his addiction.

He surged to his feet and splashed out, tugging her onto the bed.

"Do you know why men chase after women? Why they pay for them?" Michael's emotions churned in hectic cadence, mocking him. He knew his answer. He would pay any price for Kit like this, pliant and willing beneath him. He hungered for her as he pictured at Bonita's—no complications, no emotions. No caring. Forgetting the in-between time.

"Because they enjoy making love?" she asked.

"Because women make men forget everything else. They don't think straight. Except what women repeatedly forget, as you told me, is it lasts merely a few minutes." He prayed pure carnality would lessen his hurts and doubts, seeking and reaching blissful oblivion.

Michael rolled aside, breath heaving, and stared through the window into blackness. What was he doing? He couldn't purge her from his system with a quick tumble in bed. If they didn't stop, they would create a child soon. A baby would be a joint responsibility. Was he as happy today accepting proof of their passion?

Was she?

Kit curled into a ball next to him. A single tear spilled onto the wrinkled bedclothes.

Evidently not. He grappled with his guilty conscience in silence.

"Are you still willing to be my protector?" Her somber question floated into the dim room.

Relieved to continue their business arrangement, he cleared his throat. "Of course. We had a deal until we found your father."

"I'll hunt for Papa tonight, and I must blend in so I can ask for him in the Chinese area of town. I don't think the other guests will take kindly to a coolie coming down the stairs. I need you to sneak me out."

"You're dressing in your old clothes and walking dark streets asking for your father? Yes, I'll be there protecting you."

"Unfortunately, I don't think the Chinese will be thrilled seeing a Californio. They may not open up to me if you're there. Won't you wait for me here?"

"No. It's either with me at your side or not at all." He grasped her arms and rolled her flat, staring into her mutinous face. "No extra risks."

"Because if I'm not in court as your pretend wife it will hurt your claim?"

"Because I don't want you in danger, even to find your father," he said through gritted teeth, nerves raw at her pointed reminder of his very odd request. "Don't you remember what it was like to be almost killed? It's happened to you often enough. You will run out of luck sometime."

In turmoil, he rose and crossed to the window. He'd failed as her bodyguard many times already, and here she was, putting herself into another chancy situation, relying on him to keep her safe.

"I don't intend to get killed," she said. "I'm looking for Papa. Besides, I think I've used up my luck."

"Another reason not to take unnecessary chances. I'll be as inconspicuous as possible, but I'm not letting you go alone." He calculated the drop to the alleyway, and smiled at the latest quirk of fate. "Who knows, maybe I'll be more of a help than you believe."

"Why do you think that?"

"I seem to have a knack for helping you jump from windows," he said.

Kit rose, stepped to his side, and peered out.

He slid an arm along her hips. "It's a long fall down, so I'll catch you at the bottom—again. And boost you up afterward." He swatted her backside, turning the pats into lingering caresses.

"Evidently I will need you," she said. "Thank you."

"May we eat first? Those sounds you're hearing are my stomach clamoring."

"If you stop distracting me." With a demure smile, Kit stepped away and rifled through the saddlebag.

"Let's picnic on the bed." He spread their remaining food on the tangled sheets.

"And have dessert when we return," she said, winking.

Michael's mind raced through possibilities, flooded with sudden anticipation and happiness. God help him, he needed Kit. Needed her sweetness, her acceptance of his foibles, her enduring optimism.

CHAPTER 44

"Keep low," Kit hissed over her shoulder. It was no use. Michael towered over the Chinese men in the packed saloon. He crowded behind her, creating a void of silence before and after.

She pushed the door open and entered another decrepit neighborhood along I Street. The stench from the compressed humanity crammed onto meandering riverbanks rose in choking waves.

"This isn't working," she sighed. After two hours of searching, not one person would talk to her. A renewed sense of urgency to reunite with Papa pushed her. Any dream was better than having none. The present was her only future—unless she re-earned Michael's belief in her.

Unless that, too, was a hopeless dream.

"Can't we search for him during the day?" Michael's testiness was palpable. "We won't get answers at night."

She shot him a withering glance. "People may assume you bought me from him and want your money refunded. Is that what you want?"

He clamped his lips together, the twitching muscle in his cheek resembling an angry cat's tail.

Kit scanned the alley and shacks in this distant section of China Slough, identical to every other winding lane through the squalid ghetto. Crowded and noisy, it still showed a sense of order, a desire for self-respect injected into abandoned lives.

Old men squatted on rickety stools, talking in hushed voices. They scrutinized Kit and Michael, yet focused elsewhere as they approached. Dogs, pigs, and chickens ran wild, their incessant racket adding to the drone of constant indoor chatter. Opium's rank smell drifted in the night air from some outlying hovel, an irresistible siren call to those forsaking ambition altogether. Kit suspected poor slave girls inhabited those vile shacks, servicing wretched hundreds paying for sexual consummation.

Her bravado slipped away. This was far worse than any place her parents settled. Maybe Papa expected her to care for him here as he aged, marrying an old Chinese man he would attain for her, as befitted a fallen woman.

No!

She wouldn't live here, although she must take care of Papa. Somehow. She would earn a living using her woman's brains and talents. Except...would any man take her seriously if even Michael didn't?

"Let's go." She couldn't abide this place.

Fingers resting on her waist, Michael escorted her toward the inn, politely aloof. Apparently, the slum's conditions didn't sicken him. Of course, he owned that wonderful property while she had—

Nothing.

Reaching the deserted alleyway under their window, Michael hoisted her into his arms, his hot breath warming her backside. He shifted his hands, cupped her buttocks, and lifted her high. She leveraged her elbows onto the sill.

"I'll be up in a moment," Michael said.

His sultry promise gave her the strength to haul herself inside the room. She removed her loathsome trousers and jacket, and waited by the bed dressed in her threadbare camisole, trembling with anticipation.

The door opened. With a rueful smile, Michael eased the door closed, crossed the room, and tugged her into his arms.

"I forget my good intentions when I'm near you." He punctuated his complaint with fervent kisses.

"Which intentions are the good ones?"

"I don't know anymore," he said. "You've upended my world. I had my life figured out already, and it didn't include anyone like you."

Kit stilled at his anguished confession. Between Diego's conniving and her unexpected presence, she wasn't surprised he was tentative. So was she. Especially if he already decided to desert her after confronting Diego.

No matter, she would take what she could get. From him. With him. Her fantasy life had disappeared into a permanent, terrible detour. Even having a bastard child couldn't ruin that future. She certainly no longer worried about her past.

"Then let's forget our intentions for a while and enjoy each other." She wrapped her arms around his neck.

"That's all? Fun and games?" Unhappiness warred with relief on his face.

"I want you, Michael Rivers, no matter your intentions...or the repercussions. This is the most fun I've ever had."

"Me, too." Michael's whispered breath tickled her ear.

"Then let's play."

CHAPTER 45

Michael blinked awake as morning sun lightened the room. Kit's naked form lay cozily in his arms, and he remembered his repeated vow to kiss her awake.

He'd been happy then, assured of her fine character, unlike now. His body raged, urging him to take her, and dull the persistent stings of her lie. No, he should absolve her, instead. He took a quavering breath, yet couldn't force forgiveness past his lips. Such an amazing woman deserved that much. What still bothered him?

She wanted her freedom—without him.

Once he owned the land free and clear he would talk to her. Yes, that was it. He couldn't decide anything with Kit until his own direction cleared up. She was right—they should simply enjoy the wonderful and precious. He fondled the curves filling his embrace, tempted.

No distractions. Not today.

He rolled from bed and splashed water on his cheeks. His first priority—dig for information to cut Diego's local power out from underneath him. If good luck smiled on Michael, they'd confront him over lunch and put him on the offensive.

Luck—bah! Michael loathed the thought of seeing Diego. However, since his thugs failed their assignment, his stepfather might become sloppy in his obsession to beat Michael. And that's when he could vanquish Diego.

Kit lifted her head from the pillow. "Do you need me?"

"You stay in bed a while longer. I'll fill you in on my plan before lunch with Diego." He gave her a quick kiss, ignoring the delicious invitation of the rumpled bed. Later. She yawned and closed her eyes with a whimper. Gathering his strewn clothes from the floor, he dressed in haste before he changed his mind.

Michael clattered down the inn stairs and started up the street looking for the courthouse. Tradesmen bustled throughout the marketplace. Dozens labored at the railroad depot and wharves, transferring cargo and people. He spotted a flyer advertising an upcoming horse race at the track, pressing gamblers to strike it rich with easy systems instead of through the backbreaking effort of mining. A young man hawked innovative business ventures, hustling California as a destination for personal wealth and a supplier to the world. Michael's aspirations surged at the multiple opportunities.

The U.S. flag waved from the capitol building in the distance. Its wings were still under construction, its granite columns soaring heavenward. He wondered when California would grant him, and Kit, the equality they sought under the nation's Constitution. Or would their racial heritage forever determine their fate?

He steered from the imposing structure toward the new courthouse at Fourth and J Streets, forgetting everything but winning this endless battle against Diego. It was past time to get on with his life.

Entering the cavernous records room, he approached the sole clerk and inquired if anyone else laid claim to his land besides his stepfather. No, only Diego—ostensibly ant squatters moved on. And nobody claimed the adjacent lands, either. Michael realized he would be very, very isolated on his property, especially if Kit left him.

Rather than lamenting that reality, he concentrated on outsmarting Diego. Following his instincts, he requested records on other cases involving Diego's business in Sacramento. Despite tossing speculative glances at him, the clerk cooperated and unearthed documents relating to those cases from a shelf below the counter. A tangle of relationships involving other attorneys, state politicians, and judges surrounded Diego.

Michael noticed this week's case dockets tacked to the wall, topped by the name of the presiding judge. Stepping closer, he found Diego's name and his own penned in for that afternoon. No surprise. Diego always worked fast.

He approached the clerk once more. "Excuse me. Do you know other information about Diego Salazar that isn't included in these documents?"

"What is your purpose for asking?" The clerk's intelligent voice cued Michael of an interest beyond that of a gossipy clerk.

Michael maintained his friendly smile, hoping the clerk would remain helpful as he pushed the bounds for public information. The old Chinese man's thin chest stooped badly forward, probably due to filing these papers all his adult years. His eyes were razor sharp behind round glasses. The traditional blue jacket hung in loose folds off his shoulders and reached to his knees. Inwardly, Michael applauded that at least one Chinese man had a good job, instead of the privation Kit's father undoubtedly faced.

"I'm defending myself against Salazar in court this afternoon," Michael said. Maybe a play for sympathy would sway the clerk. "He's attempting to cheat me of my land. Is there other documentation that might help me?"

The clerk curled his lip and muttered foreign words under his breath. Dropping to his knees, he rifled through a sheaf of haphazard papers, removing ones from the pile and setting them aside. He bent to his left and tugged open the middle drawer of an old wooden desk, jammed to the brim with yellowed sheets. The clerk dug to the bottom and unearthed a neat stack. Gathering the papers together, he tidied them on the counter, glancing over his shoulder toward the open door.

"These are cases of Diego Salazar's business partners," the clerk said. "They usually file land claims under a joint business name. An individual partner defends the property owner in opposition to his own company. In either situation, the partners win." He ruffled the pages and gave Michael a stiff bow. "That might not surprise you."

Michael scanned the documents, noticing a pattern of names and incidents adding up to a Diego-style fraud.

"Have you scheduled a case concerning Abigail Jenkins recently?" Michael asked, hoping for blind luck.

"Yesterday. The claimant did not appear. Mr. Salazar and his friends won title to the land. Judge Hancock was very obliging to their situation."

Michael caught the wryness in the clerk's voice. "Is that judge one of his partners?"

The clerk pulled a paper from the stack listing business owners, and pointed to identical names from yesterday's court records. Judge Joshua Hancock's name showed up on both documents.

His gut roiled. Hancock would preside over Michael's case today.

"Do you know anything regarding Judge Hancock?" Michael asked.

"Not as much."

Michael rubbed his jaw. There must be a solution here somewhere.

A compassionate look settled over the clerk's features. He reached behind the counter, extracted a paper, and slid the official document under Michael's nose.

Judge Joshua Hancock's name topped the page. Michael skimmed the formal words declaring Hancock's run for the U.S. Senate in September. Confused, he waited for an explanation from the impassive clerk.

"Perhaps the judge should account for his past deeds when asked for his qualifications to represent all Californians," the clerk said in a biting tone.

"What past deeds?"

"He recently arrived here from New York, and is devoted to establishing a sterling reputation in California to further his career. The newspapermen are not acquainted with him yet, and are bound to investigate his most recent court rulings."

Michael stared at him, puzzling over the inscrutable clerk's nuanced message. Ideas tumbled around in his brain. This line of reasoning opened novel possibilities to foil Diego and his partners.

"Thanks, old timer. I owe you if I win this case." Grinning, Michael extended his hand across the counter.

"If you win, I would consider it an honor to hear by what means you did so." The clerk shook Michael's fingers, casting a worried glance toward the door. Apparently, few rarely bestowed such a simple gesture of goodwill to this Chinaman, despite his elevated position.

Michael belatedly remembered Kit's quest, and decided to take a risk. "By chance, have you heard of a fellow named Juan Lee?"

"No." The clerk stepped backward and re-jammed his own into his opposite sleeve, bowing his head deferentially.

Michael hesitated at his sudden withdrawal. He'd been forthcoming until he asked about Kit's father. Now he seemed…distant, suspicious.

He shrugged away the mystery. He might be simply protecting a fellow Chinaman from an outsider's scrutiny. Kit had searched for her father in Sacramento's meanest quarters. Most likely, he'd reverted to illegal means for survival over the past year.

Even so, Michael regretted his inability to carry good news to Kit. Added details might win the clerk over.

"That's too bad," he said. "I have business to discuss with him regarding a land claim south of here."

The clerk's gaze shot upward. Surprise flashed across his face and disappeared as quickly. He bowed. "Sorry. Good luck versus Salazar."

"Thanks, old man." Michael strode from the courthouse and trotted down the steps, devising alternative tactics.

A shop's window display of colorful women's fineries captured his attention. He studied the selections inviting purchase, and an unconventional plan formed in his mind. It would work. Confident Kit would agree no matter what he asked of her, he pushed open the door.

CHAPTER 46

Kit awoke and found Michael perched at the foot of the bed, sporting a sheepish expression. A bundle of cloth rested across his thighs, and he juggled a brown-paper wrapped package in the air. She hoped today would be better than yesterday to re-earn his trust.

She sat up, the blankets pooling at her waist.

Thump—the package dropped onto the bed. Inwardly gleeful at Michael's fixated stare, she slowly arched her brow.

His cheeks tinged a dull red. With a quick shake of his head, he pulled an ivory-colored dress from the pile of clothes. An emerald green ribbon trailed across the covers. "Happy Birthday."

Kit gasped. "Your mother's?" Touched he remembered, she was doubly astounded at his consideration early in their trip. Love crept through her body, soothing her heart.

"The tie matches your eyes. And your clothing choice is limited. What better way to celebrate than with a new gown?" He deposited the entire bundle into her hands, and began unwrapping the beige package. "There's more."

"Michael, you shouldn't be spending your money on gifts for me! You have a ranch to develop."

"Listen to the whole plan, and then you'll understand these clothes are crucial."

He laid a lacy white scarf and gloves across her lap. She fingered the exquisite handiwork. Tears blurred her vision.

"These are the most beautiful clothes I've ever had," she said.

"They're not as beautiful as you are. And what I have in mind for you, you may not welcome."

"What do you mean?" Apprehension tightened her spine.

Michael's eyes flickered. "Beyond masquerading as my wife, I want you to pretend to be a Spanish señora to Diego. These clothes should clinch the image."

"Whatever for?" she asked.

"So he won't accuse me of owning a Chinese slave girl."

"This mixed breed Chinese-Irish woman isn't good enough to marry, is that it?" Cynicism chased away gratitude for the gifts.

"No! Not me, my stepfather. And you're simply pretending in order to eliminate one of his weapons. Don't you see that?" He scrubbed his jaw and glowered. "You're so unique and pretty Diego will want to accept you as my wife."

"It's only in front of your stepfather I'll pretend to be a señora?"

"Yes, including in court against him. Your fluent Spanish should reinforce your false identity." He paused, looking guilty and defiant. "You promised you would do whatever it takes to fight him for my land."

She sighed in resignation. She still wasn't good enough for Michael. Nevertheless, he was perfect for her, and she wouldn't give up yet. "I said that, and I meant it. Now what?"

"I fill you in on my plan," he said. "Then, we meet my stepfather for lunch, and fight him this afternoon in court."

"This afternoon? Already?"

Michael grunted. "Diego moves mountains to win, and he pushed this case to the front of the court docket. It's lucky we're here to defend the land claim. Otherwise, he would win without a fight. However, we don't have much time. Here's my strategy."

She focused on his words, grasping what was at stake today, and gulping at the price of failure.

Michael's entire future.

When he finished, Kit scrambled from the bed and pulled on the filmy underclothing. She studied the camisole in the mirror. A narrow pink tape spiraled up the front, pulling the lacy bodice edges together and creating snug, unfamiliar cleavage. The snowy white pantaloons used a similar strip, cinching at the waist and flaring a gauzy curtain over each leg.

"Is this really how these are worn, tied by just two flimsy ribbons?" She motioned from chest to knees, her cheeks warm.

Michael wiped off the soapy remnants of his shave. Without the bristle, only a yellowish tinge across his jaw hinted at the pounding he suffered at Diego's behest. He flipped the towel onto the bed and stepped behind her.

"A señora dresses slightly differently than a Chinese woman," he said with a roguish smile. "And before you put on more clothes, you need to change your hair."

"What's wrong with my hair? Don't chop it off!" She clutched her locks. Papa's favorite Chinese fables described hacking off the long, braided queue as punishment for sinners and criminals. Had her lapses in judgment truly offended Michael?

"I would never cut it." Michael raised the heavy mass high. It cascaded over his fingers like a satiny veil. "Señoras wear it high to indicate to society they're taken." He pulled a currycomb from his pocket.

"Señoras share their toilette with horses?" she asked, flabbergasted.

He burst out laughing, breaking the comb in half. "No, they use outsized combs to lift their hair up. I figure we'll use what we have. The scarf will cover it, anyway."

"Still, I don't know how to arrange my hair the style you describe. Mama insisted I keep it braided."

"I watched Mother countless times." He ran the comb through her silky mass, untangling the strands and crimping it around his fist. "I think I can create an acceptable bun."

Kit relaxed into the soothing pleasure, fluttering her lids shut. She swayed backward toward his bare chest. Gooseflesh rippled across her arms, and she hummed in surprise.

Muttering an oath, he stabbed the comb into her hair.

She caught his heated gaze in the mirror. Michael's heavy, angled brows created a perfect foil in contrast to his brown skin and wide cheekbones. Dear heavens, he was good-looking, all wiry strength and rugged sharpness.

"These fancy linens sure earn my vote," he murmured. Untangling the camisole's ribbon, he traced its deep neckline with rough fingertips.

"Is that the reason you prefer a señora?" With a demure smile, Kit tapped his wandering hand and re-tied the loosened knot. "In that case, I'll stay one a little longer and explore other clothing options."

Michael grinned and lifted a stray hair from her neck and into place. "You're a delightful señora, a fascinating Chinese girl, an exquisite Irish-American woman, or any female you wish to be. You're simply beautiful as you."

His warm sincerity carried away Kit's remaining qualms.

"Thank you, Michael. You're the nicest thing that ever happened to me." She rose on tiptoe and wrapped her arms around his neck.

"Don't tempt me, you witch," he said. "We have to hurry or we'll be late. Put your clothes on before I change my mind."

Giggling, she pulled the gown up to her shoulders. It draped in a billowing mass of tiered ruffles to the floor. She tugged the gloves on and lifted the scarf over her swept-up hair.

Michael gave her attire a critical once-over. Adjusting the scarf around her shoulders, he overlapped the front ends against her chest in perfect symmetry.

"You are the most exotic señora in California," he said. "Diego will be smitten. If we convince him to believe us, we'll be a step ahead."

"You clean up good, too." She nodded her approval of his white shirt and polished boots. "Let's get this over with."

CHAPTER 47

Michael snatched open the Capital Hotel doors, Kit clasping his arm. They were late. Even a few minutes tardiness put Diego in a bad mood. Michael's entire future depended on this meeting, yet he'd lost track of time when Kit melted at his lightest touch.

Her unfaltering support today gave him another chance to prevail. What would his future be if she left? Maybe he could convince her she belonged at his side—permanently. Assuming he also convinced Diego to give up and go home.

He stared across the luxurious hotel lobby, spying Diego hobnobbing with a circle of well-dressed gentlemen. Top hat in hand, one leaned close to Diego's ear, his lips moving and his other fingers wagging in the air. If Diego's smug bearing was any indication, the man no doubt sought a favor. Michael wondered if the supplicant understood Diego exploited his network of contacts for his personal gain, not anyone else's.

Waving indifferently at the petitioner, Diego strolled toward Michael, folding his white gloves inside his silk hat. Not a gray hair fell out of place. His footsteps rang in measured cadence on the polished wooden floor. Not too haughty, not humble in the least, but strong. Commanding—no, demanding—respect here in Sacramento. His rotund belly stretched the waist of creased trousers, and peeked from the bottom of his vest under a tailored jacket. His eyes measured them, and narrowed with a ruthless, skeptical gleam.

Michael glanced at Kit, wondering if her first impression of Diego matched his own repulsion.

Incredibly, Kit notched her chin higher. She plastered a confident smile on her face. Her graceful carriage and exotic appearance enhanced their pretense, as if she could buy and sell Diego at will.

"Good afternoon, Diego." Michael dipped his chin, keeping his fist at his side. "This is my wife Katerina, or Kit, as she prefers to be called."

Kit curtseyed and presented her fingers to Diego for the customary kiss. Lip curling, Diego pulled her erect instead. Kit's nostrils flared at Diego's insult.

"Señor Salazar, it is my honor to meet you at last. I hope I have not offended you in any way." She hid her temper, following Michael's lead and speaking Spanish in a placid voice.

"Not at all." Diego patted Kit's hand, continuing the ruse of a jovial family reunion in front of his colleagues. "Miguel, you look fine considering your swift journey. Is everything well with you?"

Michael rankled at Diego's hypocrisy. "I now go by the name Michael Rivers. I would appreciate it if you would remember that."

"A leopard can't change his spots, Miguel, and neither are you able to hide your heritage, no matter how hard you try. Your señora understands that, doesn't she?" Diego slanted his head at Kit.

"I think Michael may be whomever he wishes," Kit said. "He is a grown man, ready to begin his own family. Here in America that is respected, is it not?" Her serenity was perfect, as if no one expected further of her than to defuse rivalries.

Surprise raced across Diego's features, replaced by disbelief. "Of course. Shall we go to the dining room? I reserved a private table to celebrate your…nuptials."

"And yours, too, Diego, is that not true? I met Isabel before coming north, and she informed me of your pending happy union. Congratulations." Michael didn't bother disguising the sarcasm dripping from his voice.

Kit dug her nails into his arm. She was right—angering Diego would do no good. Engaging him so he would lower his guard was their goal. She transferred her grasp to Diego's sleeve.

"I would be honored if you would escort me inside the restaurant," she said. "I am eager to understand my new father's successful law practice. You are obviously greatly respected by your colleagues."

Kit beamed with disarming grace at Diego and displayed her winning smile at the group of fascinated spectators. The gentlemen bumped elbows sweeping hats off and nodding in her direction. She winked at Michael, her eyes dancing. Unquestionably, Diego's worth in their estimation wouldn't rise as much if his peers knew she was half-Chinese.

Michael doubted his stepfather believed their deception. True, Kit no longer resembled a Chinese slave girl. Yet her striking features didn't match those of a traditional Spanish señora, either. From Diego's perspective, Kit's hoax afforded Michael a temporary air of propriety, while she sought the next bidder for her charms. A whore, in other words. Exactly what he hoped to sidestep.

Diego led them with a confident saunter to the far corner. Of course. Diego would hate airing a family squabble in the open. Bad publicity weakened his business and political objectives. Let Diego think he outsmarted them by playing along with their charade. This time, though, Michael wouldn't be intimidated.

They sat around the circular table and Diego began his charm offensive. "My boy, I wish you would consider returning Midnight to me, and ranching at home."

"Midnight is mine. I won't return him."

"So you say," Diego said. "It is considerably more appropriate to begin your marriage around civilization, and not subject your pretty wife to the harsh rigors of the wilderness."

Michael tautened his jaw at Diego's opening gambit. At least Diego didn't allege horse theft. Yet.

"Actually, Kit is excited by the challenge of our new venture as property owners," Michael said. "We both believe in America's laws encouraging people to develop their own land, instead of working to increase its worth for a landlord, as they do in Mexico and Spain."

A solicitous waiter approached and hovered near Diego's elbow. Michael waved him off.

"That's idealistic, Miguel," Diego replied. "You'll soon find that this country, identical to others, prefers its property owned by moneyed citizens. There is no value in simpletons establishing a home merely for the sake of ownership. People should leave that to educated gentlemen who turn land into productive assets for the greater good. Besides, working your individual ranch like a slave is not a pathway to become influential in society."

Michael itched to pop Diego's smirking ego. "Why would I want influence in your piddling circle? From what I've seen, the corruption of these so-called gentlemen is worse than among common prisoners. If your great society continues demeaning the hard-working folk, how will you and your kind find more to exploit?"

Kit nodded her discreet approval.

Michael rested his forearms on the tabletop, drilling Diego with his gaze. "Who will work the land for you, produce your food, and build the railroads so you can travel quickly to Washington in comfort? Or build your fancy homes and take care of your children so you can entertain lavishly to impress your powerful friends? Who will you be influencing but each other, once people refuse to work for you anymore?"

"You think you're able to change society from the outside by working hard on your land, instead of letting the cream of society make improvements from the inside?" Diego's loud laugh filled the dining room.

"Mistreating people will only get you so far," Michael said. "Immigrants come to this country to work for their private rewards and enjoy the fruits of their personal labors. Swaying others' opinions is not of value to them...or to me."

"Miguel, Miguel. You no longer have any other option except becoming subordinate to me because you mated with a Celestial slave." Diego wagged his index finger at Kit.

"What are you talking about?" Michael blustered.

"You pursue a decadent life, traveling together unmarried for this time, and you shall live with its outcome. California lawmakers are working hard to maintain a certain level of decency, despite the riff-raff moving into the state. You'll find that out in court today—unless you agree to settle it here. My offer is good before the court hearing begins. After that, when you lose…" He shrugged. "…you will be on your own."

Kit's emerald eyes blazed. Michael nudged her leg under the table, hardly keeping his temper in check. She scowled and compressed her lips. The anxious waiter shuffled in their direction. Michael disregarded the interruption, now that Diego had begun a negotiation dance in his high and mighty fashion.

"What are you proposing?" Michael asked.

Diego leaned forward, exuding a false demeanor of victorious goodwill. "Son, I merely want what's best for our family. I really don't care who you choose for a wife. Nevertheless, society will judge you harshly."

"And if I don't care what society thinks of my choice?" Michael hoped the polite tone cloaked his iron resolve to preclude Diego from dictating to him one more time—or beat him out of his land.

"You will eventually, Miguel, and my plan will take care of you. After you return to San Jose, I'll appoint you foreman of our expanded ranch, since we're adding Isabel's property to mine. That represents quite a prestigious concession given your dubious behavior and Celestial wife."

"How generous," Michael muttered.

"Taking care of my stepson, regardless of his wife, will reflect admirably on Isabel and me...and is the wisest choice for you both."

Diego gave Michael's arm three short taps. Michael moved it from reach.

Tutting, Diego continued. "This land of your father's will be titled over to me in court today. In time, I will trade it for land of greater usefulness, adding to my holdings. If Isabel and I are unfortunate and remain childless, then my entire estate will pass on to you when we depart this earth." Diego paused, smoothing his mustache. "The land will be mine, Miguel."

"And if I don't choose to simply wait until you die or sire children of your own?" He seethed at Diego's assumption they would go along as servants—or slaves.

"You will at least enjoy a good livelihood, son, working only as hard in San Jose as you will on this land of your father's. Plus, you will enjoy the advantage of my patronage, earning a trifling influence in San Jose for you and your wife to make the most of as you see fit." Diego beckoned the waiter.

Michael threw his linen napkin on the table in disgust and switched to English. "We don't speak the same language. Get this through your thick skull. I fought for years to ranch this land. I beat you already in San Francisco and I'll beat you here. Two can play this game."

Michael hardened his voice. "I've watched as you've taken advantage of everyone and everything in your sad life. I've learned your tricks and added mine." He pointed at Diego. "You are not getting this land from me. Not today. Not ever."

"We'll see, my boy, we'll see." Diego sneered, tucking one pudgy thumb in his vest's armhole and leaning back. He drummed his fingers in unhurried rhythm on the tablecloth. "Many of my friends in Sacramento owe me favors."

"Including judges?"

"Of course. What good is influence if it isn't in the right place at the precise time?"

"Exactly what I'm counting on." Michael shoved his chair from the table, nearly knocking the poor attendant off his feet. The loud squeak of wrought iron legs against wooden floors echoed throughout the restaurant. "We'll pass on lunch, Diego. The atmosphere is unappetizing, to say the least."

Michael assisted Kit upright. Squaring her shoulders, she stared at Diego. Anger lit her expression, stunning Michael anew with her beauty. The waiter moved aside, a respectful gaze riveted on her face.

"You may have earned the admiration of your colleagues, but you haven't earned mine." Kit's gloved thumb touched her chest. "And while you may condescend to accept me as part of your family, I won't accept you as part of mine—you're too evil to tolerate."

She swept from the restaurant at Michael's side.

CHAPTER 48

Kit halted on the hotel veranda, gathering her thoughts. The midday sun crept toward her booted toes.

"Diego hasn't changed a bit," Michael said.

"Were you expecting a different response?"

"No, not really. Now he'll feel justified lining his cohorts up against me in court, and assert I stole Midnight, I'll wager. We'll have to follow my plan to the letter to beat him at his own game."

At Michael's air of resignation, Kit finally understood the type of contest Diego and his kind pursued. Her parents fought it their whole lives—seeking unattainable justness as outsiders to a corrupt legal system. She knew people fed off the efforts of others. However, she never met any of them. Hearing Diego's triumphant proclamation of his right to destroy lives sickened her.

If Diego and his cronies won in California, in the still developing United States, after the recent war tore the country apart correcting these types of injustices, they would set a precedent for years to come. She and Michael could outwit at least one of them. It was a start. Otherwise, she wouldn't live as she longed for, or fill the secret dreams harbored in her heart. Like Papa, freedom and justice fed her very soul.

She shook Michael's arm with renewed fervor. "I hate your stepfather and what he stands for. I will do anything to stop him from taking your land. It's both of us versus him now."

"I'm sorry to expose you to such filth," he said. "It went as poorly as I feared. Diego wasn't fooled by your señora masquerade."

"We shouldn't have tried to gain his approval. He is beyond accepting you for who you are. And he already had rejected me, no matter my dress." She might be able to insist Mama's heritage gave her legal rights in America, but she certainly couldn't alter her gender. Prejudice hostile to women ran as deeply as opposition to Chinese.

"Maybe," Michael said. "Certainly he'll use our supposed immorality against us in court."

"By the court's standards perhaps we were immoral. I don't feel that way. Do you?" Kit gripped his arm and held her breath.

"No. We're two adults who chose knowingly. I accept the results."

"As do I."

"Even if that means losing my land." He worked a finger inside his collar and stared down the street to the distant river.

"It won't come to that, I'm sure." She wanted to erase his bleakness, except she was far from reassured herself.

"Thanks, only you saw what kind of fiend Diego is. He won't soften his words in court. His view regarding us is widespread in society."

"Possibly in terms of morality, but not politically," she said. "He's vying to be a puppet master, pulling strings to grab power, and undermining the spirit of the law. He's exploiting everyone by claiming his actions are for society's good. If we refute his arguments at that level, his view of us and our travel together is meaningless."

"And how do you suggest we make sure of that?" Michael trod onto the wide stair, tugging at her hand. Pedestrians strolled by in the hot sun, men's hats pulled down, ladies' parasols up.

She kept her feet planted on the porch above, for once at the same level as he. "As a matter of fact, he's a mass of contradictions already. If he claims his social circle objects to our unmarried status for propriety's sake, is he able to balk at a Chinese slave girl as a daughter-in-law if our marriage is the moral path? He must choose one or the other of those realities. He cannot escape the repercussions of our actions any more than we can, as long as he publicly criticizes us."

Michael scratched his jaw. "I'm not sure we'll have a chance to argue that point. The court case revolves around the land title."

"Maybe not. Nonetheless, I bet there is an equivalent flaw in his logic. We'll listen for it and use it against him."

"We'd better be ready for Diego's sly tactics." He pointed to the diner across the street. "Let's eat, and get to court early. We'll watch other cases and learn about this judge before our time comes. In San Francisco, it may have helped me win."

"Yes, I'd appreciate that," she said. "I've never been inside a courthouse before, and I always prefer scouting the battleground in advance."

"Who taught you to be such a knowledgeable warrior?" He nudged her forward, chuckling.

"Papa, of course. He told me stories of ancient Chinese combats and why their strategies worked or didn't. The most basic is studying your enemy and which obstacles to overcome before ever going into battle."

A cart laden with ripe peaches blocked her path. She stepped to the side.

Michael tucked her close and peered in both directions. "I hope you're a fast learner. Our case is scheduled for early afternoon."

Halting, Kit planted her fists on her hips. "Have you ever known me to hide from a challenge?"

"Never."

"I have one condition." She prayed he would not fight her on this. "I'll still wear the scarf to show respect for the court. However, I will appear just as I am, with my hair unbound—a young American woman fighting for her rights in the court of law."

"Aren't we fighting for my right to own the land?" he asked.

"Don't you see it's the same issue?" Her impassioned cry elicited curious stares of the passersby.

He led them several steps into the street. "We still need to fight within the context of our case. Otherwise, we'll be thrown from court for frivolous behavior."

Kit tugged him to a stop in the midst of the teeming thoroughfare. "I will champion your goal, if that's what concerns you. But people will judge you by the company you keep. Are you comfortable if I am simply myself in court?"

Sharp curses from draymen peppered the air. Wagons with precariously balanced goods destined for the train depot maneuvered around their still figures.

"I am comfortable in all ways, especially when you are yourself." Reaching up, he solemnly extracted the comb. Her hair unfurled like a cavalry's banner leading a battlefield charge. "My lady, may I escort you to lunch?"

Uncertain whether to laugh at being called a lady or take him seriously, she returned her hand to his sleeve. "As my husband for the day, please do."

Kit continued across the street on his arm, wishing the day could turn into a lifetime. She would follow him anywhere.

CHAPTER 49

Michael gauged the courtroom's hostile atmosphere during the first scheduled land dispute. It reminded him of the San Francisco court—earnest settlers losing to land speculators accompanied by a round of applause. The blatant injustice aggravated him.

Shiny twin windows flanked opposing walls, filtering the brilliant sunshine into dancing dust motes. Five rows of raw pine benches lined the aisle. The judge's desk sat on a raised platform above the clerk's paper-laden table. Draped in a black robe, Judge Hancock had the appearance of a scrawny crow sitting on high as final arbiter. Dark hair peppered with gray framed sagging wrinkles lining genteel features. The singsong murmurs from attentive listeners lessened only when he rapped his gavel.

Seated beside Michael, Kit mumbled under her breath and whispered frequent questions regarding the judge's logic. Michael doubted she fathomed the man's inconsistent rationales any more than he did. She had no experience in a court, and certainly none confronting Diego. The responsibility of winning rested on his shoulders alone.

The clerk rose. "The case being called before this court is Diego Salazar versus Miguel Salazar regarding a land title dispute."

Cupping Kit's elbow, Michael escorted her down the short aisle ahead of Diego. They reached the front, turned left, and stood behind a rough pine table in front of two sturdy chairs. Diego sauntered to the right, doffing his hat with informal ease to the judge, and dropped into a comparable chair.

Michael's anger at Diego's supercilious attitude smoldered like banked embers. Kit nudged his arm, and he assisted her into the seat. She sat tall, her proud, determined chin pointed toward the front. He settled beside her. Time to win.

"Do we require a Spanish language interpreter for the parties, or does everyone speak English?" The clerk peered first at Michael, then Diego.

Diego rose with alacrity. "The main parties speak English. We'll need a Chinese translator for my son's…consort."

Kit sniffed and opened her mouth. Michael placed a hand on her thigh, staying her protest. The clerk walked to a side door and beckoned.

Michael cleared his throat. "It is not necessary, your honor. Everyone speaks English."

The clerk's exasperated puff filled the courtroom as he returned to his seat. Michael glimpsed a slender figure slip through the opening and hover within the shadowed doorway.

The helpful clerk from this morning! Relieved at having an extra ally, Michael spoke up. "And for the record, legally I go by the name Michael Rivers."

Judge Hancock viewed Kit and Michael from under knitted brows, harrumphed, and faced his stepfather. "Diego, what seems to be the issue here? Surely your family matters can be dealt with outside the court of law."

"I agree, your honor." Diego sighed with melodramatic affectation. "Unfortunately, my young son has an independent streak. It seems he wishes to prove his manhood at the expense of society and the law."

Contorting his features into pretend sadness, Diego shifted sideways. "Early last week, Miguel took my prized horse without permission, and went to a court in San Francisco. He found a friendly judge, bribed him as I hear affairs are done in that licentious town, and convinced him to hand over the title to land that is legally mine. I am simply asking you to reverse that flawed decision and return legal ownership to me. After that, I will govern my family's affairs outside the purview of this court, including my son's thieving tendencies."

"Is that true young man?" Judge Hancock asked. "Did you steal from your father?"

"No, your honor. I did not steal a horse nor land from my step...father." Holding onto his temper, he resolved to set the record straight. "Nor did I influence the judge in San Francisco. The horse came from my mother's original stock and belonged to me—I raised him, trained him, and rode him. The land in question belonged to my real father, worked by him for a period of years, and bequeathed to me on his deathbed."

Michael clenched and unclenched his jaw. "When my mother married Diego, she clarified the land was mine, kept in her name until I attained adulthood. The court in San Francisco stipulated the land should pass directly from father to son, and not from husband to widow to new husband, since a blood relative lived."

"Your honor, he is claiming falsehoods already," Diego said. "The land was not worked by his father after the Mexican government gave it to him. Not developing it meant he forfeited all rights to it, under Mexican, United States, and California law."

"Young man, are you lying to this court? I do not countenance perjury."

"No, your honor, I swear it is the truth." Michael raised his right hand for emphasis, wary of the breadth of Diego's legal expertise and Judge Hancock's obvious favoritism. "Acres of mature trees are yielding a full harvest. The orchard was planted while my father still lived, qualifying it as developed property."

"Can anyone else corroborate this claim for the court?" the judge asked.

Kit inched to the edge of her chair. "Yes, your honor. The orchard is exactly as he represented."

"Your honor, her word is unreliable." Diego thumped his tabletop. "I have it from a reliable witness she is a slave, purchased by my son at auction in San Francisco as an illicit crony for his journey. Plus, one of my long-term San Jose employees implicated her in horse theft. Given her questionable character, I wouldn't be surprised if she is being paid for her testimony."

"Well, young lady? Were you bought by this man, or are you being paid, in any fashion or by any means, for your statement?" Judge Hancock asked.

Michael's hackles rose at his overt leer. How dare he?

"No, sir, I am not," Kit answered. Michael was amazed she managed a respectful tone. "Nor am I, nor have I ever been, a slave. I was born in this country, and am a law-abiding American citizen, the daughter of an Irish-American woman and a Chinese scholar."

Michael released his held breath. She could report truthfully that she rejected his offer for payment. Yet another example where Kit's innate wisdom proved better than his.

She continued, aiming a ridiculing glower at Diego. "And regarding the other accusations, I wish to challenge Mr. Salazar's wonderful employee who is inventing lies about me."

"Then, your honor, what exactly is the relationship of this young girl to my son?" Diego asked. "She traveled alone in his company for the past week and at present shares a room in this very city. This kind of dissolute behavior, whatever you name it, undermines their claim of being upstanding citizens. Nor does it reflect acceptably on my son's moral character." He conjured up an air of simultaneous smugness and disappointment. "Surely California deserves landowners who respect our laws, including the marriage law."

Michael seethed at Diego's underhanded tactics. "Your honor, the truthfulness of our testimonies is unrelated to the reason we have been in each other's company for the last week."

Judge Hancock faced Kit. "How old are you, young lady? Do your parents approve of you traveling unchaperoned?"

Kit's cheeks became a fiery red. "I am eighteen years old, sir. My mother is dead, and I'm looking for my father who I haven't seen in a year. I am solely responsible for my actions."

"Young man, what conceivable excuse is there for your sinful behavior?" Judge Hancock eased into a relaxed slouch. "It offends this court and society."

"It is our full intention to legalize our marriage as soon as we stand up in front of a judge," Michael said.

"Then I pronounce you man and wife." He rapped his gavel and tossed Diego a broad smile.

Michael swore under his breath. He hadn't meant for it to get this far. Diego undoubtedly clued in his partner earlier, plotting a spiteful revenge for their lunchtime playacting. Nonetheless, a feeling of rightness came over Michael at the official pronouncement.

Kit's muted squeak caught his attention. Blood drained from her cheeks. She inhaled as if to protest. Michael caught her rigid arm and squeezed, pleading for her continued silence. She subsided, nestling her brow into her palms.

So much for not letting his stepfather dictate the terms of his life.

CHAPTER 50

"Thank you, your honor, for removing that moral objection." Michael rose from his chair and nodded. "I believe my wife and I will be good stewards of this land, as my father was before me."

Diego sprang to his feet and pounded his fist on the table. "Your honor, surely a wife's testimony on behalf of her husband is suspect. Without another witness, we cannot confirm the land is indeed developed. Therefore, the issue is simply whether the court in San Francisco had justification to re-title my land."

"Can anyone else confirm your story?" Judge Hancock asked.

Michael's hopes plummeted. Diego just outmaneuvered him, gambling he had no further allies. "No, your honor."

"I can." The voice came from the rear of the courtroom.

Michael spun around. That orchard farmer, Ivan Sankovitch, saluted him. Michael glanced at Kit. She shook her head, looking as puzzled as he felt.

Trail powder covered Ivan from top to bottom, puffing into the air each time his boot struck the aisle floor. Tossing up additional dust, limping next to him, was a young man who found a seat halfway. He reminded Michael of someone. Michael stared for a long moment, but couldn't place him. Whoever he was, maybe he was the reason Ivan popped up like a welcome trout at dusk after a long day fishing.

"And who might you be?" Judge Hancock eyed Ivan's unkempt appearance.

"My name is Ivan Sankovitch, and I knew this young man's father. I'll vouch fer a fact the property is sure enough developed and has been fer years, includin' a workin' orchard. I rode through the property yesterday, and there's a right smart dwellin' and the beginnin's of a first rate horse ranch. I reckon those qualify to claim the land." He delivered his testimony in a firm, clear voice, sending a reassuring smile toward Michael.

Diego harrumphed. "Your honor, should we take the word of a stranger to our community? It is possible my son paid for his testimony in advance, too. And if his horse ranch is beginning with purloined horses..." Diego shrugged, his barbed reproof persisting in the stagnant air.

"I do not use the tactics you readily employ to win my battles," Michael said with a low, menacing voice." If you continue calling me a liar, I will file a lawsuit for slander. You have no basis for your allegations."

The crowd's muttering backed up Michael. Judge Hancock rapped his gavel. "Mr. Sankovitch, has this young man paid you for your testimony?"

"No, he didn't know beans I'd be comin' here today. I took matters into my hands after I met him last week and fer sure connected him to the man I knew. His father worked the land to leave to his son, and told me so a lotta times. I figgered the court oughta know that."

"And if my stepfather had not been disputing my right to own the land, I would have worked it for the last six years." Michael battled his inner turmoil. Even if Ivan had been friendly with Father, Michael didn't breathe a word of his land dispute during their brief conversation. It didn't add up.

Unless Ivan was acquainted with Diego, too. That still didn't explain the uncanny coincidence of showing up in court today.

Michael gathered his thoughts. "Possibly the court should consider the motivation underlying the title dispute, such as simply to delay mandatory improvements."

Judge Hancock blanched, darting a suspicious glare at Michael. He gazed at Ivan for long moments. "This man's testimony is accepted as the truth, and therefore the qualification that the land be developed is met." He tapped his gavel on the benchtop and turned toward Diego. "Have you another reason that demonstrates you are entitled to the land instead of your son?"

Diego stuck his thumbs in his vest. He paced in front of the courtroom as if intensely troubled. "The law of the land needs to be upheld here. The fact is that the San Francisco court erroneously awarded title to my son, bypassing the normal chain of bequest. When my poor wife perished a few years ago, I included this land as part of a larger inheritance to pass on to my future children. All my lands are developed to their full potential for the good of society at large, as well as my family." Diego's sonorous voice rang with pomposity.

He rotated, addressing the full courtroom, in his element as the center of attention. "Miguel will surely benefit from this land and from my lifelong efforts to provide for him. It is a sad state of affairs that the San Francisco court interjected into a family tiff, ruining the wishes of his dear departed mother and the relationship with his sole living relative."

Michael fumed at Diego's obvious ploy to influence the court. Unfortunately, the spectators nodded agreement.

One last chance remained open to Michael.

He cleared his throat and shook his head in his best Diego imitation. "Your honor, I dispute the altruistic motivations of my stepfather. While he would like us to believe he has my interests at heart, his past actions lead me to conclude otherwise."

"We are not getting into petty family quarrels in my courtroom." Judge Hancock rippled his fingers on the bench, twitching his nose and mouth in counter rhythm.

"No, sir, not his past actions regarding me. I mean his past actions regarding other lands he acquired, the methods he used to acquire them, and their ultimate disposition." Michael threw a challenging look at the judge. Speculative whispers reached his ears from the court watchers.

Heaving a long-suffering sigh, Judge Hancock settled into his chair. "Explain yourself."

"Your honor, I possess evidence that Diego Salazar was involved in a scheme to unscrupulously wrest land from the rightful owner by abusing the law." Michael brandished the thugs' documents. "Diego offered to represent Abigail Jenkins in her title claim, and then delayed getting a fair hearing to resolve the dispute. During the drawn-out process, he charged fees for his time, which eventually became more than Mrs. Jenkins could afford, thus resulting in her land being titled to Diego as payment for his so-called services." He paused, gauging the effect of his words on Judge Hancock and Diego.

Nothing. Their faces remained impassive. This tactic wasn't working!

Michael's heartbeat accelerated. He faked an outward calm. "This is one of many times Diego acquired land by this method—including through my mother. I've uncovered in this court's records specific instances proving he and his business partners colluded illegally." He met the judge's gaze squarely. "Other lawyers are involved who are in a position to influence the outcome of the ownership of the land."

"Your honor, he is calling me a land swindler." Diego banged his fist so hard the table skittered on the wooden floor. "I am not."

"What do you call it when you flagrantly take land you had no role in developing, and deny the rightful claimant what they worked years to achieve?" Michael asked, girding for the worst.

"I charge fairly for my services as an attorney," Diego said. "It is not my fault the title process takes a long time to reach a decision. If my clients wish to hire me to help keep their land, that is their business. And if I accept payment in land, that is mine."

Michael pursued the logic with dogged relentlessness. "And if you flip the ownership of that property to another man in return for a favor he does for you—for example, in politics—that is also your business, is that correct?"

"Yes, it is."

Michael restrained a gratified smile at Diego's hasty retort. "Your honor, I believe California has an interest in keeping speculation at bay. The law states its intention to keep the land for settlers to develop as homesteads. If my stepfather's interest here is to line his pockets with money or favors, doesn't that fall into the category of land speculation?"

Judge Hancock appeared disquieted. "Have you proof of these charges?" he asked. "They are certainly very serious ones to ascribe to an officer of the court."

Michael walked forward and laid the document on his bench. "This is the contract between Diego and Abigail Jenkins. The rest is a matter of public record, simply requiring a clerk to pull the corresponding information to prove the pattern of abuse." He returned to his seat.

Strolling to the bench, Diego swiftly inspected the document and gave a loud humph. "Your honor, this is irrelevant to what is before the court today. Besides, you settled that case yesterday —the claimant failed to arrive. If you have a valid concern regarding the fees I charge my clients, I am happy to discuss that in your chambers later. The matter in front of us today is regarding an entirely different plot of land."

"Your honor?" Ivan's distinctive accents drifted to the front of the courtroom.

Michael peered over his shoulder.

"I expect I can share some thoughts on that other land issue Mr. Rivers mentioned." Ivan gave a half-salute, pointing at the young man sitting next to him.

"Your honor, this court hearing is regarding a specific parcel of land, and is not meant to explore other disputed claims." Shooting Ivan a sneering glance, Diego raised his voice. "May we please address the subject in front of the court?"

"Yes, you're right, Diego." Judge Hancock shoved the contract toward Michael. "This is irrelevant."

Michael shuffled to the bench and retrieved the paper. He had moments left before the final ruling. There must be something else to say. Something to argue. Something…

Or someone?

He looked at Kit, hoping against hope. She nodded once, appearing resolute. What else could he lose?

He slouched into his chair, fighting an overwhelming feeling of defeat.

Kit held his life in her dainty hands.

CHAPTER 51

Kit stood, determined to mask her nervousness in the wake of Michael's obvious discouragement. "Your honor, since I am now his legal wife and therefore have a vested interest in this case, may I speak?"

Judge Hancock nodded and swabbed a kerchief along his glistening forehead. Good—Michael's and Ivan's inside knowledge had unnerved the pompous jackass. Launching his political career might not be easy, even with Diego's sponsorship.

"I was not in the San Francisco court when it granted Michael his land title." Despite her effort, Kit's voice quavered. Michael may not want her help, but he needed it. He needed her. And for once in her unorthodox life, she might beat the odds and change her future.

"Yet I have had many chances to consider how some people are able to own property and others not," she said. "It seems the only approach for laws advocating land ownership to succeed, no matter who lays title to it, is if we have trust in an objective court. In the end, if the courts don't follow their explicit rules, is it fair to expect citizens will?"

Kit paused, anticipating a testy response from the judge, including cutting her off. Instead, he cringed. Fear settled over his dour face.

Michael's damp fingers eased across her palm and enfolded hers.

She repaid that small, trusting gesture and withdrew, clasping her hands at her waist. "While I don't agree the current law is correct in denying some people land ownership, I do believe in enforcing all laws equally and in the spirit in which they were created."

Kit indicated Michael and herself. "In this case, for the land to belong to people who are willing to work it, contributing to our country's overall wealth. This Homestead law also sets forth that land ownership should not be concentrated in the name of a few, while the rest of the population labors for token wages."

"Your honor," Diego sneered. "What relevance is this to our case?"

"I'll let her continue." Judge Hancock waved Diego off.

With ruddy cheeks, Diego tugged on his jacket lapels and glowered at her.

Judge Hancock spun the gavel on his desk, his gaze fixed on its movement. Kit imagined the thoughts whirling in his mind. Michael's contention of unethical conduct seemed to catch the judge unawares. And undoubtedly, no one warned him of the acumen of this Chinese slave. If the judge needs a moment to consider the implications on his political career, she'll seize every minute and speak her mind.

Confidence strengthened her spine. She leveled her finger at Diego. "If you allow this officer of the court to bend the law to increase his personal wealth by virtually robbing people who trust in its fairness, you will undermine the entire country's homestead system." She aimed her thumb toward the rapt courtroom listeners. "Then what's the point in anyone respecting the law? Why won't each person claim land at gunpoint, spending the rest of his years defending the land instead of working it? Where is the promise of this country if we allow the legal system to be abused in this manner by a lone individual?"

Even if the law couldn't help Papa, her insights might—just might—bear out Michael's case if she presented a clear argument. Heart pounding, Kit slid the scarf from her shoulders.

"The San Francisco court kept their decision uncomplicated: a son should inherit the land his father claimed and worked," she said. "Is it proper that this court simply overturns that court based on the testimony of a solitary man whose motives are suspect?"

"Your honor." Diego hammered his knuckles on the wooden surface in a continuous beat.

She ignored his interruption. "What will keep another court from overturning this court? Won't it only end when the courts themselves respect the rulings of their fellow judges upholding the true spirit of the law?"

Sweeping her arm toward the agape crowd, Kit raised her voice. "Otherwise, the rest of us will simply function outside the law, developing special rules to suit our situations. Only if you ratify the rulings of other courts will we be able to rely on uniform justice. Then we can work our land, trusting that a wealthy individual with political connections we don't have, cannot take it from us capriciously. Isn't that what this country is about?"

The court observers burst into applause. Michael's lips curved up at the tangible validation. Unfortunately, Diego looked daggers at her.

Murmurings from the crowd repeating her words pervaded the air. Heads nodded. Smiles wreathed too many faces to count. Maybe she succeeded in bringing the community over to Michael's side. Next time she and Papa might win, and achieve their dream.

Returning to her seat, Kit shot a smug look at the judge. Now he had to justify a decision in the context of broader issues—if possible. Michael said he had proof of inside connections being part of Diego's plans. Judge Hancock won't dare have his ambitions questioned with his political career in jeopardy.

"Please enlighten us on your plans for this land, Mr. Salazar." Kit suppressed her chuckle at the judge's sudden formality and prodding.

Diego rose to his full height. "Your honor, this woman admitted her ignorance of the San Francisco decision. Therefore, her opinions are immaterial."

Kit sifted through possible arguments he might use to re-establish his credibility and control. She never met anyone so villainous.

"Nevertheless, to answer your question..." Diego bowed to the judge with perfect dignity and courtesy, "...I unfortunately have not had time to explore this specific property. I have been very busy managing my extensive ranch in San Jose. I enjoy business associates who wish to purchase it from me directly. In fact, they categorized it as swampland, useless to develop on its own, yet available to be converted by the state to irrigate surrounding properties."

"Does that mean if you win title to this land you will sell it to someone else?" Judge Hancock asked.

"Your honor, if I possess a good offer for the land, of course I'll give it due consideration." Diego dropped his eyelid in the barest hint of a wink.

A ripple of laughter spilled over Kit from behind. She glanced at Michael, and prayed he was alert for retaliatory tactics, since Diego essentially admitted his land dealings.

Diego flushed and his posture stiffened. He strode to the front.

"Your honor, let's end this farce. My impulsive son's claim is baseless, championed by a woman of questionable virtue, despite your efforts to mold her into an honest woman. The unfortunate fact is my son's morals are of the lowest kind, since he kept company with her this week, flaunting marriage conventions."

Diego paced to his right. "When Miguel was in San Francisco, he apparently bribed a local judge to commandeer my property. Now he has the unmitigated gall to attempt to defend those actions here by accusing me, a man of excellent professional reputation, of nefarious dealings and outright theft."

Pivoting, he paced to the left, stopped in front of Kit and Michael, and thundered over them to the crowd. "Without proof of these declarations, is he believable? And distracting the court with an idealistic view of the real world is simply a reflection of this Celestial woman's ignorance of our legal system." He wiggled a rebuking finger under Kit's nose. She sat on her hands, awfully tempted to grab and wrench it until he squawked.

Diego continued. "That's not surprising given her obviously inadequate upbringing. We know better. Please consider the actual evidence and community standing of the parties involved."

Kit's heart tripped into double time. If Judge Hancock agreed to Diego's clear appeal and kept the scope of the case very narrow, they would lose. And why wouldn't he? Either approach was justified within the law. And clearly, Diego will pay splendidly for deciding in his favor.

Judge Hancock remained silent, and twirled his gavel in circles.

"I'll offer additional proof." A clear voice rang from the side of the room.

An elderly man stepped forward from the shadows. Kit gasped. Papa! He was safe. She started to rise. Michael's strong arm wrapped around her waist and halted her.

Of course—he didn't realize this was Papa. She opened her mouth, and he laid a finger across her lips.

"Listen!" He whispered in her ear. "He may help us."

Kit stared at him, perplexed. How did Michael recognize Papa? And how could Papa help Michael? Oh no, Papa knew she was wedded to Michael—and what prompted their marriage! Heat suffused her neck and cheeks.

Michael was correct—she should listen to Papa first. And pray he didn't disown her.

CHAPTER 52

Michael leaned forward, curious what prompted the Chinaman's public testimony. Crossing the room, the clerk stopped in front of the judge's bench and bowed from the waist. A stray sunbeam lit his distinctive features and long, gray braid. The crowd quieted.

"What is your business here, translator?" Judge Hancock's voice boomed in the intent silence with the impact of a thunderclap. "This case has been conducted in English. Your services are not required."

"I beg to differ, your honor. My name is Juan Lee. I am this young woman's father, and wish to dispute Mr. Salazar's claim her upbringing was inadequate."

Michael's jaw sagged at the pronouncement. He glanced from Kit's stricken face to the old man standing proud. Why hadn't Lee admitted it to him this morning?

Like a tenacious raccoon, his habitual distrust clawed to the surface. He shoved it down. For once, he'd be open-minded and heed the whole set of facts before he jumped to conclusions. He owed Kit loyalty to her father unless he proved otherwise.

After all, Michael never divulged to Lee that Kit was in town. He was justified in not admitting he was Kit's father to a total stranger. Regardless, he helped Michael this morning, and was coming to his defense.

Serenity enveloped Michael. He had more allies and friends than he realized.

Judge Hancock pursed his lips, and gestured for Lee to continue.

"She received a superb education from her mother, including knowledge of the laws and customs of this land, as you already heard." Lee's voice was strong and clear. "If she elected to travel with her husband in advance of legalizing their marriage, she had her reasons. Besides, that is a moot point."

Kit breathed a huge sigh, and her eyes shut for a brief moment. Her shoulders relaxed, her fist uncurling and resting on top of the table.

"How nice that you approve of their marriage, now that you have no say in the matter," Diego said. "She obviously got the better of the match."

Lee scrutinized him. "If you say so. As is the custom in my culture, even with such an impromptu marriage—welcome to our Chinese family." He grinned at Diego, his resemblance to Kit unnerving.

Diego paled, and staggered to his chair.

"Your honor," Lee turned toward the judge, his bow long and respectful, "in addition to my personal interest here, I am in a unique position to verify this young man's statements. Mr. Salazar has a pattern of accepting payment from his clients of the disputed land he is supposedly defending. He is most certainly speculating on land. If it will help in your decision, I will bring pertinent documents and enter them into the official court record...including the names of his business partners."

Lee bowed again. His fingers, shaded by his long sleeves, swiftly crossed and uncrossed in Michael's direction. Michael knew the judge could ill-afford any of those documents to see the light of day.

Judge Hancock twisted his chin upward and cleared his throat. "Do you swear as an employee of the court that the information you are providing is correct?" His nervous gaze darted between Lee and Diego.

Lee straightened and squared his shoulders. "Yes, sir." He notched his chin higher, identical to Kit's mannerism. Both were plucky and tenacious. Michael had no doubt Lee would use the files if need be. He prayed the judge was as astute and understood Lee wasn't bluffing.

"Then I declare the legal owner of this disputed land to be Michael Rivers, as the San Francisco court declared. I discern no compelling evidence to overturn its decision in favor of Diego Salazar." Judge Hancock drummed his mallet. "We will take a short recess before the next case." He hastened from the courtroom.

Michael whooped and leapt to his feet. He swung Kit up in his arms, spinning her around. From the corner of his eye, he spied Ivan picking up his hat and exiting. His mysterious pal limped after him. Too bad, he couldn't follow and solve the riddle of Ivan's timely arrival. Weighty issues required his attention first. A new wife. And the best father-in-law in the world. He stopped swirling and tucked Kit into his side.

Diego stormed over to Lee, his face beet-red. "You have no job to return to. You've compromised the integrity of the information entrusted to you. I'm going to demand your yellow hands never touch court documents again. The gall of you using your position against us, when we gave you a chance to better yourself."

Clapping his hat on his head, Diego trailed Judge Hancock through the door. He looked intent on immediate retribution. And salvaging a doomed career.

CHAPTER 53

Shrugging, Papa extended his arms in greeting. Kit rushed into them, tears flowing at his typical loving support. A matching tear slipped from behind his spectacles and down his cheek. He must have been as worried as she had been during their year of separation.

"How are you?" Papa pulled away, inspecting her from top to bottom. "A messenger told me he was unable to discover your whereabouts in San Francisco. I was not sure you could locate me on your own." He hugged her once more.

Kit squeezed his waist, noting grayer hair and a more pronounced stoop. Remembering what he'd witnessed, her cheeks flamed.

"I'm fine, Papa. I'm sorry you had to hear those nasty tales from Diego. Most of them aren't true." She pleated her fingers in the folds of her gown, unable to meet his eyes.

He nudged her chin up with his knuckle. "Are you saying you were married under false pretenses?"

"No, that part of it was true."

"Should I move to annul the marriage? As your father, I may be able to reverse the judge's pronouncement if I demand it immediately."

Hesitating, she peeped at Michael from under her lashes. He stood apart at the table, gathering his papers, honoring her request for a private reunion. His thoughtfulness warmed her.

"No. Yes. I don't know what I want," she said.

Papa steered her toward Michael. "At the least, I beg a formal introduction to this brave young man. He asked such strange questions! I confess I was suspicious of his motives. Nevertheless, he proved his intentions were fully noble—at least regarding his land." He halted mid-stride. Cupping her jaw, he compelled her eyes up until they met his. "We'll talk later and determine what to do then."

What did Papa mean about Michael's questioning? She clutched Papa's arm and approached Michael with trepidation. She had a hard time thinking of him as her husband instead of her traveling attendant. Or lover.

"Michael, I'd like you to meet Papa. I guess you held up your end of our bargain in spite of everything."

"I can't thank you too much for your help, sir," Michael said.

"Is that not what families are for?" Papa grasped Michael's extended hand and held it longer than customary, studying him.

"I used to think so. As you see by my stepfather's actions, I'm accustomed to an adversarial family relationship," Michael said. "You pointed me in the proper direction this morning. I don't think my bluff would have worked if you hadn't been willing to corroborate the information."

"This morning?" Kit interjected, stupefied.

"Remember the clerk who helped me? It was your father who showed me Diego's weakness."

"I performed my job." Papa shrugged. "I simply took my oath seriously, unlike these officers of the court."

"Did you really lose your job because of your testimony?" Michael asked.

"I risked much." Papa nodded. "I am tired of such abuse and travesty by public figures. I have been awaiting someone to challenge these illegal methods and shed light onto their tactics. Little did I know I could be this useful, or a member of my family could benefit from their downfall." A grin split his face. "Actually, it felt wonderful to rout those thieves. I would not trade this feeling for the world. It has been too long since I won anything meaningful."

Michael smiled. "Then I won't say I'm sorry. How can I return the favor?"

"I ask for a kindness, which I hope you, as a generous man, will grant." Papa bowed low.

"Of course."

"I ask simply for the pleasure of my daughter's company for a few days before she returns to you and your land. We have much to talk over, including her marriage."

Michael's cheeriness receded. Kit burrowed her hands in the dress ruffles and stared at her toes.

"Is that satisfactory to you?" Using a gentle touch, Michael tilted her chin up.

Kit was torn. Part of her wanted him to refuse leaving her side for a second. The other part realized their marriage was a sham, and he deserved his freedom. She examined his guarded expression for any clue, fumbling for a fitting way out.

"You know it was important to reunite with Papa. I certainly wish to visit a while, especially since my life was turned upside down by that judge."

"Each of our lives was altered today, yours no more than mine. We are married now."

Tears welled at his matter-of-fact tone, tears she refused to let fall. She couldn't tell if Michael was happy or angry. Chewing on her lip, she waited.

"Kitten, we have a lot to resolve—together." He tugged on a stray end of her hair. "I'll pay for the room for another two nights. Then I need you—no, I ask you—to come to the mine. Promise me?" His gaze pinned hers, full of concern and trust, not disdain or that hated aloofness.

A profusion of mixed emotions assaulted her. He was such a gentleman—unless he was just saying that because he cared for her out of obligation. She might be simply a responsibility he tended to, no different from his horses. No, he was being sweet and considerate, remembering her wish to talk to Papa alone. Maybe they could salvage their relationship. Except she needed certainty he loved her before she would spend the rest of her days by his side.

With a tremulous breath, Kit brushed her fingertips along his cheek. His eyes darkened. Her memories of their time together wakened in response.

"I promise," she said.

"Thank you. I trust you won't get lost." Michael brushed a kiss on the sensitive flesh peeking from the glove. "And thank you for today, Kitten. If it weren't for you, I don't think I could have won. I owe you a lot for that."

"Let's call us even. I'd rather come up with a means to start over than worry about who owes whom what."

"Deal," he said. "Agreed, partner?"

"Deal." Kit wondered what kind of partner he might truly prefer. "If you hurry, you might reach the ranch tonight. Assuming you don't lose your way." She dared a teasing smile.

Michael winked at her, faced Papa, and bowed. "I'd like to see you afterward, as well, if you will escort Kit. I believe you will be very interested in my land claim."

"It is my honor to do so," Papa said.

"Thank you. I'll arrange a horse for you at the stable." Michael paused, darting a warm glance at her. "Please take care of my wife for me."

He left the courthouse without looking back.

CHAPTER 54

Michael's pent-up emotions jarred free with each trotting step. Home! And all his. He loosed a hurrah, and welcoming echoes from his very own hillside replied. He hadn't been this excited since that last day in San Francisco. When he was ready to conquer the world.

Before he met Kit.

She added unexpected dimensions to his life—joy, hope, and love. She also made him run the gamut of despair, animosity, and betrayal...then repaid him with unmatched loyalty and respect.

Maybe, just maybe, he wasn't doomed to solitude.

Over the years, Diego's malicious tactics taught him to fight and avoid emotional ties, not seek them. As a husband, he had to learn loving, fast, and win Kit's heart.

The orchard's sweet redolence surrounded him as daylight ebbed into dusk. Bless Father for his long-ago effort developing this land, while simultaneously working the ranch in San Jose. He spent many more days away from home than Michael ever realized.

After seeing to Midnight and the three horses left fending for themselves, Michael ducked inside the lean-to. The fir branches still carried double impressions from the night they slept here. Settling his body over her spot, thoughts of Kit flooded him.

She had many chances today to manipulate the explosive situation to her benefit and yet didn't. Instead, she defended his right to the land with staunch conviction, and without mentioning her family's previous claim. Her actions more than compensated for any misunderstanding. Frankly, he simply cared about building a future together—if she agreed.

He groaned, recalling his outright rudeness after distrust got the better of him. She never deserved that. It was his blind stupidity preventing him from seeing her innate goodness. He prayed that same decency would give him one last chance.

The judge hastening the process didn't help, either. Michael cursed his foolhardiness. Why didn't he ask Kit her feelings regarding their forced marriage before he left?

Because he wanted her forever at his side, and didn't dare provoke a refusal.

He needed a plan that would entice her to stay, no matter her feelings. A plan to re-earn her trust, and prove he deserved it. A plan to buy him time and convince her to love him as much as he loved her.

He fell asleep seeking a solution.

In the morning, Michael tackled reinforcing the mine entrance. The blazing sun climbed to its zenith, eliminating all except the smallest pools of shade. Sweating, Michael straddled the nearby log and swigged water from his canteen. A faint whinny carried on the breeze, accompanied by squeaking leather. He reached for his rifle, holding it at the ready.

Ivan Sankovitch rode into the clearing, along with that same mysterious young man from the courthouse.

"Howdy!" Ivan added a salute to his hearty greeting.

Michael stood, waved, and set aside his firearm. That stranger was a young kid, not a danger like those hoodlums.

Striding over, Michael waited until Ivan swung from his horse. He caught the old man's grasp. "Welcome, and thanks for your aid yesterday."

"I couldn't let your father's land get switched over to a schemin' thief, could I? Besides, I worked this parcel too. I expect to visit now and then, just like I used to."

Michael clapped his shoulder. "You'll always be welcome. And before you journey home, I insist you recount more of Father's past. Apparently he kept me in the dark concerning an entire portion of his life... and his friends."

"I'll take you up on that offer. First, I have someone to introduce to you." Ivan pointed to his fellow traveler slumping in the saddle. A battered hat provided minimal protection and a threadbare shirt hung loosely on his shoulders. "This Peter Jenkins is one of those hooligans who jumped you—the only good one of the lot, and sure enough grateful to be alive. I agreed to help him set matters straight between him and your stepfather."

"Why are you helping a common criminal?" Michael barely got the words through his gritted teeth.

Wait.

Jenkins was the name on that contract he found. Was he married to the woman?

"It's a long story, and I'll be happy to fill you in over a meal," Ivan said. "We've been ridin' hard since meetin' with Salazar this mornin'."

Michael watched Jenkins dismount, every movement slow and deliberate, favoring his wounded leg. He had no pangs about shooting the man. His fading aches reminded him still of that night. And he'd never forget how they battered Kit. He jerked his chin at him and turned toward Ivan.

"I was setting down to eat," Michael said. "Please join me. You can fill me in on our mutual acquaintance and explain why I should be hospitable to him."

Jenkins limped forward and extended his arm. "I'm truly sorry for the harm that befell you and your wife. I took a bunch of rash actions to win back my land from Salazar. Things got out of control."

Michael crossed his arms over his chest. Jenkins' contrite words resonated—they both battled Diego's thieving ways. Glancing at Ivan, who nodded his approval, Michael briefly shook the still-extended hand. "I'm all ears. You two make yourselves comfortable while I ready the grub."

They lounged in the inviting shade, escaping the hot sun's blast. Michael chewed a bit of jerky. The others gnawed on stale biscuits. He draped one arm over his knees and thrummed his fingers impatiently.

"What really brings you here, Ivan? And with this thug?" Michael asked.

Ivan wriggled his shoulders against the tree trunk. "Son, I think the most useful way to start is by chattin' about Salazar's career. By chance, do you still have Abigail Jenkins' contract? You referred to it in court."

"I have no further use for it." Michael retrieved the paper and gave it to Ivan. "Why do you want it?"

Ivan passed the document on to Jenkins. "Peter here had some unfinished business with Salazar over his family property. Even though the judge didn't see fit to take it up in court yesterday, we convinced Salazar to accept a fair-minded trade fer his services rather than pinchin' Peter's land."

Michael contemplated the two smug men. "It took me forever to beat him, and I had to use the entire legal system to win. How did you manage to convince him to roll over?"

"Your court hearin' lit a fire under his greedy butt." Ivan laughed, slapping his thigh. "He tore his copy of the contract into itty-bitty pieces right in front of us, swearin' it was a misunderstandin'. He all but paid Peter here fer the bother, and seemed awful desperate to fix his reputation. From the scuttlebutt I heard around the courthouse, that ain't gonna happen. That judge is stirrin' up a first-rate hornet's nest and winnin' votes. The newspaper is blamin' Salazar fer any land speculation gone bad."

"Couldn't happen to a better man." A fierce stab of pride and elation ran through Michael. He finally beat Diego where it hurt most—his powerful status and prestige. "Let's talk about you…and Jenkins here. What brought you to Sacramento? And to court at such an opportune time?"

"I got to thinkin' over you and your pint-size lady after we met." Ivan grunted and loosened his belt. "You reminded me of your father, only it took me a day to figger that out and recognize the English version of his name. I followed you to make sure you arrived safe, stoppin' overnight in Angels Camp. This fella here had the whole town on fire with his tale. Once I heard him out, we decided to trail you to Sacramento, if need be."

Michael confronted Jenkins reclining on the hard ground, rubbing his wounded leg. Lank blonde hair fell across sky blue eyes, which met Michael's squarely.

"What's your rationale for jumping an innocent man and woman?" Michael couldn't keep the fury from his voice.

"There's no excuse for the harm I put you and your wife in, and I am sorry." Shame crossed Jenkins' face. "Believe me—that was not my intention. I fell in with the wrong kind of men. They tracked you down because some angry San Jose gambler promised them good money."

"That's what they told me while they kicked the stuffing out of me," Michael said. "Why did you join them?"

"I met them after the War Between the States when returning home to California. My mother wrote me that our land was being taken over by squatters, and she employed a lawyer to fight them."

"Diego?"

Jenkins nodded. "Those no-accounts decided to start fresh in California, and paid me to be their guide. One of them found a land warrant buried in a box at a burned-down plantation. They planned on claiming land and working it together. We split up before I reached home. They continued on to San Jose, and I never expected to see them again."

He paused, brows raised, as if asking permission to continue. Michael dipped his head in acquiescence.

"When I got home, I found out Salazar had won the title dispute for my mother, and then demanded payment in our land," Jenkins said. "I was so plumb hopping mad I couldn't see straight. Then those other three showed up dogging the bounty on your head. I figured the quickest path to fix Salazar was to join them hunting you."

A flush painted Jenkins' sharp cheekbones. "They forced me to jump you first to see if you were dangerous. After you shot my leg, I don't recall much. But I swear I never touched you or your wife."

Michael replayed the events of that night in his mind. Jenkins told the truth. His worst crime was reaching for his gun. The facts didn't warrant holding onto resentment. Ivan obviously believed Peter was worthy of his friendship. Michael should at least follow his lead and become a more forgiving, trusting man.

"I remember," Michael said. "And if we commandeered your favorite horse, Peter, swap it for the mount you're riding now. It's grazing a mite farther down on my land."

Ivan smiled at his overture of truce. "In Angels Camp this young fella was rantin' and ravin' on losing his mother's papers, not his mount. Everyone else wanted to hear how his pals jumped some Californio horse thief with a Chinese slave gal, and got themselves killed."

"They deserved it." Michael spat in the dirt.

"I believe it, especially since I figgered it was you," Ivan said. "I knew Peter here had it wrong. Once I heard his account of what he was up against, I decided to help you both. We followed you here to your spread, but you already vamoosed. We knew Salazar was in Sacramento, and it was easy enough to figger where you might be and why. Whew, that man worked awful fast to get your land case heard by the court. We only just made it in time."

"For that I am eternally grateful." Michael smiled. "And I'm glad my case put Diego in a bargaining mood, Peter. I sure hope you got his agreement in writing."

Peter patted his pocket. "Yes, the title is officially in my mother's name once more. I'm on my way home with the good news." Digging his good heel into the ground, he hoisted himself to his feet. "In fact, I'll move on and take advantage of the rest of the daylight."

Michael rose, extending his hand and shaking Peter's. "If you ever come in this direction another time, stop on by. I can use every friend I can get."

"Me, too. Thanks for the offer." Peter flashed a grin. "And keep the mare—she's from Carolina stock, steady and strong. Probably drop spirited foals with a quality stallion." He clambered into his saddle, favoring his injured leg, and galloped south with a farewell salute.

Ivan waved until Peter's figure disappeared behind the tree line. "That boy felt terrible fer the harm that came to you. I blame it on Salazar's gold bounty. I'm sure glad you fergave him."

"He didn't do me lasting harm," Michael said. "We all blunder sometimes in the company we keep." At least he proved to himself that he knew how to forgive and forget. Now to convince Kit for the same. Unless Kit felt that he was a colossal mistake, and that's why she wanted to stay in Sacramento without him.

"Since your dear father is gone and your stepfather is a no-good lawbreaker, I'll give you a piece of fatherly advice. Are you listenin'?"

Michael reclined next to Ivan with a wry smile. "Don't you think I'm too old to need a father?"

"Nobody is so old he can't learn from someone else's experience, and in this case I know what I'm talkin' about." Ivan wagged his finger at him. "You figger a way to hold on to that gal. She'll turn this place into a home. Trust me."

"I'm not sure she wants me. Judge Hancock didn't give her a chance to say yes or no."

"Your hands sure are full resolvin' family business, that's certain." Ivan's eyes twinkled. "Now, that judge did you a favor, seein' what a fine job your wife did defendin' you. Give your marriage a chance. I wish I had. I tried doin' it on my own and it's not worth it. A good woman will help keep your sanity here."

"We have a few problems —my fault entirely," Michael said. "I'm worried Kit will only be happy on land in her name only. Not mine. Not even ours."

"That wife of yours has a clever head on her shoulders. A good compromise will make your marriage work."

Michael stared up into the crystal blue sky, wishing his future were as clear. "We could use that land warrant and claim the neighboring acreage. Kit might bring her father here to live. To the extent he is able, he can work this old gold mine to his heart's content. I don't want it. Kit told me that's been his goal for years. I'm willing to help him achieve it."

"That's a fine gift fer your new family, son." Nodding, Ivan stroked his beard.

Tapping his toes in excitement, Michael raised a fine layer of dust. "Although the law still prohibits Chinese from owning land, and taxes them on gold they unearth, we should be able to share in any wealth if I claim it under my name." He sobered. "Of course, that's assuming Kit will come and live here." His energy drained away.

"Son, it seems to me you have a pretty good plan worked out. What's holdin' you back is your belief in it."

Michael jolted upright. "I'm not sure—"

"Hogwash! Only death is certain, and you're too young to worry on that. Life is full of choices. You won't be certain any of them are right 'til you're my age and see your past mistakes."

"But—"

Ivan lifted his hand. "You spent your adulthood focusin' on gettin' this land. Now it's yours. If it was worth that effort, then your next choices should be good ones. You gotta be willin' to risk everthin' again fer happiness."

Michael stifled his instinctive defensiveness to Ivan's common sense advice. Plot a different course if he wanted a different result, exactly what he told Kit. The rest of his years should be very different than he planned—they should be better. Kit pursued her dreams, no matter how quirky or dangerous. Why not mimic her? He rolled his shoulders, shaking off the chains of his past.

"Thank you." Humility suffused Michael. "I guess I could use a good father, if you're willing."

"Are you kiddin'? I listened to every teeny detail your father told me as you grew. I already feel as if you're my son."

Michael smiled at Ivan's earnestness. "Speaking of which, thank you for helping Father start the orchard. Given his infrequent visits, it must have been tough working it alone."

"Don't thank me, son. Your father didn't plant that orchard. He seen the half-grown trees on his land, and came to me fer advice. He was thrilled the land was developed, ready to pass on to you."

"He always thought of me first. This is proof," Michael said, uplifted by Father's love.

"He was a good man. I helped him when I could, and pruned the branches myself in seasons he didn't show." Ivan threw his arm wide, encompassing the grove below. "Whoever started that orchard was right smart. The trees get the perfect amount of light and water to keep them healthy without much help. You've got a great start on turnin' your land profitable."

"Who on earth develops an orchard and then abandons it?"

"Maybe the squatters who also worked the mine."

Michael dropped his jaw. "You think Kit's parents planted these trees?"

"Someone loved this land, sure enough, and invested a lotta effort to make it produce." Ivan's gaze swept the mine, the fruitful trees, the pastureland below, and the protective slopes. "They probably figgered the orchard could earn them a livin' once the mine played out. Whoever it was counted on claimin' the land."

Michael's long exhalation fluttered his pursed lips. Kit's random tidbits of her childhood didn't shed light on the mysterious orchard. He will ask Lee himself. And thank him, too. Already Father's absentee ownership misled Kit's family into working land they could never own. Lee's years-ago labor might keep Michael fed while he got his ranch up and running. He owed Lee more than gratitude.

He owed him his future.

CHAPTER 55

Kit stuffed the last of her belongings into the burlap bag and scanned the rented room. Two days since Michael won the title to his land and left. It seemed like weeks. She missed him so, especially his arms wrapped around her at night. As true partners in the courtroom, they won. Would that success carry over to other aspects of their marriage, or was it a fluke?

Married! Beyond just pretending, that judge ordered it legal. Unbreakable. Forever.

And confirmed ownership of Kit's Mine to her husband, not Papa. That was eternal as well.

Buttoning her riding jacket, she faced the mirror and ran fingers through her long tangles. She recalled that Spanish author Cervantes' words. *"Destiny guides our fortunes more favorably than we could have expected."* Might Michael prefer a señora?

It was no use—her Chinese and Irish blood controlled her destiny. Pretending to be someone else got her nowhere. She plaited her hair into the usual single braid and left for the stables, hoping she would not return to Sacramento any time soon.

Trotting alongside Papa toward Michael's land, she mused over the last two days' bittersweet conversations with her father in his pathetic hovel. Thin partitions crudely joined couldn't keep the cold winter squall or summer heat out. His pitiful furnishings—thin mattress, wobbly chair and table, chipped washbasin—jammed Papa's cramped living space in the rat-infested Little China slum. Yet on the far wall, displayed with obvious pride, hung the detailed map of Gold Country. His dedicated labors relegated to a symbol of his life's dream, instead of a path to its reality.

"Papa, let's talk," Kit said yesterday, urging him over to the table holding their tea. Sitting at his feet, she clasped his bony hands between hers.

"What is it, daughter?"

"Remember your promise to us concerning Kit's Mine?"

"I do not go a single day without remembering it." He sighed, distress clear on his aged features. His chin drooped to his sunken chest. "I tried to give your mother everything while she was alive. It was never as much as she deserved. She only asked we return to the mine to live free. And now I cannot see to that, either."

His whispered confession tore at her heart. "Papa, you gave me what matters most—your love."

He didn't look at her.

Frustrated, she raised her voice. "You cannot fight these damn laws by yourself, but I just bet you tried."

"Daughter! Your language."

"Papa!" She imitated his disapproving tone and smiled. "That's precisely what they are. I have good news for you, anyway."

"What good news?"

"Kit's Mine is on Michael's land, Papa. When you helped him win in court, you kept your promise to Mama. My hus-husband owns the mine." She plucked at the fabric of her riding pants, uncertain whether this was truly good news or fate laughing at her. Her dream came close enough to touch. Would it flit away like a gossamer butterfly?

Joy flickered across Papa's face. "Is that not good for you?"

"I'm not sure. He thinks I merely helped him to reach my mine."

"And was that true? Is that why you gave yourself to him before marriage?" Shrewdness gleamed in his wise old eyes.

Her cheeks flamed. She stared at the earthen floor.

The lulling trickle of pouring tea filled the awkward silence. Papa slurped the hot liquid and smacked his lips.

"No, Papa, that's not why." She hugged her knees, rested her chin on top, and stared at his hand-drawn diagram. She mentally saluted his conscientious accuracy. Without it, she wouldn't have offered to guide Michael, or be at Papa's side today. "I suspected the mine was on his property. I wasn't sure until I actually got there. I figured he might distrust my motives, except that's not why I...well, you know—"

"Kit, look at me."

His harsh command cut through her embarrassment. She obeyed, and met sympathy, not censure. Surprised, she quashed threatening tears.

"Do you love him?"

"Yes, only I'm not sure he loves me," Kit said. "He'll feel trapped into staying married because it's honorable."

"Honor is of the essence, yes, in every action we take."

Hot tears began an errant journey down her cheeks. "I'll offer to annul our marriage. I won't turn him into a slave, dictated by societal propriety. Is that what he deserves after treating me as an equal? I simply led him to his property in return for protection. He's the first person that didn't belittle me because I'm a Chinese woman. And for that, he has to live an existence of misery? That's not fair."

"He more than protected you," Papa said. "He made you his. Michael strikes me as a man who pursues what he wants. Perhaps he does love you."

"I thought he might." She shrugged, sniffling and swiping her nose. "Once he discovered I lied to him…he changed."

"Do you doubt your love for him?"

"No." Although if this was love, why did she feel dejected?

"The answer is simple, then, my daughter. Work for your love and your marriage. That is the pathway to happiness."

"Even if he doesn't love me, or blames me for that judge's pronouncement? No matter what I've done to earn his trust, he cannot push beyond past hurts." Her husky cry carried her concealed anguish.

"You need to determine the truth of his feelings, of course. Marriage requires honesty. From what I observed, he was not upset. You are."

"What if I don't make him happy?" Kit pounded her fists together, doubts plaguing her. "It would tear me apart if he were miserable because of me."

"Then bring about happiness, no matter what."

Papa seemed calm and resolute that love was so easy.

"Trust me, it is worth it," he said. "As much as your mother and I struggled, neither of us would have chosen differently. It was our fate."

"And you think it was fate I met Michael?"

He chuckled and tousled her hair. "Your mother would scold you to use the brain God gave you. Really, daughter, what are the odds that the very man who rescued you in San Francisco was the landowner of the property you lived on as a child, the very home you sought in your quest? The poetry in the universe brings us together in harmony. Call it fate, call it God's will, or call it good luck—it was clearly meant to be."

Sipping her tea, Kit wasn't convinced Michael would see life as simply as Papa. She had no other honorable option besides offering to annul their marriage. At least that gave Michael a choice. That horrible judge never should have taken it from him.

Forget whimsical fate. She would still pursue her dream of land ownership on her terms. Michael deserved his freedom.

True, if Michael agreed to an annulment, her future with Papa would be dismal since Diego followed through on his threat, and Papa lost his prestigious government job. His opportunities as a Chinese were minimal. At his age, manual labor would soon kill him. The other viable alternatives fell outside the law. Her throat tightened at the depressing possibilities to earn sufficient income for two. Papa's lot rested entirely on her decisions.

Papa rose and puttered around the confining space, wiping the cups and pot and placing them with care atop the empty shelf.

"Your young man impressed me. Is it that hard to believe he has the mettle to forget your deception and forgive you?" He laid his hand on her crown. "The circumstances of your marriage are not ideal, true. Nevertheless, they could be worse. He can manage it if you let him."

She remembered Michael's outrage at her lies, a stark contrast to his comforting behavior early in their journey. "Michael spent all his energy fighting his stepfather. He has nothing left."

He snorted. "If he is a man, he will constantly battle obstacles. That is no excuse for him, or you, to be a coward. Besides, why are you giving up living on our land?"

"Because I cannot bear challenging Michael for it."

"What if you oppose yourself instead of him?"

"What do you mean?" Kit scrambled to follow his logic.

"I mean grow up and cope with your problems as a married woman. Not every day will be as glorious as the first. Hardship will enter your days, that is certain. You can live on the land you dreamed of, with a man you love at your side. Why are you unwilling to stand up for this life you desire?"

His severe voice raised her hackles. Kit glared at him. "I won't earn my happiness at the expense of anyone else's. I'll figure out a different path."

"And what would that be, eh? Have you eternity to choose?" Papa gripped the sides of his eyeglasses and shook his head. "Bah! You are as intractable as your mother ever was. Unless she accomplished the goal in the manner she envisioned, it was no good. What foolishness! Is a flower less beautiful because it grows in a field of weeds instead of a manicured garden? Of course not. And your time on this earth will be no better because you create the field in which it will develop. What is foremost is that you mature and your purpose is meaningful."

The horse stumbled, shaking Kit from her musings. Papa's strong disapproval of her decision for annulment unsettled her. Trailing him, his form ramrod straight in the saddle, she pondered his arguments, interlinking them with the dreams she clung to during her darkest nights in San Francisco. The dilemma was similar to mining. If you keep digging in the same direction, never striking on a different bearing, you may miss a spectacular gold deposit a mere inch away. Unseen, but oh, so close.

She urged Lucky alongside. "Papa, tell me more of Kit's Mine. Did you ever dig out gold?"

"Why ask now?"

"I'm trying to get a sense of the prize I held out for myself. Was it real or was it in my mind?" Chastened, she lifted a shoulder. "I guess I want the truth, finally."

"Hmm." He stared at the distant horizon, his features inscrutable, making her wait for his answer as usual. "Your mother and I worked that mine for months. When we left, we carried gold to feed us one week. What do you think?"

"I think I was convinced owning the mine would solve all of our problems," Kit said. "I never stopped to ask if any gold remained."

"It is good to stop and ask the precise question." Long seconds passed, broken by the deadened footfall of hooves trampling the tall grasses. "Gold is often hidden in places—and ways—that are unexpected, even for the most experienced miner."

Wistful memories of her childhood welled up inside Kit. "Why did you and Mama stay if the mine didn't yield enough gold?"

"We fled Hong Kong with nothing except our love to live on—and that was a bounteous fortune to survive our toughest years." He slowed his horse to a standstill.

Kit reined in, subdued by his cheerless demeanor.

"Your mother and I tried to settle down, to call any place our home." Papa said. "I came to this country for the opportunity to succeed and thrive, to be more than a scholar or cartographer or common employee—or slave."

His voice became gravelly, and he cleared his throat. "We were too early. California had to grow up first."

"It's been decades, though," she said. "People still hate the Chinese...and Californios. Why? What have we done to them besides want our freedom?"

"Men such as Salazar and Hancock will soon lose their power, and old Chinese men will have their chance to prosper," he said. "We accept the times into which we are born. Your mother and I prayed you would have fond memories of a home, instead of the prejudices we encountered every day. I hope we succeeded."

His forlorn attitude wrenched her heart. "Yes, Papa, you did! In my dreams of a perfect home, I envision the land around the mine. Mama's laughter as she called me to lunch, your teachings by the fire after sunset. I wish for that all over again."

"Remember, child, work hard for your dreams, and do not chase old memories. You will never recreate the past. It is gone."

He kicked his mount into a gallop. She chased after him, topping the rise at his side. Recognizable terrain spread before them. The mine opening emerged as a gaping slash aligned with the golden slopes. She caught her breath at the fertile promise of the land.

"Ready?" He reached across the gap between their horses and gripped Kit's hand, his strength reassuring. She prayed the future would turn out favorably. Releasing her, he loped down the hill to his land of lost dreams. She followed, wondering if hers were as futile.

CHAPTER 56

Ivan jogged across the clearing to Papa's side. "I'm Ivan Sankovitch, an old friend of Michael's father and newly adopted family after this commotion. You must be Kit's father."

Papa dismounted in the hot, still air and shook Ivan's extended hand. "Yes, I am Juan Lee. It is my honor to meet you. I remember you from court. I am grateful you helped my daughter and her husband." He bowed at the waist.

Husband! Where was Michael? Kit caught sight of him in the distance. His familiar presence thrilled her, yet their upcoming confrontation scared her, too. She alighted in haste, preempting his certain assistance.

Michael's long stride ate up the ground between them, a quizzical expression on his face. Her heart pounded in her breast, thankfully hidden by the dusty riding jacket. She peeked up at him but extended her fingers to Ivan, smiling.

"Thank you for your testimony," she said. "Who would guess meeting you in your orchards would help Michael win?"

"Little miss, you have no idea how glad I am to see you in good health." Ivan wrapped her in a giant bear hug. "I spent long hours worryin' you would make it this far, let alone to Sacramento. I guess I never should have doubted your navigation skills."

Touched, Kit squeezed him in return. "Thank Papa for that. I spent hours right here learning from him." She twinkled up at Ivan. "I don't suppose you stashed extra fruit in your saddlebag, did you? I've been craving more since we finished the first delicious batch."

"Daughter!" Papa hissed. "It is not polite to beg a guest."

Ivan guffawed, tugging her braid. "Sorry to disappoint you. I finished mine long ago. Guess you'll have to visit me at my place after you sort things out here."

Kit's answering smile dissolved. Too many issues needed resolution before she went anywhere—or nowhere. She hastily removed Lucky's saddle, and staggered under its weight. Michael steadied her, Papa's saddle cradled in his arm.

"I'll take care of the horses, Kit. You go rest." Michael hefted her heavy burden.

"I don't need rest, silly. The horses do." She cringed at her childish tone and ungracious words. So much for taking Papa's advice to grow up. She corralled her unruly tongue. "I do appreciate your help. Thank you."

Habits from their traveling days fell into place. In effortless tandem, they groomed the horses, set out food and water, and hobbled them in the field. Putting the combs aside, Michael reached a hand to Kit. She hesitated, still cautious, but finally accepted his friendly gesture.

"I'm glad to see you, Kitten." He escorted her up the slope toward Ivan and Papa. "It seems like forever since we had a chance to talk."

Slowing, his gaze captured hers. She faltered at the vibrant heat, managing a mute nod. They crested the hill and strolled toward the mine. Emotion bubbled up in her, demanding release.

"I missed you," she whispered, glancing up at him.

His eyes flared with hunger and intensity. She tugged him forward the remaining steps and focused her attention on the old men chatting around the fire. A succulent aroma saturated the warm air.

"Figgered you two might be hungry and it wouldn't hurt to eat an early supper. Trapped these this mornin'." Ivan balanced two long sticks of skewered rabbits over the blaze. "Chores will wait 'til tomorrow. Tonight we talk."

Kit braced for her coming challenge—gaining their understanding and acceptance of her decision. She eased from Michael and perched on the log next to Papa. Michael trudged to the other side of the fire and slumped onto the ground.

The expectant silence grew longer, broken by the hissing of fat spraying into the flames. Were the three men letting her speak first out of courtesy, or because they sensed whatever she said would change Papa and Michael's worlds?

Papa nudged her knee. Taking a breath to slow her pattering heart, she met each man's impassive gaze in turn.

"I have waited all these years to live free on land I can work and call my own," she said. "Usually only men enjoy the luxury of that dream. But it's mine, too. I won't give it up—at least not yet. That may seem selfish, except it's my life. My freedom. It's as elemental for me as breathing."

Ivan snorted and poked the rabbit. As usual, Papa wore an indecipherable expression. Michael peered into the mine entrance. A frown creased his forehead.

She braced herself. She didn't care what they thought—she wouldn't back down!

"Besides, Papa is dependent on me since Diego got him fired." Kit ignored Papa's flush and Ivan's challenging stare. "I'm Papa's only family."

Further silence greeted her blunt pronouncements.

Unnerved, she drew random patterns in the soil with her boot heel. "I need to be sure my decisions are best for him."

With a stifled choke, Papa's torso sagged.

How arrogant she sounded! She squashed embarrassed tears and sighed.

"Obviously you all disagree," she said. "Do you have better ideas?"

Ivan kicked Michael's shin. Michael flinched and glared at him. Shifting sideways, he faced Kit across the dancing flames. The skin across his cheekbones grew taut.

"The way I see it, you are seeking viable land, titled in your name, and a means to provide for your father. You'd be happy then?" Michael's tone was flat and businesslike.

Kit dipped her head in partial agreement and twiddled her fingers in her lap. Something more, and of course someone in particular, would bring her true happiness. "I think so. However—"

"If I were to present to you, free and clear, the 160 acres of land adjacent to mine, owned by you and you alone, would that qualify?" Michael asked.

Eyes wide, she stilled.

"The land warrant belonging to that thug who jumped us is yours for the asking, no strings attached," Michael said. "You saved my hide that night. You deserve it. Your father may live on it, if you choose. That would be your privilege to grant as the property owner."

She began to reject that warrant again and hesitated, reminding herself of the promise to Papa to be less prideful. Cautious, she met Michael's gaze.

"Yes, that warrant represents a wonderful opportunity for whoever holds it," she said. "It would certainly meet one of my criteria. I guess it would depend on whether the land was workable."

Michael rolled his shoulders in a loose circle and released his held breath. "It is. Ivan and I rode it yesterday, and your father helped me research it in Sacramento. It's as good a piece of property as mine, and available to claim."

Had Michael really identified an escape from her vagabond existence? She nodded. Calm peace permeated her soul. A landowner—finally!

Michael chucked a stick onto the fire. The cooking rabbit hissed, and waves of fragrant smoke enveloped them.

"That brings me to my next proposal," he said. "I'm a rancher. I have no idea what's involved in working a gold mine. However, your father has vast experience."

He turned toward Papa and bowed. "I would be honored if you would consider a business proposition. Half ownership of the yield from the mine in return for your expertise in working it." Fleeting doubt shadowed Michael's features. "That is, if in your opinion any gold still remains to be mined."

"I would be honored to go into business with you, Mr. Michael Rivers." Papa tipped his head in return and grinned. "And yes, when my wife and I stopped working the mine, ample gold remained. It simply was not worth excavating due to our high taxes."

"Stupid, unfair law." Ivan gripped his knees and glowered in the direction of Sacramento.

Papa sobered. "We also feared a squatter might strip the mine of its value if anyone knew except us. The land was not ours, and the onerous laws kept me from submitting a claim. We did not dare inform Kit before she reached maturity to claim it herself."

Michael shot Kit a sympathetic grimace, and her heart lifted. He understood her father's plight, and offered a different choice.

"Unfortunately, my age prevents me from doing the physical labor involved in working that mine." Papa raised his bony hands toward the flames. Unmistakable tremors shook them.

Kit swallowed past the lump forming in her throat at the realization that Papa's dream came too late.

"Uh, sir, then I'm not sure what kind of yield we should count on from the mine, if neither of us works it," Michael said.

"I have a rather...progressive...suggestion, if that is appropriate," Papa said.

"Shoot, Lee, you're talkin' to family." Ivan poked at the meat. "There's no law stoppin' bangin' ideas around. Let's hear it."

"Many unemployed, hard-working Chinese are rotting their lives away, praying someone will give them a chance to succeed," Papa said. "I propose we hire the most proficient men to work the mine. They would be glad to leave Sacramento and live with me on our adjacent land. I introduced this possibility to many Chinese during the past year, yet I found no cooperative landowner. Unless you...?"

"That's an excellent idea, except it's not actually my decision," Michael said. "The mine itself belongs to Kit, as befits its proper name."

He stepped behind a tree and revealed the old sign, newly blackened. "We'll have a re-christening ceremony once you start mining." Michael laid the board at her feet and returned to his seat.

Kit gasped. "You're giving the mine to me?"

"I am giving you ownership as a wedding present. However, I propose half the yield belongs to your father by virtue of his work developing it. Surely you won't object to that?"

"No, of course not." Kit never expected such generosity from Michael. Or that he would link that kindness to their marriage, not past obligations to her. Maybe she could trust his strategies, and accomplish her dream. His ideas were far more enticing than any she considered.

A radical idea struck her, and she scooted forward. "Papa, we can set up a company and give the mine workers ownership stake in it as a reward for their efforts! If Mama taught me right, California law doesn't prevent Chinese from owning a share of a private company."

Considering the hardship Papa's friends endured, displaced from their mines, this was the ethical resolution. She gave a vigorous nod. "Yes, I will give half my ownership to the other miners."

"Daughter, you fill me with pride at your benevolence and loyalty." Papa's voice quavered. He wiped the corner of his eye. "I believe Kit's Mine will be the first enterprise to offer that kind of opportunity. I pray it will not be the last."

Delighted, her mind raced. What other possibilities were open to her? She spun to face Michael, flushed and excited. He raised a hand, forestalling her. What next? Her birthday may have been days ago, but she felt like a child again, anticipating bigger surprises as the hours flew by.

Michael looked straight at Papa. "I am quite fortunate. A mature orchard grows on my land, planted years ago by a very far-sighted man. Is that possibly you, Lee?"

"Colleen begged me to plant those trees." A single tear glided from behind Papa's eyeglass, dampening his cheek. "She collected seeds during our travels. I never expected to be able to see them again, let alone eat from them."

"I hope you also have the expertise to help the trees flourish and reach their full potential. I intend to be very busy raising horses," Michael said with a half-salute.

Gratitude replaced the faint remnants of sorrow on Papa's face. "I will develop our orchard into the finest in California, in memory of Colleen and the roots our family planted here."

Ivan chortled. "Whoa, Lee. Who says you'll be able to produce better than me?"

"I am prepared to compete with you for buyers," Papa said. "I will work very hard so our trees yield more and better fruit than yours. I am curious. Did you also plant nut trees, Ivan?"

"No, just fruit," Ivan said. "Why do you ask?"

"Because half of the harvest from our trees will be sold before we pick them," Papa said. "Eastern merchants pay higher prices for quality nuts. Plus, there's no spoilage during the long train trip. I have contacts in Sacramento who will welcome premium suppliers."

Ivan scratched his jaw with a rueful grin. "I'll keep pluggin' away growin' fruit. At least your daughter recognizes quality."

Enthralled by Papa's animation, Kit fought the dampness pooling on her bottom lids. Because of Michael's wisdom, Papa finally would earn the self-respect he yearned for, and control his destiny.

"Yes, Ivan, your fruit is wonderful," she said. "Since I haven't yet had a chance to taste Papa's harvest, I would be a wise and prudent daughter to keep my opinions to myself until I compare fairly." She winked. "I'll require plenty of samples first."

The three men laughed. Ivan and Papa tore charred pieces off the cooking rabbit, swapping techniques for growing an outstanding orchard, chattering like the greatest of friends.

Chin cupped in her palms, she stared into the fire, relieved yet uncertain. The mine was hers as a wedding present—and she still didn't know whether Michael wanted to be married. Accepting her lifelong dream would entrap Michael! Her thoughts darted in chaotic tempo to the dancing flames. If he bothered offering this plan, he must want her happiness. That meant he cared.

How much he cared, and why, she doubted.

CHAPTER 57

A heavy pressure lifted from Michael's chest. Somehow, Kit learned open-mindedness. Of course, her obvious amazement at his thoroughness left him a mite disgruntled. She hadn't trusted he would do everything in his power to bring her happiness.

Kit giggled at the old men's banter, looking hopeful instead of strained. The burden of her father's welfare never should have weighed on her young shoulders.

Michael shifted his legs, impatient for time alone with Kit. She seemed in no hurry.

Lee glanced between the two of them. A discerning smile crossed his face. "Michael, have you had a chance to examine the roots of the orchard trees?"

"Aren't they prospering?" Michael asked. "Is there a problem?" Luck was never on his side, even with his grand plan.

"Not unless you think having extra capital to start your ranch presents a problem," Lee said, his face glimmering with humor.

Unnerved again by his resemblance to Kit, Michael shook his head in mute wonder and confusion.

Kit frowned. "Papa, stop joking. What are you talking about?"

Lee stared at the distant orchard. "Your mother and I hid most of our gold at the base of the trees rather than letting it be taken in taxes."

Kit's mystified gaze met Michael's. He shrugged.

Lee pointed to the expanse of flourishing trees. "The result of our years of struggle is protected by their roots. If worse came to worse, we had our gold hidden, awaiting a different opportunity, or the chance to live here again."

"Did you ever return?" Michael asked.

"We tried to come back after my railroad job ended. Colleen never made it." Tears thickened Lee's voice. In moments, grief aged his features. "Daughter, I am sorry that you had to live in privation until your inheritance was available. Perhaps your mother and I erred, given what happened. Until you were an adult at eighteen, I was afraid they would seize it from you. Once your mother died, you had no proof of your American heritage. Besides, we risked the owner of the land finding it."

Lee faced Ivan. "Did Michael's father ever mention finding any gold, Ivan?"

"No siree, not to me, he didn't. Michael?"

"No," Michael said. "He would have told Mother, and she would have told me after he died."

"How much gold is buried?" Kit interrupted, and Michael silently echoed her breathless question.

"Ample for the two of you to follow your dreams without ever worrying over money. As I will be able to follow mine, thanks to Michael's wisdom and generosity. Now that Michael has claimed legal ownership, the required taxes on his finds are minimal."

"I think you are very wise, sir," Michael said. "And my Mother would agree. This is her favorite line from *Don Quixote*: *'time has more power to undo and change things than the human will.'*"

Lee nodded. "That is so. I am pleased my new son is so well educated." He waved dismissively. "Go! Walk through your orchard and leave Ivan and me to gab as old men do. This may be my last chance to relax for years. I look forward to a lifetime of work to accomplish, starting tomorrow."

Grateful, Michael helped Kit to her feet, keeping her fingers encased within his. He led her down the hill. The evening sun bathed their swinging arms in a golden aura.

"We have another issue to resolve, don't you agree, Kitten?"

She pulled free and stared at the horizon. Crickets alone answered his question.

"Kitten?"

"Thank you for your wonderful consideration of Papa," she said. "You have almost guaranteed he will be very happy the rest of his days."

"And you? Will you be happy?"

"I could be." Turning away, she kicked a stone at her feet, keeping her face lowered. "Michael, what the judge decreed was unfair to you. We have to fix it."

"No, thank you." Michael strove for a matter-of-fact tone, ignoring the sudden tension coursing through him. He sensed a torrent of seething, illogical emotions ready to spill from her. "Judge Hancock affirmed ownership of my land, and I intend to keep it."

"Oh, you know that's not what I meant."

"Really?" Michael pretended ignorance. "Then what is so urgent to fix?"

"The marriage should be annulled." Anxiety suffused her features. "The judge had no call to marry us without our permission."

Michael folded his arms across his chest and looked at her, guarded. "We gave him that right. We didn't deny our travels together, nor that it was our intention to marry eventually. Did he or I get that part wrong?"

"You never asked me to marry you." Her voice quivered.

"True, not in those words. Nonetheless, you know better than anyone which actions spoke my intentions." He spanned her waist and pulled her close. "Remember the line from *Don Quixote*? *'Where there is great love there is often little display of it.'* We got caught up in each other's nightmares, and never took the time to shape our dreams."

"I won't be shoved on you merely because we spent a few nights together." Kit's cheeks colored a rosy pink, and she tossed her head. Defiance firmed her chin. "You deserve better."

"You were not shoved onto me, and I am not unhappy with our marriage," Michael said.

She tugged against his clasp.

Despairing, he loosened his grip and eased back, resenting every inch of separation. "You are, aren't you?"

"Do you expect me to forget your anger and distrust when we left here?"

"I forgave you after I realized what I fool I was. I understand why you kept the mine a secret from me. I would have done the same." Michael tensed his fingers at her waist. "I never apologized for my behavior, did I? It's considerably past time. Kitten, I am sorry for treating you poorly, for not trusting you. You proved yourself countless times. I promise to be a better man, someone you can be proud of."

Kit stared at his chest in silence, her fists clenched against his shirt. Michael nudged her chin up with his knuckle, caressing her jaw tenderly with his thumb. Her bemused gaze locked onto his.

"Kitten, I wouldn't have anything without you. You've been the partner I never realized I wanted, let alone needed. My single goal before I met you was to ranch this land and succeed, all on my own. Now, that's not enough. I want you here at my side. As my wife, raising our children, sharing the stories of our parents and grandparents. Reading to them from *Don Quixote*, so they dream, too. Please forgive me."

He melded her into his embrace, seeking her physical response, desperate to reconnect in that elemental sense.

"What about—"

He slanted his lips over hers, cutting off her words. Moving in gentle sweeps, he coaxed her to forget their past except this, this hot fire consuming them whenever they succumbed, pulsing with life, with anticipation—with love.

"I've missed you so much." He loosened the tie binding her hair, and it tumbled into his hands. He stroked the nape of her neck. She trembled, but remained passive.

Unnerved, Michael slowed his caresses. She still hadn't agreed to build a future together.

He gathered his courage and humility for words he once thought impossible to utter. "I love you until I hurt. I need you here by my side, on my…no, on our land. Don't you feel what's between us? Will you be mine?"

His anxiety must have shown. Kit smiled, reassurance wreathing her features. She twined her arms around his neck and pressed a tender kiss to his lips.

"I love you too, Michael. And I'm proud to be your wife." She paused, her cheeks reddening. "But…I'm not sure I know how to make you truly happy. I'm stubborn and opinionated…and I cannot bear letting you go."

He embraced her. "For your information, I think you are a beautiful and fearless woman, who showed me a way to live that I never knew before. Thank you for that. I wanted you the first time I saw you, and I'm positive I'll want you always."

"Really?" She caught her bottom lip between her teeth.

"Really. I can't wait to imagine... and experience…every possible dream with you." He nipped at her tempting mouth.

"Whatever they will be, we'll weave them together," Kit said, love shining through her glorious eyes. "I'm yours forever."

They rambled into the discreet arms of the welcoming orchard, their rapid heartbeats pulsing as one.

If you enjoyed reading *Kit's Mine*...

...won't you please take a moment to leave a review at your favorite retailer? And don't forget to tell your friends!

Thanks for your support.

Ann Bridges

Author's Note and Acknowledgements

As the old adage says, "History is written by the winners." Therefore, little is contained in California's historical records on many of these issues, especially documenting property rights of single women, Chinese, and the plight of the native Californios during the infamous Gold Rush of 1849 through the completion of the Transcontinental Railroad in 1869.

An interesting addendum to the categorization of Chinese immigrants as sojourners: even with the acclaimed Burlingame Treaty in 1868 granting China equal status as a trading partner and fair treatment of Chinese subjects residing in America, Chinese couldn't become naturalized citizens of the United States. A series of additional "Chinese Exclusion Acts" went into effect starting in 1879, with the stated purpose of controlling the number of unskilled laborers entering the U.S., and were not overturned until late 1943, almost 100 years after the California Gold Rush. In 1944, the first Chinese person became a naturalized U.S. citizen, just prior to Mao Zedong's rise to power and emigration prohibition.

It is no wonder that most Americans are woefully ignorant of Chinese traditions, or their contributions to the development of this country. Racial bias continued because it was codified. As a result, most Chinese didn't integrate or inter-marry as so many other immigrants did. Nor is it surprising that there might be animosity still from current-day Chinese political leaders on this blatant discrimination of their country's citizens alone.

I want to thank the numerous reference librarians at San Jose Public Library and the California Room for helping me find pertinent resources, especially of the history of the Californios. Elena Smith, from the California State Library, provided invaluable assistance tracking down maps and photos of Sacramento in its earliest days. History San Jose and the Chinese Historical Society of America provided authentic exhibits helping me picture life in the 19th century. And heartfelt gratitude goes to the many journalists, biographers, diarists, and authors who dared to explore these taboo topics contemporaneously.

A special thank you to all my cheerleaders, early readers, critique partners, and other supporters as I wrote and re-wrote this story over the years. I couldn't have done it without you all.

Read More from Ann Bridges

Discover the chase for California's modern wealth in her Silicon Valley Series:

Private Offerings: A Silicon Valley Novel (#1)

Silicon Valley entrepreneur Eric Coleman hires public relations consultant Lynn Baker to accomplish his dream of a successful Wall Street Initial Public Offering, unaware they are jumping into a morass of behind–the–scenes deal making threatening both their companies. Eric's past commitments run headlong into Lynn's secrets, and thrust them between competing Chinese and American interests to control his innovative technology—and the global power it brings.

Praise and Acclaim for *Private Offerings*:

Named **BEST BUSINESS FICTION FOR 2015**: "...This novel captures the intensity of the Silicon Valley business world and its arcane financial practices with appealing characters, unrelenting action and depictions of high finance and corporate boardroom dynamics that ring true."—*John Kador, Wealth Management Magazine*

"...a timely fictional page-turner...she can tell a story..."—*Scott Herhold, San Jose Mercury News*

"...a high-tech tale of international intrigue, populated with promiscuous characters of dubious integrity...demystifies Silicon Valley with a story of love, greed and financial shenanigans."—*George Koo, New America Media, former U.S.-China business consultant*

Rare Mettle: A Silicon Valley Novel (#2)

When China threatens to withhold critical rare earth metals from U.S. defense contractors and high-tech firms, American undercover agents and rogue operatives step up with unorthodox methods to procure the needed components. First introduced in the acclaimed prequel, Private Offerings, military veteran and staunch patriot Paul Freeman joins forces with Silicon Valley entrepreneurs, cutting-edge technologists, and elected officials to rescue an undercover operative with key intelligence. His team forces him to face past ghosts, current enemies, and future desires, in a courageous hero's journey taking from Washington D.C. to China, and home to Silicon Valley.

Praise and Acclaim for *Rare Mettle*:

"...a gripping fictional account of a serious real world problem..."—*Robert H. Latiff, PhD., Major General (retired), United States Air Force, Technology Consultant*

"...a chilling tale..."—*Anthony Marchese, Chairman, Texas Mineral Resources Corp.*

"...[Bridges'] depiction of the current commercial and National Security situation is accurate, valid and deeply relevant to U.S. economic standing in the world..."—*James C. Kennedy, President ThREEConsulting.com, St. Louis Missouri*

"...captures the dragon spirit of both Silicon Valley and China--bold, ambitious, and intelligent..."—*Margaret Zhao, former Enemy of the State in Mao's China, Award winning author*

"...as fast-paced and exciting as a Dan Brown thriller..."—*William DeVincenzi, Executive in Residence, Director of Gary J. Sbona Honors Program and Thompson Global Internship, Lucas College of Business, San Jose State University*

About Ann Bridges

Ann Bridges is a native of Chicago who fell in love with Northern California while earning her B.S. degree from Stanford University. Settling in San Jose, she embarked on a challenging career spanning operations, finance, and marketing executive positions in the exploding convergence of the technology, communications, and entertainment industries.

Years of intimate business experience earned in the diverse world of Silicon Valley form the foundation of Ann Bridges' addictive, intelligent fiction. She captures real-world elements and balances complex plots with genuine characters and provocative twists in a literary style that appeals to both sexes.

Her debut novel, *Private Offerings*, was named Best Business Fiction of 2015 by *Wealth Management Magazine. San Jose Mercury News* and *Upside* journalists, as well as fellow businesspeople, acclaim it for its authenticity and timeliness. Its sequel, *Rare Mettle*, tackles the controversial issue of global free trade juxtaposed against rising political tensions. Ringing endorsements from industry experts and military insiders validate her fictional account of the critical significance of rate earth metals to our 21st century lifestyle and national security. Her latest novel, *Kit's Mine*, exposes the plight of immigrant Chinese and native Californios fighting injustice in 1870 post-Gold Rush California, another in a series of untold stories.

Ann Bridges is a featured speaker at leading business conferences and universities, talking about the impact of technology worldwide and the need to better understand the role of China in our past, present, and future. She is also a frequent guest on national radio shows sharing insights on today's Silicon Valley and the issues affecting today's consumers and investors.

Connect with Ann Bridges

For more information, including an in–depth interview,
please visit her website:

https://AuthorAnnBridges.wordpress.com

Or, connect on **Facebook**, **Twitter**, or **LinkedIn**

Made in the USA
Middletown, DE
15 March 2019